THE
BRIDE RAFFLE

BY

LISA PLUMLEY

First published in Great Britain 2012
by Mills & Boon, an imprint of Harlequin (UK) Limited.
Large Print edition 2012
Harlequin (UK) Limited, Eton House,
18-24 Paradise Road, Richmond, Surrey TW9 1SR

© Lisa Plumley 2011

ISBN: 978 0 263 23609 5

 **18 JUL 2012**

Harlequin (UK) policy is to use papers that are natural, renewable and recyclable products and made from wood grown in sustainable forests. The logging and manufacturing process conform to the legal environmental regulations of the country of origin.

Printed and bound in Great Britain
by CPI Antony Rowe, Chippenham, Wiltshire

When she found herself living in modern-day Arizona Territory, **Lisa Plumley** decided to take advantage of it—by immersing herself in the state's fascinating history, visiting ghost towns and historical sites, and finding inspiration in the desert and mountains surrounding her. It didn't take long before she got busy creating light-hearted romances like this one, featuring strong-willed women, ruggedly intelligent men, and the unexpected situations that bring them together.

When she's not writing, Lisa loves to spend time with her husband and two children, travelling, hiking, watching classic movies, reading, and defending her trivia game championship. She enjoys hearing from readers, and invites you to contact her via e-mail at lisa@lisaplumley.com, or visit her website at www.lisaplumley.com

Previous novels by the same author:

THE DRIFTER
THE MATCHMAKER*
THE SCOUNDREL*
THE RASCAL*
MARRIAGE AT MORROW CREEK*
  (part of *Halloween Temptations* anthology)
MAIL-ORDER GROOM

**Morrow Creek* mini-series

And in Mills & Boon Historical *Undone!* eBooks:

WANTON IN THE WEST

To John, with all my love,
now and forever.

Chapter One

Morrow Creek, northern Arizona Territory
June 1883

On an otherwise unremarkable day in Morrow Creek, Owen Cooper stood in the modest quarters where he lived atop his livery stable and made himself a solemn promise: he was going to learn to braid his daughter's hair, even if it killed him.

It looked as though it might. Already, Owen had made more than one attempt. He'd been defeated every time. Still, ten-year-old Élodie appeared to believe he could finish the task.

With every appearance of certainty in a braiding prowess Owen strongly doubted he possessed, Élodie stood with her back to him. With pint-size eagerness, she wiggled on her tiptoes. Then she craned her neck, trying to glimpse one of her pigtails.

"Are you done yet, Papa? Can I look?"

"Not yet. Keep holding still."

"I am! I'm pretending my feet are glued to the floor!"

Hmm. For an instant, Owen contemplated the potential merits of *actually* gluing Élodie's high-buttoned shoes to the floor, then allowing her to step into them like a pony in a stall. Such a tactic would doubtless make mornings like this one easier. As it was, Élodie had been fidgeting nonstop, even before she'd begged Owen, over breakfast, to take on this delicate maneuver. He squinted, newly determined to master this task.

"Remember, both braids are supposed to be exactly the same!" Élodie reminded him earnestly. "Nice and neat, too."

Nice and neat. Frowning at the twin fistfuls of coppery hair he'd been bundling and twisting in his hands for the past fifteen minutes, Owen shifted his feet. He felt his frown deepen. What he'd accomplished so far was poor, he realized. And raggedy. The horses he boarded at his stable sometimes boasted fancier plaits than the ones he'd created for his daughter.

He'd have to try harder. He could do it. After all, he'd already learned to do so many fatherly tasks that had fallen to him in the years since he'd lost Renée. Owen was proud of the progress he'd made, too. So when Élodie had begged him to braid her hair in a new fashion today, he'd thought the undertaking would be simple enough to accomplish, especially for a man like him—a man who was reasonably intelligent, occasionally clever and always skilled with his hands.

Years ago, Owen had earned a good living with those hands. Not good in the sense of untarnished and pure, of course; those were concepts Owen had had only a passing acquaintance with until he'd met Renée, and she'd begun to reform him. What he'd earned with his hands and mind all those years ago had been a *profitable* living. A frivolous, fun-loving, *profitable* living.

The truth was, Owen had always enjoyed a talent for the disreputable. Minor thievery had come easily to him; so had running a swindle or delivering a punch or seducing a woman. These days, Owen regretted his rapscallion's past—but he saw it for what it was, too: a cockeyed blessing. If he'd been a better man, he knew, he might never have met Renée outside his favorite gambling house in Baltimore. As it was, he and Renée had taken instantly and wholeheartedly to one another…never mind that the woman had been crusading to shut down the place.

Renée, scarcely nineteen and staunchly naive, hadn't known then that the sizable nest egg Owen had brought to their marriage had been the result of gambling, conning and generally charming the world at large. Owen, already a hell-raising bachelor at twenty-two, had been too smitten to risk enlightening her. She'd discovered his faults quickly enough, though—and had set out to reform him of them straightaway. Two years later, Owen and Renée had taken those savings with them from Baltimore, intending to start a new, more respectable life together with their toddler daughter in California.

Instead, his wife's journey westward had ended in the Arizona Territory, in the picturesque mountain town of Morrow Creek. After losing Renée, Owen had decided to stay there, too, with tiny Élodie. In the years since then, he'd done his best to care for his daughter the way Renée would have wanted him to.

That meant fancy pigtails and ribbons were his duty.

They were damnably difficult to master, though. Far more so than he'd imagined they would be. But Owen was not a man who entertained the notion of defeat. Not when it came to Élodie.

When it came to his daughter, Owen *had* to succeed. He was all Élodie had…and she was all he had. He would have died before giving up on her—even when it came to inconsequential matters like intricate braids and froufrou ribbons.

"Maybe this is too much for you, Papa." Élodie's narrow shoulders slumped. She tapped her toes, pondering the issue. "Maybe I'll ask Mrs. Archer to do these braids for me instead."

"No, you won't." At Élodie's mention of the neighboring woman who looked after her while Owen was at work in his stable, he felt his resolve strengthen. He didn't want to give Mrs. Archer—or any of the other local womenfolk—any more reason to mollycoddle him. Owen appreciated their help. He did. But whether they were flirting with him, admiring him for raising a daughter single-handedly or offering him their assistance with any one of the domestic matters that arose daily, they could be a little too... *interfering* for his liking. "I'm almost finished."

With his breath held, Owen gave a few more twists. He peered in fierce concentration at Élodie's hair, then twisted again. He bit his lip. Cautiously, he examined his handiwork.

Yes. That might suit. The braids he'd produced weren't exactly prizewinning quality. But he reckoned they would appear much improved after he wrangled on the ribbons. Probably.

He tried. Unfortunately, the moment Owen wrapped one of the slippery pink ribbons Élodie had enthusiastically provided for him, he lost his hold on the braid he'd fashioned.

It unraveled instantly. He bit back a swearword.

Élodie knew what that meant. Swearing was one of the few disreputable habits Owen hadn't been able to break. Prompted by that stifled expletive, his daughter sent her gaze toward his. She tried to give him a smile. It looked wobbly.

"It's all right, Papa. I don't need those fancy pigtails today, after all. I've just decided it."

The disappointment in her eyes just about killed him.

If Owen had had anything left to gamble, he would have wagered it, just to win a talent for fashioning acceptable pigtails. He'd have promised anything to make Élodie happy.

Unfortunately, he'd already left behind his debauched past—and with it, all his leveraging ability. With Renée's pristine example in mind, Owen had done his best not only to raise Élodie as his wife would have seen fit, but also to live his own life commendably. That meant cussing was off-limits to him. So were gambling, cigar smoking, wanton spending, partaking of the territory's (reputedly) excellent mescal and enjoying…well, pretty much anything at all that was strictly pleasurable.

If it felt good, Owen refused it.

That was his simplified method of living a laudable life. The tactic hadn't steered him wrong yet. Of course, in Morrow Creek, true temptations stood few and far between…which was part of the reason he'd remained there. It was better, he'd learned during his early (and sometimes failed) attempts to be a truly *good* man, to avoid undue enticement at all costs. After all, if he slipped once, who knew how far and fast he'd fall?

Squaring his shoulders, Owen returned his attention to the matter at hand: Élodie's pigtails. Briefly, he considered asking the Almighty to grant him the favor of braid-weaving dexterity. But then he realized the sorry truth: the Lord had undoubtedly washed his hands of the entire Cooper clan years before.

There'd be no help from that quarter. Not for him or his brothers. In this, as in everything else, Owen was on his own.

"One ordinary braid would be fine," Élodie assured him.

"One?" Decidedly, Owen shook his head. One auburn braid was all his daughter usually sported. Today, she'd asked for two. "You asked for two pigtails today. That's what you'll have."

Regrouping, Owen planted his feet. With painstaking precision, he parted Élodie's hair. He handed her the leftmost bundle to hold—a deviation from his previous attempts, when he'd tried to wrangle both handfuls of tresses himself—then got to work plaiting the other bundle. Almost there…

"But the horses will be wanting to be watered and fed!" Élodie insisted. "They're probably very hungry by now."

Her stated concern for the beasts didn't fool him.

While his daughter *did* have a strong affection for the horses they boarded, she knew her papa would no more set aside responsibility for those horses than he would wear a pair of pigtails himself.

At the notion of his own overgrown, shoulder-length dark hair plaited in twain, Owen felt his lips quirk. *That* would be a sight and a half. The whole town would be in an uproar.

Which was saying something, when it came to sleepy Morrow Creek. Around here, the liveliest action that ever took place happened between the banks of the namesake creek, during its typical springtime flooding. Unlike the rowdy Western towns of tabloid periodicals and dime novels, Morrow Creek was sedate and settled. It was *not* given to shenanigans or uproars of any kind.

Owen doubted the townspeople even knew how to cause a ruckus. That's why this place was perfect for him. Because he *definitely* knew how to cause a ruckus…and refused to do so. For Élodie's sake.

"Gus will take care of the horses." Owen's hired stableman might be wiry and full of jokes, but he was reliable. "Don't you worry about that." Owen reached the end of Élodie's braid, then pinched it between his fingers. With his free hand, he motioned for the pink ribbon, then thought better of it. "Hold still."

Contemplatively, Owen glanced around their quarters' humble kitchen. On the tabletop stood a lamp, a pair of books and the harness he'd been mending last night. Nearby lay an awl, a set of leatherworking tools and a few scraps of rawhide. Eureka.

A few ticks of the clock later, Owen stepped back. He gave a masterful flourish toward his daughter's hair. "All done."

"Really?" Élodie bit her lip. "You mean I can look?"

"After all that hard work I just did?" Owen crossed his arms over his chest. "I'd be plumb disappointed if you didn't."

With no further nudging, Élodie ran to her bedroom's cheval mirror—one of the few keepsakes she'd inherited from Renée. By the time Owen caught up to her, his daughter stood examining her pigtails with awestruck eyes. Carefully, she stroked her hair.

"These are nice, Papa!" Smiling, Élodie turned in a circle. She wrapped her arms around his middle, then squeezed. "Not even Maman could have done better! I'm sure of it!"

At Élodie's mention of her mother, Owen couldn't help feeling his heart turn over. Not for the first time, he wished he could give Élodie more. He wished he could give her the warmth and caring Renée would have given her.

Owen could be gruff at times. Taciturn. He knew that. Hell, the whole town knew that—all his friends and neighbors and customers alike—and had for years. Why else would Mrs. Archer and everyone else keep pestering him to get remarried?

Because they rightly loved Élodie and wanted the best for her. They wanted a *mother* for her, plain and simple.

Owen wanted that, too. But he refused to marry a woman he didn't love, simply to find a caretaker for his daughter. Besides, he was doing fine on his own. He'd mastered pigtails, hadn't he? He could wait to find someone of his own to love.

"What's wrong, Papa?" Élodie touched his arm, gazing up at him with concern. "You look so sad. Don't you like my hair?"

"'Course I do." Owen couldn't quite smile. But he could still reassure Élodie. So he did, as best he could. "And I'm not sad. I couldn't be—not with my favorite girl here with me."

To prove it, he gave Élodie's braid an affectionate tug. It had been a stroke of genius to bind those plaits with fine strips of rawhide *before* fastening the ribbons on top. He'd have to remember that trick for later, he told himself, for when Élodie moved on to even more elaborate hairstyles—ones designed to capture men's eyes and win their hearts.

At the thought of his loving, trusting daughter putting herself in a man's hands—any man's hands—Owen narrowed his gaze. He knew, more than most, the dastardly deeds men were capable of. He didn't want Élodie to be at the mercy of a scoundrel.

A scoundrel…like him. Like the man he used to be.

It took a thief to catch a thief, Owen reasoned. So it probably took a heartbreaker to stop a heartbreaker. That meant—

"Now you look scary, like a big black bear!" Élodie said.

Owen didn't doubt it. Thinking about his daughter's future left him feeling decidedly protective. And a little growly, too.

Thankfully, he had years ahead of him before he needed to worry about Élodie being courted by scurrilous beaux with questionable intentions. For now, his daughter was a ten-year-old innocent, well pleased with her appearance in the mirror.

"*You* look prettier than a field of flowers," Owen told her.

"See there? That was a very kind compliment. Thank you." His daughter swept into an elaborate curtsy—doubtless learned from the Morrow Creek ladies who'd taken her under their wing. "I can't imagine why Mrs. Archer insists that you have 'a heart of stone and no verifiable sign of a working smile.'" Playfully, Élodie grinned. "See how wrong she was?"

"At least about the heart. Mine's tin."

"*And* about the smile. I know I've seen it at *least* once!"

"Just once?" Owen asked. Could that be true?

Surely he'd smiled more than *once* in all these years…

"Well, your smile *almost* came out just then, too!"

Mischievously, Élodie poked him. Owen paused, struck by the frolicsome expression she wore. For an instant, he glimpsed the shadow of his own fun-loving tendencies in his daughter's impish face—and it worried him anew.

Could he have bequeathed Élodie some unstoppable bent toward ruination? Could Élodie, like her ne'er-do-well father, find herself drawn toward irresponsibly pleasurable pursuits? Or, just as alarmingly, toward irresponsible suitors?

If so, Owen didn't know how he would forgive himself.

Renée had rightly disapproved of Owen's less-than-admirable qualities. She'd considered him an imperfect husband—at least she had, once she'd gotten to know him better. His rakish and reckless tendencies were supposed to have been cured by their migration west. Unfortunately, Owen had never had a chance to prove himself to Renée—to prove he could be the good husband she deserved. And now, seeing Élodie behave so mischievously...

Well, it was like being visited by the ghost of his own past. A ghost who charmed freely, squandered its money, wasted its time and never quit laughing over its own carefree ways.

Owen frowned. Allowing those selfsame unfortunate traits to flourish in his daughter would be an affront to his wife's memory. However much he didn't want to admit it, Owen realized, he *might* need further help with Élodie, now that she was growing older—the kind of help only a good woman could provide.

Looking at his daughter as she danced out of reach toward the mirror again, Owen vowed he'd do what he could to get that help. Lord knew, the womenfolk of Morrow Creek were more than keen to give it.

Starting today, Owen promised himself, whatever suggestions they had for him, he would do his best to follow them. He'd listen closely to their chatter—even though it made his head ache sometimes—and try to glean whatever bits of feminine wisdom he could. For his daughter's sake, any sacrifice was worth it.

Turning to the kitchen table, Owen snatched up Élodie's canvas satchel. It contained her rag doll, extra clothing, books and whatever other necessities she might need at Mrs. Archer's. "Enough admiring your braids. It's time to leave."

Élodie frowned, as though wounded by his abrupt tone.

"We're late, *mon petit chou,*" Owen said in a softer voice. "Mrs. Archer will be wondering where we are."

And she'll never let me hear the end of my tardiness.

Sometimes it was downright tiresome living in one of the most wholesome and upright towns in all the territory. But an instant after Owen had that mutinous thought, Élodie smiled at him, and he found he didn't mind living a wholesome life all that much. Not if it was good for his little girl.

"That's what Maman used to call me," she said. "Isn't it?"

Owen nodded. *Mon petit chou* had been Renée's favorite endearment. She'd whispered it over and over again to their tiny daughter. Doubtless, he mangled the accent. But he didn't care.

"*Mon petit chou,*" Élodie repeated. She sighed. "It's so lovely. I wish I could remember hearing her say it."

Struck by her wistful tone, Owen felt his heart turn over again. He clenched Élodie's satchel. "I do, too. But I guess you'll have to make do with my version." In a deep, extra manly tone, he boomed, "Let's go, *mon petit chou!* Time's a-wastin'!"

Giggling, Élodie hurried to the door. Just like that, the wistfulness between them vanished—squashed beneath the weight of workaday responsibilities and the dependable routine Owen had established to keep himself on the straight and narrow.

God forbid any disruptions to that routine should crop up. He didn't know how he would fare without the tether of good habits to rein him in. He didn't want to find out, either.

For now, though, distractions weren't a problem. As long as Owen stuck with his proven routine for him and Élodie, they never would be. He felt absolutely sure of it.

Chapter Two

Near Flagstaff, Arizona Territory June 1883

Standing in the middle of the private train car that her manager, Conrad Parish, had helpfully engaged for the Western portion of her speaking-engagements tour, cookery-book author Daisy Walsh rocked sideways. She nearly toppled. Flustered, she righted herself, rearranged her skirts, then lifted her chin.

"What do you think?" she asked. "Will this do?"

In the plush seat across from her, Conrad did not look up. He *did* continue reading his newspaper, though. He gave every impression of being more interested in the happenings of the day than in Daisy's question. That was typical of him. Conrad liked to do one thing at a time—and to do it flawlessly. She'd simply have to bide her time until he was ready to attend to her.

Still swaying in the moving train car, Daisy waited. Conrad's hat sat at a jaunty angle, she noticed. His suit fit perfectly. His shoes were spotless, even though the train car's floor decidedly wasn't. Gallingly, Conrad seemed unaffected by the wavy, ocean liner–like effects of train travel. As far as Daisy knew, he hadn't experienced a moment's queasiness during their months-long cross-country excursion together.

Daisy wished she could say the same. Just a quarter hour ago, she'd lost her battle to keep down her meager breakfast of toast and coffee. Recovered now, Daisy shook out her blue-gingham dress. She smoothed her bustle. Unfortunately, even that much vigorous motion brought on a fresh wave of nausea. She needed to get Conrad's approval on today's attire quickly, before something regrettable happened.

Conrad hated it when she was ill.

"No one wants to be subjected to someone else's sickness," he'd told her, not unkindly, the first time she'd found herself struck by that fearsome nausea. "*Try* to be a little stronger, won't you? Everyone at Barker & Bowles is depending on you."

"I know they are." Panting, Daisy had nodded, even as her belly had roiled. She hadn't wanted to disappoint anyone who was relying on her—least of all poor, beleaguered, patient Conrad, whom she knew had her best interests at heart. He hadn't asked to be assigned to her speaking-engagements tour—a job which, given that it dealt with home keeping and cookery, certainly wasn't in Conrad's area of interest. "I'll try harder. I promise I will! Just please, don't tell Mr. Barker or Mr. Bowles about my travel sickness. I don't want them to think they chose the wrong woman to represent them on the speaking tour."

"Well…I'll do my best," Conrad had promised her.

But the doubt in his usually self-assured voice had made Daisy feel even queasier. Because she simply couldn't fail. Not now. Not after Barker & Bowles, the renowned publisher, had selected *her,* unbelievably, out of hundreds of students at New York City's School of Cookery. They'd singled out *Daisy,* of all the other eligible candidates, to author and promote the *New Book of Cookery and General Home Keeping: with Recipes and Formulas for All Occasions, Both Informal and Grand.*

Wobbling anew in the rocking train car, Daisy put her hand on the seat back to steady herself. Outside the window, flat terrain flashed by, dotted with scrubby bushes and faraway mountains. The Western territories were austere, compared with New York. She wasn't sure she liked them. She *knew* she disliked Conrad's cigar, which he puffed idly as he read his newspaper.

"I'm quite fond of this blue gingham," Daisy said,

daring to nudge him into acknowledging her. This wardrobe-checking routine was tiresome, but Daisy had to accede to Conrad's greater experience in these matters. He hadn't guided her wrong a single time, not through her entire sold-out series of engagements. "Or would you prefer the green plaid?"

Frowning, her manager finally glanced up. His gaze flicked over her. "Maybe. That blue dress makes you look a bit stout."

"It does?" Concerned, Daisy looked down at herself. The blue gingham *did* strain a bit over her midsection. Probably she'd been eating too much rich food at hotel restaurants and the like. She *had* been on her speaking tour a while now....

"It might not be the dress." Conrad's scrutiny increased. He even lowered his newspaper. "It might be your figure."

With a practiced eye he took in her appearance, seeming to glimpse beneath her dress and petticoats and stockings, all the way to her skin and flesh and bones beneath. Standing alert for his necessary inspection, Daisy felt herself flush. Most likely, Conrad *could* imagine the way she appeared while naked. After all, there had been that one impetuous time when they'd—

Well, *that* had never happened again. And never would.

It didn't bear thinking about.

"Come now, Daisy. Don't look so churlish. You'll ruin your attractiveness with those frowns." Her book-tour manager tsk-tsked, his voice interrupting her thoughts. "You know I don't *enjoy* criticizing you this way. It's my job. My responsibility."

She inhaled deeply. She nodded. "I understand."

"This wouldn't be necessary if you would obtain a firmer grasp of what suits you and what doesn't. For example—"

"Will this dress do or not?" Feeling her stomach lurch, Daisy clutched the seat more tightly. She didn't like to interrupt, but these were special circumstances, and Conrad had appeared on the verge of launching into a full-blown lecture, besides. "We'll be at the next town soon, and I'd like to review my speech, so—"

"Yes. You *do* have that regrettable habit of forgetting which ladies'-auxiliary group you're addressing. You probably should review your speeches a bit more carefully in the future."

With effort, Daisy bit her tongue. She'd only made that mistake once. The error had occurred because she'd been unable to sleep in her rocking train berth. Ordinarily, she had a fine memory. But she'd traveled to so many towns lately…

She could use a break, it occurred to her. For the past several weeks, she'd felt unusually weary— even to the point of growing teary eyed at times.

Fortunately, after the next speaking engagement, Conrad had promised Daisy a much-needed reprieve: two whole weeks free to visit her brother, Thomas.

She missed Thomas. She hadn't seen her elder brother since he'd emigrated west last year, but they'd always been close.

"It wouldn't hurt to review your recipe techniques, too." Conrad tapped ash from his cigar out the train window. "You made a mistake last time. The huckleberry pie was much too soggy."

"It was still delicious!" Daisy protested, emboldened by the thought of her imminent break. She'd promised Thomas she'd bake him all manner of treats—items he didn't have ready access to as a bachelor newspaper editor at Adam Crabtree's *Pioneer Press* in Morrow Creek. "Every bite disappeared!"

She shouldn't have argued with Conrad, though, no matter how eager she was for her time with her brother. Arguing with her tour manager only brought on lectures…and disapproval.

Daisy hated being the subject of disapproval. Knowing she'd disappointed someone else made her feel awful.

Predictably, Conrad's stern expression met hers. "If *you'd* possessed the judgment to discern that pie's quality yourself, Barker & Bowles would not have hired *me* to monitor you."

Miserably, she hung her head. Conrad did have a point.

"You need guidance and supervision, Daisy." Conrad tapped his cigar again. "Even more than most females do, I'm afraid."

He made her sound downright hopeless. She believed she was capable. Evidently Barker & Bowles did not. Not yet. But they would, Daisy vowed, before she was through. In the meantime…

"Ugh. You're not going to *cry* again, are you?" Conrad wagged his finger. "As I've told you before, the fact that you feel so prickly over my helpful remarks only demonstrates that you need to grow a thicker skin. I merely wish to enlighten you—to give you the benefit of my greater wisdom and proficiency."

Of course. He'd mentioned that to her before. Maybe, despite Daisy's misgivings, Conrad was right. Clearly, Barker & Bowles held her book-tour manager in the highest esteem. The men in every town they visited patted him on the back and bought him drinks to earn his favor. The ladies at her speaking engagements fawned over him, too. It didn't seem possible that all those people were wrong about Conrad, and Daisy alone was right.

That's why, although bothered by his blunt opinion, Daisy pressed her lips together to hold in another rebuttal.

"In any case, you should cook something else next time." Conrad eyed her tightly fitting dress again. His brows drew downward. "Maybe a healthful soup. No more pies for you."

Because of her "stout" figure, Daisy realized, and felt newly embarrassed. Even on the most personal level, it seemed, she was lacking. If she were to have any hope of remedying the problem, she'd better listen to Conrad.

At that, another wave of nausea assailed her. Oh, no.

"Excuse me," she blurted. "I'm so sorry!"

Conrad frowned. Then, doubtless prompted by her ashen complexion, he scrutinized her more closely. In a tone of mild disgust, he asked, "Are you going to be sick again?"

With a panicked nod, Daisy lifted her skirts. She rushed to the train car's rear door. It would certainly not be ideal to dispel the residual contents of her stomach between the rolling, swaying cars as they raced along the tracks. But faced with the alternative prospect of being sick in front of Conrad…

She'd rather give up huckleberry pie forever than live with the memory of Conrad's censorious gaze for the rest of her days.

"Don't worry. We'll continue this discussion later,"

Conrad called after her. "And this time, when you're sick, don't get your dress dirty!" He gave a clucking sound of displeasure. "We don't have the funds for such frequent laundress expenses."

Daisy scarcely heard the last of his admonishments. She yanked open the train-car door, felt the cooling whoosh of the fresh morning air as it buffeted her, heard the rattle and clang of the train wheels against the track…then was violently ill.

Daisy was still clinging to the railing when she heard the train-car door open again. Gratefully, she glanced up. She hoped Conrad had arrived with a cup of water or a clean handkerchief for her. Sometimes, he was kind and thoughtful and caring. She'd experienced it herself, during their earlier days together.

To her relief, Conrad *did* have a handkerchief. But he pressed it to his own nose, making a moue of distaste as he did.

"Feeling better now?" he inquired.

Shakily, Daisy nodded. She couldn't *wait* to get off this train. She sorely needed a break from her motion sickness. By now, all that kept her going was the hope of seeing Thomas soon.

"Good. Because of your tiresome argumentativeness just now, I neglected to make a necessary announcement, Daisy." Her book-tour manager lifted his chin, wearing an inscrutable expression. "I received a telegram from Barker & Bowles at the last station. I've been reassigned to a more prestigious speaking tour."

She blinked with surprise. "Reassigned?"

"Yes." Conrad gave her a gentle pat, as though rewarding her for mimicking his pronouncement. "We'll change trains in Flagstaff, after your next speaking engagement. This means there won't be time for your little sojourn in Morrow Creek, of course." He scanned the countryside as it flashed past them. "It's too bad, really. We'll probably pass within a few dozen miles of the place."

A few dozen miles. That's all that separated Daisy from her brother? She'd already promised Thomas she'd visit. She'd so been looking forward to seeing him! How could she pass by so close and not see him? It was unthinkable.

"But you *promised,* Conrad! You said I could visit—"

"I'm afraid priorities must be attended to."

"*Your* priorities, you mean."

He appeared surprised—and displeased. "This matter is closed. The decision is made. I'd suggest you align yourself with it." Conrad narrowed his eyes. "I would hate to have to deliver an unflattering report to Barker & Bowles, just when you're on the brink of being assigned a new manager. It would be…unfortunate if Barker & Bowles decide you're not worth the trouble of continuing your speaking-engagements tour."

"I understand." Reluctantly, Daisy nodded. Pensively, she gazed at the barren landscape. "I'll do my best to acquiesce."

Conrad nodded. "You always do. In fact, your compliant nature is one of my favorite qualities about you!"

He beamed encouragingly upon saying it, as though the most wonderful thing she could offer him was her compliance—and likely, in his mind, it was. Then Conrad returned to the train, leaving Daisy standing alone at the railing, wondering…

Was acquiescence really the best policy here? And if it wasn't…what else was she supposed to do?

Chapter Three

Hurrying along the raised wooden planks that formed the sidewalk along Main Street, Élodie Cooper listened to her high-buttoned shoes clomping along. They sounded funny, like horses' hooves, and she gave an extra kick and a jig, pretending to be a pony in a parade, all decked out in a braided mane and ribbons.

"Élodie! Watch out for the mud," her papa instructed.

Reluctantly, Élodie abandoned her next flight of fancy. She'd been intending to squash her shoes in the next mucky spot, just to experience the squish and slide of it. She liked moving. She liked *doing*. She liked feeling that she was exploring, like an adventurer from a storybook. She didn't even mind getting dirty…sometimes. But today, her papa appeared so somber—even for him—that she tamped down her usual interest in seeing how far she could slide. Instead, she walked like a proper girl.

Then, quickly bored with ordinary propriety, she walked like a very fancy lady, with her nose in the air. Élodie held up her arm, the better to wield her imaginary fringed parasol. Then, bored with that too, she tried walking like a saloon girl.

Fancifully, she pushed her skirts to and fro. She batted her eyelashes, giving the passersby wide, winsome smiles.

"Élodie," Papa asked, "are you feeling all right?"

"I'm fine, Papa! Just fine," she assured him.

"Good. I thought maybe you had a pebble in your shoe."

He meant because of her sashaying, side-to-side walk, Élodie reckoned. "Nope! I'm just excited to get to Mrs. Archer's place. We're planning a surprise today, at Mr. Walsh's raffle!"

Breathlessly, she peeked at him, wondering if he'd catch her hint. But her father only took her hand, then kept walking.

Élodie didn't mind. Soon enough, Papa would realize the truth—that she and Mrs. Archer had devised a clever plan to assure her papa's happy future. Today was the day that future was set to start happening, and Élodie could hardly wait.

Her papa's part-time housekeeper, Mrs. Sunley, had helped her and Mrs. Archer conceive of their clever plan. So had his laundress, Miss O'Neill, and his other neighbor, Miss Reardon.

All four women were very interested in making sure Papa was happy. Élodie thought that was mighty generous of them. Caring, too. But then, her papa *was* the best man in all the territory. *Of course* his friends and neighbors wanted him to be happy!

Although Élodie hadn't admitted as much to her papa, *the plan* was the main reason she'd requested her special pigtails today. Even though her braids had turned out a bit lopsided, with pieces of hair sticking out in a few places, she'd been well pleased with them. It was important to Élodie that she look her very best for this momentous occasion—for the event that would ensure her papa's future happiness. By the time she saw Papa at the end of today, he would be well on his way to his new contented life. Even if he didn't know it yet.

In response to Papa's knock, Mrs. Archer opened her front door and greeted Élodie's papa with a smile, then gave Élodie a wink.

"Are you ready for an exciting day, Élodie?" she asked.

"Oh, yes! I am!" Élodie vowed, nearly dancing in place.

Her papa entered the house. He had to angle his shoulders sideways to fit comfortably through the narrow doorway, with Élodie and Mrs. Archer trailing in his wake. As was his custom, Papa set Élodie's satchel on Mrs. Archer's front-room table.

"You have an exciting day in mind?" he asked politely.

Mrs. Archer waved. "Oh, you know… Just that *Pioneer Press* shindig down at the train depot. That's all. Right, Élodie?"

Eagerly, Élodie agreed. Her papa didn't seem to appreciate the significance of Mrs. Archer's comment. He only nodded, already seeming absorbed in whatever tasks he had to tend to.

"You have a nice time then," he said. "I'll see you later."

"At the train depot?" Mrs. Archer prompted, brows lifted.

But Papa only shrugged, still appearing preoccupied. He had big responsibilities, Élodie knew. He was never much for sociable small talk, in any case. Mrs. Sunley was of the opinion that Papa had been too long without the "civilizing effects" of "a good woman" and had forgotten how to engage in polite conversation.

Élodie had disagreed, on account that *she* was "a good woman"—at least in miniature—and Papa did talk with her. But all four of the older ladies had demurred. To a woman, they all believed Papa needed a wife. Sooner rather than later.

"I do hope you'll be there, Mr. Cooper. At the

train depot, I mean," Mrs. Archer hinted further. "It could be quite a scintillating event! Aren't you even the least bit curious to find out who's going to win the raffle drawing?"

Papa didn't even ask *which* raffle drawing.

"Nope. Not the least bit curious." In his usual somber but kindhearted way, he nodded at Élodie. "Behave yourself now."

"I will! Bye, Papa! I hope you'll come to the depot."

Élodie raised herself on tiptoe to kiss his cheek. Just as he always did, Papa immediately touched his clean-shaven jaw, as though trying to hold on to her kiss before it vanished. Élodie doubted Papa knew he did that. She'd mentioned it to him once, only to be greeted by a blank stare and a gruff fatherly denial.

With confident footsteps, her papa headed for the door. He didn't look back, but Élodie didn't mind. She knew he would miss her while they were apart. She didn't need a bunch of hugging and fussing to be reminded of it. That's what Élodie had told one of her friends from school one time, and she believed it.

Goodbye for now, mon petit chou, she imagined her *maman* saying to her, had she lived to see Élodie as she was now, growing tall and elegant.

It might have been nice, Élodie thought longingly, to have been fussed over once or twice. Just to experience it, in the same way she experienced mud puddles and rainbows and, every autumn, the first delicious apples of the season. Nothing more.

That wasn't so much to ask, was it?

The front door shut behind Papa. His footfalls clonked down the steps. The moment the sound dissipated, Mrs. Archer turned to Élodie with her hands pressed together. She gave Élodie a coconspirator's grin, her eyes dancing with anticipation.

"Well! He doesn't seem to suspect a thing, does he?" Mrs. Archer's smile broadened. "Not even after those hints I gave!"

Again, Élodie felt compelled to come to her papa's defense.

"Well, his mind is usually *very* full of chores and rules for good behavior." *Both Élodie's behavior and his own,* she suspected. "So I doubt there's much room for picking up hints. Papa has lots of important business to tend to, you know."

"Yes. As do we!" With a gentle hand, Mrs. Archer shepherded Élodie to her tidy kitchen, where their fellow schemers—Mrs. Sunley and the Misses O'Neill and Reardon—were already waiting by the stove. "Come along, then! There's more still to be done!"

Happily, Élodie complied. Grabbing her satchel, she took her place at the table with the other women. She wanted today's plan to go off without a single hitch. For Papa's sake.

And—just a smidge—for her own sake, too.

Because if this plan didn't work, Élodie didn't know what to try next. She was running out of ideas. Whatever else happened, she did not want to run out of hopefulness too…the way Papa seemed to have done. His happiness relied on this plan.

That meant Élodie *had* to succeed. No matter what.

At the train depot in Flagstaff, Daisy hurried along the platform, finished with her last obligatory talk. Things had gone well with the members of the ladies'-auxiliary club, but Daisy still felt troubled by the detour she *wouldn't* be making to Morrow Creek. She'd promised Thomas she'd arrive today.

"Perhaps I should send my brother a telegram," she ventured, trotting to keep up with her manager. "Otherwise, he's bound to wonder what's happened to me."

"I wouldn't worry too much about that." Conrad offered her a preoccupied smile. He peered at the railway schedule. "For all you know, he's forgotten about your visit altogether. You're not the center of the world, you know, Daisy. Here. Hold these."

He handed her a bundle of items—his overcoat, a pair of leftover cookery books that hadn't sold at the ladies' group she'd spoken to, a fancy placard advertising her talk and an easel to place the placard on. Wounded by his suggestion that her brother might have forgotten her, Daisy accepted them all.

Perhaps Thomas *had* forgotten her. He *had* been curiously evasive in his last letter, Daisy recalled, regarding his specific plans to meet her at the Morrow Creek train depot...

"Ah, yes. There it is!" Spying the correct train, her tour manager guided Daisy across the platform. Although ordinarily Conrad took pains to be gentlemanly, it didn't seem to occur to him to take back the items he'd entrusted her with. "Our train to San Diego awaits—and at the end of it, my new assignment!"

Silently, Daisy dogged his footsteps. She didn't want to lose sight of Conrad. He'd managed all their travel thus far, appropriately shielding her from the logistical and financial details. Women, he'd told her, weren't rational enough to manage such things for themselves. Barker & Bowles agreed with him. That's why Conrad made their travel plans and collected all her money himself, taking out his agreed-upon percentage, of course.

"Well?" Conrad prompted in a slightly perturbed tone. "Aren't you even going to ask me to whom I've been assigned?"

Halfheartedly, Daisy obliged.

"It's Astair Prestell!" Conrad crowed. "The man himself!"

Daisy recognized the name. Astair Prestell packed

lecture halls the world over. This was a momentous step up for Conrad.

"Congratulations!" Momentarily, Daisy forgot about her own concerns. She gave her tour manager a genuine smile. "That's certainly more prestigious than escorting a cookery-book author across the country."

"I'll say it is!" Eagerly, Conrad eyed the waiting train. "It's about time, too! I've slogged through the *worst* assignments while waiting for an opportunity like this one."

While Daisy pondered the potentially insulting implications of that statement, her tour manager boarded the train. Wholly unaffected by her undoubtedly creased brow and morose demeanor, he offered her his hand to help her up. Through force of habit, Daisy took it, still awkwardly holding on to the items in her possession as she ascended into the dimness of the train car.

Once aboard, she immediately felt faintly nauseated. The train wasn't even in motion yet! Whatever was wrong with her?

It was almost as though her entire being was rebelling at being denied an opportunity to visit her brother. But mutiny was hardly Daisy's forte. Wasn't her presence on the San Diego–bound train proof enough of that? If only she had more courage…

"You'll make sure Barker & Bowles assigns me a

new tour escort once we arrive in San Diego, won't you?" she pressed. "Perhaps my new escort will allow me to double back to Morrow Creek—to allow a short break before my tour resumes."

"Perhaps." Irritably, Conrad snatched away her placard, easel and unsold books, leaving her with his overcoat. "Frankly, Daisy, there's no point hectoring me about it. Once I reach San Diego and meet Mr. Prestell at the Horton House Hotel, you and your cookery book won't be my problem to deal with anymore."

Surprised, Daisy gaped at him. She was…*a problem?*

Grudgingly, Conrad's expression softened. "I'm sorry. I really should try harder to remember how oversensitive you are."

Daisy lifted her chin, trying her best to rise above that flaw. Instead, she only demonstrated another one: stubbornness. "I want to go to Morrow Creek, Conrad. I promised I would, and I'm going to." Clearly, she had to look out for herself from here on. "So if you'll give me my allotment of today's speaking fees, please, I'll just disembark and buy my own ticket."

Her first attempt at independence didn't go well.

"Give you your 'allotment'?" Conrad chuckled. "Impossible."

"It's my money, isn't it?" Daisy crossed her arms.

"And I'm capable of buying a train ticket. I'm a grown woman."

"You're not acting like one. You're acting like a petulant child." Conrad spoke in measured tones, as though rationing out his patience by the dollop. He sighed, shaking his head. "Don't be daft, Daisy. You won't last a day without me telling you where to go and what to do. You know that as well as I do."

"Are you refusing to give me my earnings?"

Conrad's expression of incredulity was impressive. "Yes. I couldn't forgive myself if you spent the whole lot on bonnets."

"Bonnets?" At that, her book-tour manager finally pushed her too far. Squaring her shoulders, Daisy lifted her chin. "I have enough bonnets, Conrad. What I don't have is freedom—the freedom to keep my word to my brother!"

Fueled by righteous indignation, Daisy headed for the train car's door. She reached it. Still holding Conrad's overcoat—and all of the day's earnings she'd tardily realized were still in its pockets—she yanked open the door.

She might regret this...but she'd regret staying put even more. She knew that now. Thomas was depending on her!

"Goodbye, Conrad," Daisy said, feeling quite magnificent and brave and giddy as she did so. "And good luck to you!"

She stepped through the opening, onto the platform.

As she landed, unsteadily, she couldn't imagine what the future might hold. But it had to be better than this—better than broken promises. Better than criticism. Better than lies.

Better, even, than the sight of Conrad's startled face, gawking fishlike at her through the window. Upon glimpsing his patently surprised expression, Daisy almost laughed.

An instant later, the train left the station.

For the first time ever, she was entirely on her own.

Chapter Four

Standing in the shadowy recesses of his stable, Owen drew in a deep, hay-scented breath. He wiped his brow on his sleeve, then squinted at the busy street that fronted his business.

Outside, horses and wagons shuttled past, kicking up dust and causing a ruckus. Passersby dodged the traffic and went about their dealings, moving in groups of twos or threes. A scraggly-bearded man strode down the street with a clear sense of purpose, holding a half-full bottle of cheap Old Orchard whiskey and a copy of the *Pioneer Press*.

Hmm. That was, it occurred to Owen, the umpteenth copy of the newspaper he'd glimpsed today. That was peculiar. Because while Adam Crabtree's broadsheet was popular, it wasn't typically read by wild-eyed loners just in from the surrounding mountains. Owen had glimpsed at least a dozen such men—miners and trappers and vagabonds—in the few hours since noon.

All of them had been carrying copies of the *Pioneer Press.*

Curious about that anomaly, Owen gave the horse he'd been grooming a few reassuring words, then a pat on the withers. The beast shifted, then nuzzled him with its big old head. The gesture caught Owen off guard. It almost made him smile.

Then a pair of customers rode into the stable, looking for boarding for their horses, and Owen forgot all about that foolish notion, lickety-split. Owen didn't need smiling. He needed money to ensure Élodie's future. Money to make certain she'd never rely on a wastrel like him. Money to protect her.

Money to be there if Owen couldn't be…the way Renée couldn't be. He couldn't risk Élodie's future for anything.

The only way to get that money was to work hard for it. Fortunately, today had brought an unusually large number of people to his stable—people like the two men waiting for him.

Briefly, Owen considered wondering about the uptick in his stable business, then dismissed the idea. Things generally picked up in summertime. That wasn't uncommon. When the weather was agreeable, people liked to get out. They liked to travel and visit the neighboring towns, where they required boarding for their horses during their overnight stays.

Even Mrs. Archer, he recalled, had a trip coming up soon. She'd be leaving Morrow Creek to visit her sister in Avalanche, she'd warned him, and wouldn't be able to watch Élodie. He'd have to make other arrangements for the duration of her absence.

Too late, it occurred to Owen that he *hadn't* made such arrangements yet. Damnation. He'd grown accustomed to relying on Mrs. Archer for Élodie's care. But surely another of the women in town would look after his daughter for him. It was rare, indeed, that any of the local ladies refused Owen a favor.

One of the men tipped his hat. "Afternoon. You Cooper?"

"I am." Owen nodded. "What can I do for you?"

"I'll need a night's boarding." The man dismounted, then withdrew something from his saddlebags—a much-read copy of the *Pioneer Press* newspaper. An impressive firearm swung from the holster on his hip. "Maybe more, if I win the raffle." He winked. "With my luck, I'm bound to win it."

"The hell you are!" The man's companion—sporting a pair of shooters himself, along with a sheathed knife—waved his own creased and folded copy of the *Pioneer Press*. "I aim to win *me* that bride for a week! I plan to work her but good."

His friend gave a ribald chuckle. "That's my

idea—to put my bride straight to 'work.' But I reckon she'll like it."

At a loss to figure out what they were talking about and not liking their bawdy tone, Owen frowned. "Mind if I see that broadsheet of yours?" He held out his hand. "I haven't been following the raffle, but you've made me plumb curious."

"Not at all, Cooper. You aiming to enter the drawing?"

Making a noncommittal sound, Owen took the newspaper. Whatever was going on in town today, it had to be described in the paper. If Owen didn't miss his guess, it had to be Thomas Walsh's doing, too.

When that scholarly easterner had assumed editorship of the *Pioneer Press,* he'd instituted some pretty outlandish changes. He'd launched some crazy promotions and contests, too. But none of those schemes had been as nonsensical—and as potentially harmful—as the "raffle drawing" Owen read about next.

He handed back the man's newspaper. "Thanks for the loan of your broadsheet. My helper will take care of your horses."

With a shout, Owen summoned Gus. His stableman came at a run. Gus ably assessed the situation, then promised to take charge of the horses and ensure they were stabled properly.

"Much obliged, Gus." Owen grabbed his hat from its hook. He stuck it on his head, then nodded a goodbye to his latest customers. "Gentlemen—" On the verge of saying more, Owen stopped. *Good luck* would have been polite and expected, but he couldn't muster up the sentiment. Not given what he now knew about the raffle drawing—and these men's intentions toward its "prize." Instead, Owen settled on, "May the best man win."

Then he headed out to the train depot to find that addle-headed fool, Thomas Walsh, and put a stop to these shenanigans before someone got hurt—or worse.

It was a good five miles of steady train travel before Daisy realized that Conrad wasn't going to follow her. He wasn't going to follow her, stop her, berate her or even try to sweet-talk her out of going to Morrow Creek. Instead, he was simply going to… let her muddle along on her own, with nothing to rely on but a middling dose of courage and the paltry earnings she'd cadged from her manager's overcoat.

Brazenly wearing that selfsame overcoat right now, Daisy gazed out the window as the territorial scenery passed by. The train had changed course a while back, moving from forested terrain to craggy bluffs and back again. Now, the fast-moving landscape outside her window appeared dappled in shades of green and blue and brown, filled with majestic ponderosa pines and distant mountains. The sky hung cloudless overhead.

Its expansiveness gave Daisy a sense of dizzy possibility. She didn't know where that opportunity might lead her, but she was hoping for the best. Already, she'd managed to purchase a train ticket and board the correct train. She hadn't done either of those things before—not out west, at least. The fact that she'd succeeded so far emboldened her. Conrad couldn't stop her. No one could. She was going to see Thomas, and that was that.

If her parents or friends could have glimpsed her just then, Daisy thought as she put one hand in the overcoat's big pocket to assure herself her money was still there, they would not have believed their eyes. Everyone knew that Daisy Walsh was naturally easygoing—*too* easygoing, some would have said. Daisy rarely refused a favor and even less frequently said no. But today, Daisy had learned exactly where her boundaries lay.

Her boundaries lay at her family. At Thomas. And at being refused a chance to see her brother when she'd already made a promise to him. Truth be told, Daisy felt a bit astonished at her own behavior, even now. Earlier this morning, she would not have believed herself capable of defying Conrad and striking out on her own. She would not have been able to conceive of a situation where she would *want* to do such a thing.

Now everything had changed. From here, the only thing to do was to just keep going…and to hope for the best, besides.

Chapter Five

Torn between outright worry and gleeful exuberance, Thomas Walsh paced across the crowded
train-depot platform in Morrow Creek. By now, he
knew, Daisy should have arrived. The first westbound train had already come and gone. There'd
been no sign of his sister aboard it. He hadn't had a
letter or a telegraph wire contradicting their plans,
either. So where was she?

Wondering exactly that, Thomas peered through
his spectacles at the train track. Not even a puff
of smoke drifted along the horizon, foretelling the
imminent arrival of the next train. All that stood
between him and the apparent raw edge of the territory were dozens of Morrow Creek residents, a large
quantity of festive bunting, several painted signs and
the town's amateur musical troupe, which Thomas
had employed to—

Well, the specifics of the greeting he'd arranged

for Daisy didn't bear thinking about right now. The important thing was, everything had gone off without a hitch…even if it *had* gotten a bit out of hand, the way things sometimes did for Thomas.

He didn't really mind that, though. The plain truth was that the festivities surrounding him were responsible for his current state of exuberance. He'd pulled off another coup at the *Pioneer Press!* Since he'd begun writing about the imminent raffle drawing, circulation had gone up over two hundred percent. The presses were working overtime. Thomas—and his boss, Adam Crabtree—couldn't be anything but cheerful about that.

At least *he* couldn't…until he spied a certain broad-shouldered, dark-haired, dauntingly familiar Morrow Creek resident moving toward the depot: the livery-stable owner, brawny Owen Cooper. Owen surveyed the assemblage through his unnervingly perceptive gaze, joined the throngs on the platform, then examined the crowd again, clearly searching for someone.

Whoever it was, Thomas felt sorry for them. Owen's presence was naturally intimidating. The man was pleasant to him—if a bit reticent. Still, it was impossible to mistake the stable owner's assured stance, agile movements and sheer strength for anything less than what they were: elemental shows of raw, male primacy. Women felt that dominance; men respected it. Even Thomas, whose naturally high spirits suddenly felt somewhat quashed by Owen's presence, had to admit he was intrigued by the man.

Curiously, Thomas leaned sideways for an improved view. He watched avidly as Owen stalked through the assemblage. If not for the fact that Owen was a devoted father and a capable businessman, it occurred to Thomas he might have feared the man. As it was, he *liked* his neighbor. He had no reason to—

Oh, no. Owen turned his head. He'd spied Thomas.

He squared his shoulders and headed directly for him.

Gulping back an apprehensive breath, Thomas made himself hold his ground. Surely Owen Cooper had no quarrel with him! During his time in Morrow Creek, they'd scarcely exchanged more than pleasantries on the street. More than likely, the stable owner didn't even know who Thomas was. Not precisely. That meant that his formidable gaze couldn't possibly be directed at Thomas himself. There had to be someone nearby him. Someone else, who—

"Walsh!" Owen's voice boomed across the platform.

Thomas discovered an urgent need to be elsewhere. He swiveled, searching for an escape route. But by now, more than a few inquisitive Morrow Creek residents had stopped what they were doing to watch the unfolding drama between their eastern newspaper editor and their steadfast local stable owner.

"Walsh!" Owen's sure-footed strides rapidly consumed the space dividing them. Their neighbors scattered to make way, but he didn't seem to notice. "Don't pretend you can't see me, Walsh. I have a bone to pick with you. I intend to be heard."

One of the women near Thomas nudged her companions. The three women exchanged avid glances, the kind of glances filled with feminine interest and fluttery flirtatiousness that Thomas himself, as a bookish editor, rarely received. The realization discouraged him. Why should Owen Cooper have all the fun?

Bravely Thomas turned to confront the stable owner. Instantly, he realized exactly why Cooper had all the fun—at least in a manner of speaking. The man might not be prone to frivolity or chitchat, but he *was* handsome, tall and probably possessed of a decent income, thanks to his thriving stable business. No wonder the women in town were all aquiver over him.

Not that Cooper appeared to notice. Neither did he appear to discern the respectful glances he drew from the men on the platform, all of whom watched their exchange with interest.

Nervously Thomas smiled. He'd fought hard to be

respected here in Morrow Creek. He didn't intend
to back down now. "Mr. Cooper!" he exclaimed. "I
didn't think you were coming down to the depot for
today's celebration. What can I do for you?"

"You can call off this harebrained raffle drawing.
Right now."

Thomas blinked. That was the last thing he'd expected to hear. "Call off the drawing?" he repeated.
"But I can't possibly—I mean, so much has gone
into it! The signs, the band, the bunting… Surely
you can see how much effort I've put in."

Vigorously, Thomas gestured at the ever-increas-
ing crowd. When Daisy arrived and saw all the
hoopla he'd arranged for her, she'd be downright
thrilled. He just knew it. He loved his younger sister. He wanted dearly for Daisy to be happy.

"If you go through with this raffle drawing," Owen
said in an unwavering tone, "I guarantee you'll regret it."

"Wh—" Feeling dry-mouthed, Thomas yanked his
collar. Owen probably didn't intend to be so scary,
he reminded himself. The man couldn't help looking so big and tough. At least he sounded civil. So
far. "Why would I regret it? Exactly?"

"Because your little 'bride raffle' drawing has
pulled in every unsavory character from here to
Tucson." Owen's signifying nod encompassed everyone on the depot platform. "You must have noticed

them—they're the ones carrying whiskey bottles down Main Street, packing six-shooters and looking for trouble."

"Trouble?" Thomas swallowed hard. He glanced around the platform, looking for those rabble-rousing gate-crashers whom Owen had mentioned. He felt certain all of a sudden that Owen Cooper was the kind of man who recognized trouble when he saw it. Even though, as far as Thomas knew, Owen had never been in a lick of trouble himself. "They're looking for trouble?"

"Or for a 'bride for a week,' whichever comes first." Hard-faced, Owen gestured at a nearby sign. "That's what you promised to raffle off, isn't it? A woman who would behave like—"

"Like my *sister!*" Thomas interrupted. Fraught with nervous tension, he waved his hands, giving an anxious chuckle. Clearly, Owen Cooper had misunderstood this event. "I promised to raffle off a series of lessons from my sister, Daisy Walsh! You know—the renowned home-keeping expert and cookery-book author?"

Owen appeared not to be familiar with Daisy's métier or reputation. His dark brows only drew down even farther. "Some of the men have...*misinterpreted* what you're offering."

"I don't see how that's possible. I've been writing about Daisy for weeks now." Thomas felt relieved to know what the problem was. "I'm duly proud of her, of course, and, well, one thing led quite naturally to another. Before I knew it, I was fashioning a contest to coincide with her arrival here in—"

"A 'contest.'" Owen's uncompromising stare made Thomas feel suddenly uneasy. "With your *sister* as its prize?"

"You make it sound so…insalubrious!" Thomas laughed. He dared to poke Owen in the ribs, man-to-man style. He nearly dented his finger in the process. Owen didn't so much as crack a grin. "I didn't mean any harm by it. I'm sure Daisy will approve of the raffle drawing, once she gets here. Speaking of which, where in the world is that train? The next one should be—"

Owen didn't care about the vagaries of train travel. "What safeguards do you have in mind? For your sister's safety?"

"Safeguards? I can't imagine needing any. This is Morrow Creek! We all know one another. At most, Daisy will need protection from all the eager women who won't win the raffle drawing but will nonetheless want lessons from her."

At his quip, the ladies nearby nodded. A few of them even carried treasured copies of the *New Book of Cookery and General Home Keeping: with Recipes and Formulas for All Occasions, Both Informal and Grand,* which they'd brought to have autographed by Daisy. Any one of them, Thomas knew, would be thrilled to be tutored by his sister in the home-keeping arts.

Patiently, Owen waited for Thomas to look at him again. Then he asked, "What if a man wins the drawing instead?"

"A man?" Thomas blinked. "Why would a man want to win a series of cooking lessons? Men don't cook. For myself, I mostly have dinners at my boardinghouse kitchen or at the Lorndorff Hotel. I imagine most bachelors in town behave similarly."

"You're right," Owen agreed, jutting his jaw pugnaciously. "The men I'm talking about aren't interested in cooking."

Thomas reckoned that proved his point nicely. "Then it goes doubly that they wouldn't enter the drawing, doesn't it?"

"You can't honestly believe—" With apparent frustration, Owen broke off. He glanced at the ladies nearby. "You can't be that naive, Walsh. We should discuss this in private."

"Why?" Feeling better now, Thomas met the stable owner's gaze squarely. "If you're suggesting my *sister* would behave in anything less than a perfectly respectable fashion, then…"

Then I'll have to defend her honor. Somehow.

Thomas gulped, hardly thrilled with the idea of engaging in fisticuffs. While he was very skilled at editing, he was not typically the sort of brutish, hands-on man who started brawls.

"I'm not suggesting anything of the kind." Thankfully, Owen kept his hands relaxed at his sides. He didn't appear ready to deliver a sockdolager yet. Perhaps, despite what appeared to be a natural skillfulness at intimidation, the stable owner was not a born brawler either. "You're not listening."

Was Owen Cooper gritting his teeth? Thomas didn't know and just then he didn't care. Because as he stood there trying to decide, he heard the distant wail of a train whistle. It must be Daisy's westbound train, he reasoned. It was almost here!

"I'm listening," Thomas said. "And what I'm hearing is that *you* wish you'd entered the raffle drawing! But don't worry, Mr. Cooper. It's not too late. There's still plenty of time to slip your name in the raffle box. In fact, I'll see to it myself!"

"I don't want to win anything," Owen insisted. "All I want is for this tomfoolery to be ended, before it's too late."

"Too late for what?" Thomas joked. "For you to enter?"

Owen Cooper shut his mouth. He gritted his teeth so hard, they ought to have shot sparks from his clenched jaw.

Well, that answered that question. For whatever reason, Owen was opposed to Thomas's raffle drawing. But the event had to go on. Thomas refused to alter his grandiose plans now.

"I thank you for your opinion, Mr. Cooper. I truly do." In a peacekeeping gesture, Thomas held up his palms. "But I believe your worldview is a tad more...*dismal* than mine. I have faith that no one will enter into the raffle drawing inappropriately."

"Is your 'faith' going to keep your sister safe?"

Thomas frowned, having no answer to that. As it turned out, he didn't need one. Miss Reardon, one of his part-time typesetters at the *Pioneer Press,* came forward. Protectively, she wrapped her hand around Thomas's arm, startling him.

"You stop being such a spoilsport, Owen Cooper!" Miss Reardon raised her chin, appearing, it occurred to Thomas, quite magnificent in her kindness and courage. "Just because *you* always believe the worst of everyone doesn't mean it's right!"

Owen lowered his voice. "Is that so?"

Miss Reardon quailed. Then, even more magnificently, she rallied. "I'm afraid it is. You know how fond I am of you, Mr. Cooper, but a fact's a fact. You're a hard man, no mistake."

Owen tipped his hat. "I'm very sorry to have upset you, Mellie. I didn't mean to." He nodded at Thomas. "Walsh."

The stable owner turned, then headed for the other end of the train-depot platform. Feeling contrite and suddenly warmed all over by Miss Reardon's unexpected friendship, Thomas waved.

"Wait, Mr. Cooper!" he called out in a burst of goodwill. "Don't you want to meet the lady of the hour?"

Owen Cooper's unyielding gaze met his. For an instant Thomas thought he glimpsed a certain... *loneliness* in the man's face. It was affecting, even to a man who'd formerly feared him. But then Cooper scowled more deeply, the women surrounding him nonetheless swooning quite openly, and Thomas quit feeling sorry for him altogether. Owen Cooper didn't need his sympathy.

Owen Cooper didn't need anyone's sympathy.

He wasn't likely to get it, either—not with his set-apart ways, growling attitude and suspicious manner of thinking.

"My sister, I mean," Thomas clarified, cheerfully gesturing toward the incoming train. "Miss Daisy Walsh! Cookery-book author and home-keeping expert extraordinaire!"

Cooper held up a hand, then kept walking. "Not today."

Not ever, his demeanor said. But Thomas decided that was just as well. The unapproachable Owen Cooper paired with his sweet, innocent, kind-to-a-fault sister? It would be disastrous.

Watching the stable owner leave, Miss Reardon

put her head close to Thomas's. She smelled like—lilacs, he realized giddily.

"I think yours is a *wonderful* idea!" she opined with another squeeze of his arm. Confidingly, she added, "I still think you should enter Mr. Cooper's name in the raffle drawing, too."

Thomas smiled. "Oh, I intend to," he said.

Then he hastened to the raffle box to do exactly that.

Chapter Six

Something unusual was happening in Morrow Creek, Daisy realized as her train pulled in. There were crowds gathered at the depot. Banners and gay bunting decorated every surface. A small band even stood at the edge of the platform with their musical instruments at the ready, waiting for a signal from their bandleader.

Perhaps there was someone famous on the train! Eagerly, Daisy scanned the faces of her fellow travelers as they gathered their belongings and prepared to disembark. She hadn't noticed anyone of prominence when she'd boarded the train, but she'd been justifiably preoccupied at the time. Now, with a clearer head, she examined the passengers more closely.

So, it seemed, did the people waiting on the platform. Moving as one body, they surged closer, faces upturned to the train car's windows to catch a glimpse of…someone. Someone *very* important, by the look of things. Daisy still didn't know who. This must be the sort of greeting Astair Prestell received on a regular basis, she decided. How wonderful that must be!

Still curious about the hero's welcome that was going on outside, Daisy headed for the train car's exit. When she reached it, the bright sunshine outside momentarily blinded her. She stopped, awash in sunlight, and removed the overcoat she'd filched from Conrad. She folded it, then slung it over her arm.

"Look!" someone yelled. "There she is!"

Reflexively, Daisy looked around. The person of importance everyone was here to greet was a woman, then. That was even more impressive. In her experience, women weren't lauded much.

"Daisy! Over here!" someone else shouted.

Except *that* voice was familiar. Could it be… Thomas?

Daisy turned her head, squinting against the vivid Arizona Territory sunshine as she searched for her brother. At the same moment, the band began playing a rousing tune. The banners and bunting flapped in the breeze. The people on the platform pushed even closer to the train, chattering and calling out.

This was quite a welcome! The lady nearest Daisy, she noticed, waved a book in the air. So did the lady beside her. That book was…the *New Book of Cookery and General Home Keeping: with Recipes and Formulas for All Occasions, Both Informal and Grand?* But that was certainly strange. Why would someone bring her cookery book to greet a famous person?

Before Daisy could quite make sense of it, Thomas popped up from between two of those book-toting ladies. He came forward. At once, his beloved face seemed both as familiar as Daisy had remembered and as subtly altered as she'd anticipated. He looked a bit older than she remembered, of course. And also, to her gratification, much, much happier. Evidently, living in the Wild West agreed with him. So did abandoning his razor.

"Thomas! You have such big whiskers!" Daisy blurted.

"Yes. They're all the rage here." Abashedly, her brother rubbed his sideburns. "And *you*— Let me look at you!" Grinning from ear to ear, Thomas took her hands in his. He stepped back a pace, examining Daisy as she stood on the train car's steps. He sighed, shaking his head. "You're a sight for sore eyes, Daisy."

"No, *you* are." Suddenly feeling quite overcome, Daisy hugged him to her. Tears pricked her eyes as she felt her brother's lean, familiar frame in her arms again—as she felt his fine wavy hair against her cheek. In that moment, her journey to reach him felt very long, indeed. "I've missed you *so* much."

She'd been too long without her family, Daisy realized. Too long without the kind of simple joyfulness that being with Thomas brought her.

"But *what* is all this fuss about?" Speaking in a fascinated undertone, Daisy released him. She allowed Thomas to escort her down the train car's steps to the platform. The people nearby moved back to give them room. "I imagine there was someone famous on the train? There *must* have been, given all this!"

She gestured at the signs, the banners, the band.

"Yes! Isn't it wonderful?" her brother exclaimed. "You're right, too—there *was* someone famous on the train."

Thomas gave an impish smile, his face creased in that very particular way she remembered, the way that foretold mischief of some kind. Her brother had a long history of getting in over his head with some project or other. Daisy couldn't imagine what sort of project he might have embarked upon here in the Arizona Territory. Nonetheless, she felt her stomach somersault in anticipation of whatever her brother would reveal next.

"I guessed as much," she confided. "It must be someone very well-known, too." She wondered why they weren't yet walking across the platform, headed for Thomas's boardinghouse room or maybe a nearby restaurant or hotel. Then she realized that her brother undoubtedly wanted to glimpse Morrow Creek's famous visitor, too. "It's funny that we've arrived on the same train, isn't it?" she asked him. "Do you know who it is?"

"You truly can't guess?" Thomas asked, full of devilry.

"I honestly can't." Inquisitively, Daisy looked around. "Don't keep me in suspense, though! I'm as interested in famous figures as the next person. By the time you quit this guessing game, she might already have left the train depot."

She craned her neck, searching more diligently.

"I assure you, she will not have left the train depot."

"How do you know that? Honestly, Thomas, you're being so mysterious all of a sudden. If you don't want to tell me—"

Her brother chuckled. "It's *you,* of course! You, Daisy!"

"Me?" Baffled, Daisy looked around again. At once, those welcome banners seemed slightly surreal. They did, upon closer inspection, bear her name, she realized dazedly. So did the painted signs hung on the bunting-decorated depot building. That implausible sight, combined as it was with the presence of the nearby women who toted copies of her cookery book… Well, the situation seemed plain all of a sudden, if a bit ridiculous.

Stupefied, she said, "But *I'm* not famous, Thomas."

"Of course you are! You're a published author, aren't you?"

Only by the grace of Barker & Bowles…and their representative, Conrad Parish, Daisy knew. "Yes," she agreed.

"And you're a popular, respected home-keeping expert who's spent nearly the past year on a sold-out, cross-country speaking-engagements tour, aren't you?"

A tour that's suddenly come to an unexpected and abrupt stop, Daisy recalled guiltily. "That's true," she agreed. "But—"

"But nothing. I won't hear any more disagreement." Proudly, Thomas puffed out his chest. He hooked his thumbs in his suit vest. "There's no denying that your public is interested in meeting you, especially here in Morrow Creek. See?"

As proof, he gestured at the crowd. At the painted signs. At the band. As though interpreting his movement as a request, the players launched into an even more rollicking tune. All of them watched Daisy while the band played, eyes sparkling. Even the brass-instrument players, with their cheeks puffed

full of air, seemed downright overjoyed to be playing in Daisy's honor.

"If this isn't a welcome fit for a famous person,"
her brother said, beaming, "then I certainly don't
know what is!"

"But..." Daisy swallowed past a new lump in her
throat. She clutched Conrad's stolen overcoat, feeling like a veritable hoaxer. "But I don't deserve all
this, Thomas. Truly, I don't."

"You're the famous Daisy Walsh! You *do* deserve
it!"

Even as Daisy tried to come to terms with that notion, an unfamiliar woman pushed her way through
the assemblage. Dark-haired and vivacious, she took
her place quite confidently next to Thomas. Gently,
she took his arm, then smiled at Daisy.

"Thomas simply wants everyone to know how
proud of you he is," the woman said. "He's been
writing about you for *weeks* in the *Pioneer Press,*
you know. We're all quite familiar with you."

"I feel as if I know you!" another woman put in.
"Already!"

"Me too!" a third woman agreed, waving her
book. "Mr. Walsh printed several of your recipes
in the newspaper, and I've made every last one!
Those dishes were absolutely delicious!"

Overwhelmed, Daisy smiled at them. But her

knees felt shaky, and that old enemy, queasiness, threatened her, too.

More people pressed in, all of them eager to meet her.

Standing by, almost buffeted by the crowd, Thomas gazed at Daisy kindly. Then he seemed to remember the woman at his arm. Hurriedly but generously, he made the necessary introductions.

"Daisy, I'd like you to meet Miss Mellie Reardon." He indicated the dark-haired woman. "And her friend, Miss O'Neill."

Miss O'Neill was the second woman who'd spoken up. Holding fast to her cookery book, she gushed, "We can't *wait* for the raffle drawing! It's going to be the event of the year!"

"Raffle drawing?" Daisy asked, increasingly mystified.

"Yes. The welcome party isn't the only surprise I've arranged for you!" For the first time, Thomas appeared slightly unsure of himself. He shifted in place. "You see, thanks to all my high praise of you and your book in my newspaper, you have quite an avid following here in Morrow Creek."

Uncertainly, Daisy bit her lip. Conrad's earlier warning echoed in her ears: *You won't last a day without me telling you where to go and what to do. You know that as well as I do.*

"And, well, one thing led quite naturally to another! So when you decided to come to Morrow Creek for a visit with me—" Thomas seized her hands again. His gaze pleaded with her to understand. In a rush, he said, "I sort of, very *accidentally,* arranged to raffle off a series of lessons with you, with the prize to go to one lucky winner in town."

"Lessons?" Daisy asked. "With me?"

"Lessons. With you." In an adorably abashed fashion, her brother ended his hasty speech. Still clutching her hands, he peered into Daisy's face as though gauging her reaction.

Unfortunately, Daisy felt too dumbstruck to speak.

"Do you mind?" Thomas said. "I'm so sorry, Daisy, if this is too much to ask of you. After all, you are here for a family visit. So if you'd rather not do this at all, I understand."

Indecisively, Daisy gazed at her brother. He seemed so hopeful, caught on such tenterhooks, that she couldn't bear to refuse him. Especially not in front of all his friends and neighbors. Especially not in front of Miss Reardon!

If Daisy didn't miss her guess, that lively brunette was enamored of Thomas. But her brother appeared utterly oblivious to Miss Reardon's tender feelings for him.

Perhaps Daisy could remedy that while she was here.

"Of course I'll do it!" she announced. As ever,

her most natural reaction was to acquiesce. "How could I say no to you?" She hugged Thomas again, dearly hoping she'd be able to succeed at this tutoring commitment. "Where do I begin?"

"At the raffle box! It's just this way."

Her brother led everyone to a homemade raised dais at the edge of the depot platform. He tipped his hat to Daniel McCabe, the muscular-looking handyman who'd apparently helped erect that dais, then proceeded to take his place beside the raffle box. Gaily embellished with bunting and bright paint, possessed of a single ballot box–like opening in its upper quadrant, it stood locked and ready. Giving Daisy a grin, Thomas brandished a key.

The band played a rousing fanfare. The crowd applauded.

Daisy fought back a surge of butterflies. She hoped the possessor of the winning raffle ticket was hopeless in the kitchen. She hoped the winner was inexperienced and kind, the better to disguise whatever shortcomings she herself might reveal.

If Conrad had been there, he would doubtless have enumerated them. As it was, Daisy felt all too aware of them already. Apprehensively, she glanced at the gathering crowd. It was composed not only of women, she noticed abruptly, but also of men— men who watched the raffle drawing with every bit as much interest as the book-wielding ladies did. Perplexed by that fact, Daisy scrutinized the crowd more closely. A surprisingly large number of Morrow Creek residents appeared to be scruffy, surly, largely unkempt males of all sizes and ages and degrees of cleanliness. They hardly appeared capable of holding a cookery book without smudging the pages, much less reading it.

Could they *truly* have entered the raffle drawing too?

Newly ill at ease, Daisy smiled at the nearest of those men. He grinned back at her, revealing a mouthful of gaps where his teeth ought to have been. But poor dental hygiene was not a character flaw, she reminded herself. He was probably a fine man. A man who was…currently making a rude gesture at her?

Shocked, Daisy averted her gaze. But now that she'd noticed that objectionable gesticulation, and the man making it, she couldn't help observing other things about the raffle entrants…such as their overall air of familiarity with her.

Even as she watched Thomas unlock the raffle box, Daisy sensed several lecherous gazes following her every move. It seemed that Morrow Creek, which had appeared such a lovely little town at first glance, was chockablock with indecent men!

If one of *them* won the raffle drawing, she didn't know how she would manage. Couldn't Thomas see the problems inherent in his plan? Or was he, as a good and gentle man himself, simply blind to the impropriety that nearly froze Daisy in place on the dais?

Please draw a woman's name, Daisy prayed as her brother reached into the raffle box. *Please draw a woman's name.*

With a flourish, Thomas withdrew a ticket. The band members beat an anticipatory tattoo on their drums. The crowd hushed.

"And the winner," Thomas proclaimed, "is…"

Smiling, he glanced at the ticket. Then he scowled. Daisy's heart plummeted to her knees.

"Is," her brother gamely went on, "Owen Cooper!"

An excited murmur whooshed through the crowd. "Fortunate bastard," someone grumbled nearby. "Of all the lucky sons of—"

But Daisy didn't hear any more. Aware only that her home-keeping expertise had been raffled to one of those vulgar men for goodness only knew what purpose, she turned to her brother for support and guidance. Before she could get either, she handily fainted dead away on the spot.

Chapter Seven

Impatiently, Élodie pushed her way through the crowd at the train depot. While Mrs. Archer had been perfectly content to remain at the rear of the platform whispering something about remaining "inconspicuous" for a while, Élodie couldn't *wait* to catch a glimpse of the woman of the hour: Miss Daisy Walsh.

Like Misses Reardon and O'Neill, Élodie had followed the coverage of Miss Walsh's work in the *Pioneer Press.* So had Mrs. Archer and Mrs. Sunley. To a woman, they'd all agreed that her arrival in Morrow Creek presented a perfect opportunity to change things for the better for Papa and Élodie.

Eager to seize that opportunity, Élodie jumped up on her tiptoes to see what was happening. Ahead at the dais, the newspaper editor waved a raffle ticket. He spoke loudly and proudly. "And the winner is…" A pause. "…Owen Cooper!"

Excellent. Everything was proceeding according to plan. Élodie smiled, then glanced over her shoulder. As she'd expected, Mrs. Archer had followed in her wake. The two of them maneuvered through the crowd. Élodie had a slightly easier time of it, though, since she was smaller and sprightlier.

That's why she was first on the scene—first to see Daisy Walsh, standing in a green plaid dress. Élodie couldn't glimpse her face, but she could see that Miss Walsh's hair was blond. It was arranged at the back of her head, twisted and pinned in a simple style. She had a curled forehead fringe, Élodie noticed.

She came closer, then ducked between two women…just in time to see Miss Walsh go down!

A lady nearby cried out. Everyone surged forward. Élodie couldn't see a thing. Alarmed, she dropped to her knees, then crawled the remaining few feet, heedless of any potential damage to her skirts. Her knees bumped along the platform. She squeezed between a pair of onlookers, then scrambled to her feet.

Mr. Walsh, the newspaper editor, had caught his sister as she fell, Élodie saw. He cradled her in his arms even now, looking concerned. For her part, Miss Walsh only sagged against him in a clearly insensible state. Her limbs were unmoving. Her face, framed by her fetching forehead fringe, looked pale.

Ghostly pale. Élodie stopped short, startled at the sight.

For a moment, an awful thought occurred to her. Was Miss Walsh *dead?* Had being raffled off to Papa actually *killed* her?

Perhaps being with Papa was deadly to a lady, Élodie reasoned fearfully. After all, her own *maman* had not survived being with Papa. Élodie should *never* have agreed to this plan!

"Make way, everyone." With authority, Mrs. Archer arrived. She traded knowing glances with Miss Reardon, Miss O'Neill and Mrs. Sunley, then dropped to a crouch beside the newspaper editor and his sister. Mrs. Archer's gaze passed over Miss Walsh. Whatever her impression of the cookery-book author, she kept it to herself. "Well done, Mr. Walsh! You've behaved quite heroically on your sister's behalf." She nodded to the bystanders. "Everyone else, please give us some air."

Obediently, their friends and neighbors shuffled backward.

Impressed, Élodie nodded. A tiny bit of hopefulness bloomed inside her, wrought by Mrs. Archer's usual competence. She would make certain that being with Papa wasn't fatal. Élodie knew it.

"Miss Walsh?" Mrs. Archer inquired gently. She

gestured for Mrs. Sunley to fan the woman. "Miss Walsh, can you hear me?"

Miss Walsh's eyelashes fluttered. She gave no other sign that she heard Mrs. Archer. Frowning, Mr. Walsh gave his sister a gentle shake. If he'd hoped to revive her, it did not work.

A man nearby chuckled. "Looks like Cooper won himself a dud!" he joked. Liquor fumes pervaded his breath. "He won't be getting no useful wifely duties from a woman like that one."

"Be quiet, fool!" Miss O'Neill snapped. But as she crouched beside Mrs. Archer—and also fanned Miss Walsh with a folded copy of the *Pioneer Press*—her expression turned grave. "He's right, Matilda. We may have made a mistake," she confided to Mrs. Archer. "Look how delicate she is! Only a few minutes here in town, and already she's plumb keeled over! She'll never do."

Miss O'Neill let loose a dissatisfied *tsk-tsk*. Élodie glimpsed Miss Reardon, standing at the ready, wringing her hands as though unsure what to do. For once, she was not making cow eyes at Mr. Walsh. Élodie didn't know how the newspaper editor couldn't see that Miss Reardon was sweet on him. Everyone else knew it. It seemed likely to Élodie that getting silly for a man while his sister was conked out on a train-depot platform was an endeavor doomed to failure. Perhaps Miss Reardon had finally come to the same sensible realization.

"No. She'll have to do." Mrs. Sunley delivered her doubtful friend a quelling glance. "She might be puny and weak, but we knew we were getting a bookish easterner, didn't we? That was all part of the plan."

Puny? Weak? That was uncalled for! Unexpectedly, Élodie felt quite protective of Miss Walsh. After all, she'd fainted. She could hardly defend herself. Belligerently, Élodie stepped forward. "*I* think she looks nice! And pretty! Not weak at all!"

At Élodie's outburst all four of her women friends looked at her. They sighed. Then they dropped their pointed gazes to the fallen, insensible Miss Walsh. *Puny,* those gazes said. *Weak.*

"She'll do," Miss Reardon said. "If she were any better, we'd run the risk of this situation becoming...*permanent.*"

They all frowned, displeased by that idea. Their plan, Élodie knew, was for Miss Walsh and her homemaking expertise to reawaken Papa's appreciation for womenfolk...and to remind him how nice it might be to have a lady in his life full-time.

Once he remembered all he'd been missing, Papa would quite logically turn his sights to one of the marriageable ladies in Morrow Creek, Mrs. Archer had explained to Élodie. He would settle down with one of them—after Miss Walsh conveniently left town, of course—and Élodie would have a mother again.

It would be easy. And wonderful. Provided Miss Walsh woke up. Maybe she was too puny to inspire Papa's manly devotion.

"Daisy? Daisy!" Mr. Walsh moaned. He appeared beside himself with worry and altogether indifferent to the women's uncomplimentary talk. "Oh, what have I done? It was only a raffle!"

"It was a very wonderful raffle," Miss Reardon assured him. "Don't worry about a thing. I'm sure your sister will be fine."

Trustingly, Mr. Walsh nodded. His spectacles gleamed in the summer sunlight. He stroked his sister's face, his gaze full of love and distress. He was dedicated to her, Élodie realized. Any woman who could stir up such affection simply *must* be good.

That boded well for Élodie. And especially for Papa.

She began to feel excited about *the plan* again.

"Yes," Mrs. Archer added. "But we must get Miss Walsh out of this dizzying sunshine and into someplace cooler and calmer."

Instantly, Élodie recognized her cue. They had not planned this part. But there was only one possible thing to say.

"My papa's quarters above the stable are cool and

calm," she volunteered in her most innocent tone. "And Papa is the winner of the raffle drawing, too. Why don't we take Miss Walsh straight there."

Chapter Eight

Even by midafternoon, Owen had not forgotten what Miss Reardon had said about him on the train-depot platform.

Just because you always believe the worst of everyone, she'd declared indignantly, *doesn't mean it's right!*

She'd called him a "hard man," too. A *hard* man! That, coupled with Thomas Walsh's reaction to Owen's questions about the raffle drawing, had left him feeling irritable—and puzzled.

Why was *he* the only one in town who was suspicious and untrusting enough to want to shut down the raffle?

Everyone else saw no problem with the event. That much had been unmistakable from Thomas Walsh's perplexed looks. But Owen saw myriad problems— all of them stemming from men's baser natures… natures he was all too familiar with. He'd certainly given free rein to his own freewheeling faults more than a time or two.

Renée had thought she could save him from those faults, Owen recalled as he ushered the last of his boarding horses into a stall and shut the gate behind them. She'd certainly enumerated those faults to him often enough. And she'd done her best to stamp out Owen's "reprehensible character," too. But maybe his wife had been wrong. Maybe, even given more time than she'd had, Renée couldn't have saved Owen. Not from himself.

Maybe, despite all his efforts, he was beyond redemption.

Weighed down by the notion, Owen strode the length of his stable, double-checking all the horses. The beasts nickered. A few nosed him as he passed by. He found a sweet word and a pat for each one, feeling a little better as he made his rounds.

At the end of the last row, he spied Gus. "I'm closing up early," he told his helper. "Stable's full, thanks to all the thieves and miscreants in town today. If you're done watering and feeding all these beasts, you can go on home."

Gus eyed him skeptically. "Is this a trick?"

Owen frowned. "Have I ever pulled a trick on you?"

"Far as I know, you ain't never pulled a trick on nobody. You're as straight-arrow as they come. Fact is, it wouldn't go down too poorly if you cut yourself loose once in a while."

Owen liked hearing that. That meant he'd done well.

"The fella I used to work for woulda had himself a conniption if I'd gone home afore dark." Gus squinted at the sunshine streaming in. "Near as I can tell, it ain't dark yet."

"Well…" Owen thought about it. Blandly, he gazed at Gus. He shrugged. "There's always horse droppings to be shoveled. If you'd rather work all night, I won't stand in your way."

"I was joking!" Gus shook his head. "Tarnation, boss. You're about as much fun as an undertaker with a rash."

Owen only gazed at him. Work wasn't supposed to be fun.

"I know, I know. Don't say it—'Hard work today makes for peace of mind tomorrow.' So you've told me. Over and over."

Owen habitually told Élodie that, too. It was essential she understood how important hard work and good effort were. Until Élodie was capable of seeing to her own well-being, Owen meant to ensure the most providential future for her himself.

It was the least he could do. He wasn't the most effusive of fathers; he knew that. He loved Élodie; he loved her to the stars and back. But Owen didn't know if he loved her *enough*—if he loved her the way she deserved…the way Renée would have loved her. Just as insurance, Owen meant to give Élodie all the material blessings he could. That way, his own *petit chou* wouldn't be too handicapped by not having a *maman* in her life.

He crossed his arms. "If you don't like it, don't stay."

"All right! You don't need to tell me twice." His helper grinned, then jabbed his pitchfork into the nearest hay pile. "I ain't one of those numbskulls out there, all cowed by your stone face and tree-trunk arms, you know. I seen you with Élodie a time or two. And if you ain't the sweetest, taffy-pullingest—"

"I'm changing my mind about that manure shoveling."

"No need to break out them crazy eyes. I'm going." Still smiling, Gus grabbed his hat. He stuck it on his head, then hastened for the doorway. He saluted. "Tell Élodie hello for me. And tell her I hope her plan went down without a hitch, okay?"

Owen nodded. Gus probably meant the shindig down at the train depot. Élodie *had* been all keyed up about it this morning at Mrs. Archer's. Likely, Mrs. Archer and her lady friends had made a fuss over Thomas Walsh's raffle-drawing brouhaha, and Élodie had been swept up in all the excitement. It was only natural. Élodie didn't have any other feminine influences. She had to look to Mrs. Archer and her friends for guidance.

Now that Élodie was getting older, it occurred to him, she would need even more feminine guidance—help in taking on such things as sewing, cooking, cleaning and embroidery. Owen might have darned a pair of socks a time or two, but he was ill equipped to teach his daughter any of those necessary home-keeping skills. When he sewed, his big, blunt-tipped fingertips got tangled in the thread. When he—infrequently—cooked, he turned out griddle cakes, pots of beans with charred edges or bakery-bought toast. When he cleaned—well, he rarely cleaned, beyond necessary tidying. Mrs. Sunley did all the scrubbing and scouring herself, as part of her housekeeping duties, and Miss O'Neill took care of Owen's and Élodie's laundry.

That left him with embroidery. Imagining himself trying to practice that intrinsically feminine art, hunched over a wooden hoop with his resolute gaze fixed on a nightshirt or some such, Owen shook his head. Likely, he'd embroider his trouser leg to his nightshirt, then gash holes in both garments while trying to free himself with his trusty jackknife—the only implement he ever found truly handy in his ramshackle "sewing kit."

Renée had embroidered like an angel, he remembered, feeling sobered by the recollection. Renée would have taught Élodie all manner of stitchery. She'd embellished Owen's handkerchiefs with fancy French monograms. She'd commemorated their wedding by putting up a set of fine pillowcases. But that good bed linen had been lost on the journey westward, and over the years, Owen had grown as comfortable with plain cotton linens as he had with cactus patches, flat Western dialects and lonesome fatherhood.

Reminded of Élodie, Owen glanced at the closed door through which Gus had exited. Élodie would be tickled if Owen fetched her from Mrs. Archer's place early today. Deciding to do just that, he gave the closest horse one last pat. Then he headed upstairs for a washup and a fresh shirt, the better to fetch his daughter without also affronting her nose.

Cheered by the thought of seeing his little girl again, Owen took the stairs two at a time, headed for that washup, stripping off his sweaty shirt as he went.

Snugly tucked into an unfamiliar bed, being ridiculously fussed over by an assortment of unfamiliar but very sociable women, Daisy sighed. She wanted to catch Thomas's eye. She wanted her brother to step in and put a stop to all this commotion, since her own protests had gone nowhere. But at the moment,

Thomas appeared to be engaged with an animated Miss Reardon in one corner of the room. He didn't seem capable of noticing anyone else.

Wistfully, Daisy watched her brother and Miss Reardon. She couldn't help feeling entranced by them. The look of adoration in Miss Reardon's eyes appeared quite naked…and quite profound, too. It must be wonderful to be looked at in such a way, Daisy thought. It must be wonderful to be listened to, as Thomas was being listened to just then, as though happiness began and ended with the sound of your voice and the content of your thoughts.

Whatever it took, Daisy *had* to make sure her brother didn't fritter away his chances with Miss Reardon. But for now…

Well, for now, Daisy had to decide how to cope with this unexpected situation. Her cookery and homemaking expertise had been raffled off to one lucky winner. The commandeering Mrs. Archer had instructed everyone to bring Daisy to the home of that as-yet-unmet winner, Owen Cooper. And no one except Daisy had disagreed with that plan. So now it was done.

Daisy had been unable to protest with any efficacy as she'd been shepherded, woozily, through the streets of Morrow Creek and brought here, to a modestly furnished but clean set of rooms above a flourishing livery stable on Main Street. So far, all she'd been able to glean about the mysterious Owen Cooper was that he was a stable owner, a widowed father and a "hard man."

This last bit of information, breathlessly conveyed by Miss Reardon, had done little to set Daisy's troubled mind at ease.

"Is he…respectable?" Daisy had ventured during their walk to the stable. "Is he kind? Is he *very* awful at cooking?"

She hoped he was dreadful at it, so he would appreciate her skills doubly. Also, she hoped he was old, feeble and wholly unable to follow through on the lewd gestures his townsmen had seemed so fond of making during the raffle drawing.

But surely Thomas would protect her from anything like that. Wouldn't he? Thomas would never knowingly put her in harm's way. He trusted his neighbors and friends—including Mr. Cooper. That meant, to Daisy's way of thinking, she could, too.

"I daresay Mr. Cooper is *atrocious* at cooking!" Mrs. Sunley had cast Daisy—and her unsteady posture—an assessing glance. She'd frowned. "But then, you never know. It's devilishly hard to discern these things just by looking at someone, isn't it?"

Miss O'Neill had elbowed her, a movement Daisy had felt plainly, on account that Miss O'Neill had been guiding Daisy with her other arm. To Daisy, Miss O'Neill had offered a smile. "I have no doubt

Mr. Cooper's prospects will be immeasurably improved by your arrival here in town, Miss Walsh. We're all looking forward to seeing Mr. Cooper... progress in that area."

At that, all four women—and the adorable little girl who'd accompanied them—had exchanged eager, knowing looks. Those looks had puzzled Daisy then and still did now. She took their cryptic glances to mean that Owen Cooper needed improvement in some area, but she couldn't imagine what it was.

"Won't he be upset to find me ensconced in his home?" Daisy had protested as the foursome—with Thomas's flustered help—had ushered her upstairs and into bed "for some much-needed rest and recuperation." "This is fairly intrusive—"

"Nonsense!" Mrs. Archer had interrupted. "He'll love it!"

"He'll be grateful," Mrs. Sunley had added. "What man *doesn't* like to come home to find a woman in his bed?"

Thomas, blushing, had pretended not to hear that remark. So had Miss Reardon, who'd busied herself with brewing a pot of coffee and offering a cup to "enliven" Daisy after her "ordeal."

Only Élodie had answered Daisy's question with candor.

"Papa won't mind. He's as even-keeled as the day

is long." The little girl had nodded, absently hugging a rag doll. Her gaze had traveled over Daisy's face with avid curiosity. "Papa doesn't get riled up, not ever. But he does swear sometimes."

On that note, improbably, Daisy had relaxed an inch or two. Of all the people she'd met today—excepting her brother, of course—she liked little Élodie the most. Any man who could single-handedly raise such a lovely daughter simply *had* to have positive qualities, Daisy reasoned. That made her feel immensely reassured about Owen Cooper.

After all, little Élodie was lively and smart, polite and outspoken and very sweet. She was also disarmingly keen to be near Daisy at all times, even to the point of carrying her coffee cup to her...and mimicking, with her own small tin cup of water, the precise way Daisy sipped the recuperative brew.

"I'm feeling much better now, thank you." Daisy set down her coffee cup and saucer with a rattle. "I honestly don't think I need to stay abed this way!" she told all the assembled women for what must be the tenth time in a row. "Surely there are things I could be doing to prepare for the first lesson. I did make a promise to Thomas, after all. The winner will surely be counting on me! The sooner I start working—"

"Don't be silly!" Mrs. Sunley bustled over, casting a hasty glance at the bedroom's open doorway. "The first lesson can wait! You've been through quite a shock, arriving here to such a fuss. Of course it overwhelmed you!" Firmly, Mrs. Sunley tucked her in more securely. "You should stay right there in bed until Mr. Cooper arrives. Then he's *guaranteed* to take to this idea instantly! I reckon, of all the men in town, Owen Cooper ought to be the *most* persuaded by finding a woman in his bed!"

At that scandalous statement, everyone stilled. Then…

"What Viola means, of course," Mrs. Archer hastened to say, giving her cohort a glowering glance, "is that Mr. Cooper is a generous man who would be happy to assist a lady in need. Any lady, any time, for whatever reason. Isn't that right, Abbey?"

"Oh, yes!" Miss O'Neill bobbed her head up and down. "Yes!"

Everyone else averred the same thing, even Thomas. Daisy knew she should have felt comforted. Yet something still niggled at her. Something Mrs. Sunley had said a moment ago…

"Is Mr. Cooper entirely amenable to being my student?" Daisy asked. She peered at Mrs. Sunley. "You said he'd be 'guaranteed' to take to this idea… but why would he need to be persuaded?" *With the sight of a woman in his bed, no less!* "Mr. Cooper *did* enter his name in the raffle, didn't he?"

To Daisy, entering the raffle would seem proof

enough of his willingness to learn—no further persuasion necessary. But at her question, all the women went as still as statues in a city museum. Then Mrs. Archer put one hand to the brooch at her neck, sucked in a breath and gave a choked little chuckle.

"Why, how *else* would he have won?" she asked.

"Yes!" Miss O'Neill parroted. "How else would he have won?"

Something about their odd demeanor put Daisy on guard. She squinted at the women, trying to figure out why their behavior bothered her...then gave up. Conrad had always told her she was an awful judge of character. She guessed he was correct.

"The only thing that matters is that my papa won!" Élodie announced. "When he gets here and finds out, he'll be so happy!"

Warmly, Daisy smiled at the little girl. She appreciated her efforts to be welcoming, but... "None of you answered my question," Daisy pointed out, surprising herself with her own tenacity. "Mr. Cooper *did* enter his name in the raffle, didn't he?"

At first, no one answered. Then, into the silence...

"He did *not* enter his name" came a decisive male voice.

Startled, Daisy glanced toward that sound. A very tall, very disgruntled-looking man stood in the doorway. He swept the jam-packed bedroom with an intimidating look, seemed to come to the conclusion that merely *looking* at everyone was insufficient to properly cow them, then growled out a second statement in a tone as deep as the one he'd initially entered the room with.

"Furthermore," he said, striding nearer, "he'd like to know what the *hell* you're all doing in his goddamn bedroom!"

At his multiple profanities, Miss O'Neill gasped. She crossed herself, then took a step back. Miss Reardon shuffled a bit closer to Thomas. Eagerly he took her elbow. Mrs. Sunley put her hands on her hips. Mrs. Archer stiffened her spine and hauled in another deep breath, evidently prepared to do battle.

Daisy had the sensation that Mrs. Archer did that often. But she registered all those details only at the most peripheral level. Because most of Daisy's attention—honestly, almost *all* her attention—was busy with the arresting sight before her.

Improbably, the man who'd just arrived was *naked* from the waist up. He was holding a bundled-up shirt. He was wearing his trousers with his braces lowered, allowing those trousers to dip scandalously low on his frame. He was…simply put, *stunning,* from his finely honed male musculature to his intriguingly dark chest hair to the faint sheen of sweat beading on his skin.

He was broad shouldered. He was tanned. And

although his face bore the marks of a battered life, those few imperfections couldn't mar his appeal. He was as fine a specimen of manhood as she'd ever seen, Daisy decided. Unlike his fellow townsmen, he was, she thought in a dither, neither lecherous nor slovenly.

He was…*fascinating.* Simply fascinating. His face, his eyes, his mouth… She felt compelled to stare, feeling almost as though, by doing so, she could *know* him somehow, could learn his secrets, his thoughts, his every wish and desire…

He caught her gawking. His frown deepened impressively.

Into the breach came Élodie. Fearlessly she charged ahead where everyone else evidently feared to tread. "Papa!"

Élodie ran to him, arms open. At that, Daisy's heart jumped in her throat. *Papa?* Papa! That could mean only one thing.

This was Owen Cooper. And *she* was in his bed. Oh, dear.

Chapter Nine

Still baffled by the goings-on in his bedroom, Owen gaped at the assemblage of people there. Hastily, he pulled on his shirt to cover himself, deepening his scowl as he did so.

Then Élodie ran into his arms, and he couldn't help relaxing. A little. But that didn't alter the strangeness of this situation—or change the fact that he wanted answers.

"Papa!" Élodie cried. "See? You won! You won the raffle!"

Owen hugged her. Then he released her, holding Élodie by her skinny shoulders. He looked into her beaming face, belatedly recalled all the coarse language he'd just used and vowed to do better the next time. If there *was* a next time he came upstairs to find an unknown woman lounging in his bed as if she owned it.

Confused, yet unable to look away from that compelling sight, Owen sneaked a glance past Élodie's head. Yep. The blonde was still there, just as pretty as she pleased, tucked into his ordinary bedclothes as though she'd been waiting for him to find her there…and had decided to do a bit of light entertaining with the womenfolk to pass the time until he came home. Stunned by that dreamlike image, Owen blinked. But the woman remained there, just as she had been when he'd entered his bedroom, looking sweet and friendly and inexplicably wholesome, to boot.

Why did it have to be his *bed?* Owen groaned to himself. *Why* did it have to be a woman in his bed, looking so pretty?

It had been so long since he'd had a woman between his sheets. He'd almost forgotten how mesmerizing the sight could be. But now, with the winsome Daisy Walsh snug in his bed, Owen remembered. Damnation, he remembered! And he wanted more.

Determined to refuse himself that much, of course, he tore away his gaze. He settled on skewering Thomas Walsh, that interfering newspaperman, with a scathing look instead.

"I told you I didn't want to meet your sister, Walsh."

Daisy Walsh flinched, obviously taken aback by his words.

Owen didn't know if that was because she was wounded by his bluntness or surprised that he knew who she was. But of course Owen knew. He was smart enough to add up the elements: one gala train depot homecoming, plus one idiotic raffle drawing, plus one luscious woman in his bed equaled heaps of big trouble for him.

Besides, a man didn't come home to find the meddlesome foursome of Mrs. Archer, Mrs. Sunley, Miss O'Neill and Miss Reardon ensconced in his bedroom without rapidly divining there was a plot afoot. Morrow Creek was rife with gossip about their exploits and troublemaking. The only trouble was, Owen didn't yet know how Thomas Walsh and his sister fit into all this. And speaking of the sister…

Owen felt his gaze lured again, nigh irresistibly, in her direction. She appeared to be pouting, comfortably, there in his bed. She was wounded, then. Well, pretty women often were a mite tetchy. He couldn't help that. That didn't explain why he *wanted* to help her feel better. Because, God help him, he did want to help her feel better. He knew he could do it, too. A long time ago, he'd been *excellent* at making the women in his life feel all kinds of wonderful.

Ruthlessly, Owen squashed down those memories.

"I—I—" the newspaperman stammered in response. Then he pointed at Mrs. Archer. "Matilda said we should do it!"

At his accusation, Mrs. Archer drew herself up, plainly readying herself to go toe-to-toe with Owen. But before she could do much more than draw in a deep breath, Élodie spoke up.

"Isn't it *wonderful,* Papa?" Her joyful voice filled the room. She tugged his sleeve to make him look at her, then grinned. "Miss Walsh can't stay with Mr. Walsh, on account of his living at the boardinghouse and its being unsuitable for a lady, but she can stay here, right, Papa?" Élodie gulped in a breath, her eyes shining with faithfulness. "It's perfectly proper, because I'll be here to chaperone. And I already told everyone that you're the nicest and kindest and most generous man in the whole entire territory! You would *never* turn away a lady. Especially a lady who's going to spend a whole week here, teaching us how to cook, and sew, and bake, and knit—"

Well, it occurred crazily to Owen, Élodie *did* need to learn some of those things. If he couldn't help this situation anyway, then what would be the harm in indulging in… No. *No.*

"Just a minute, Élodie." Finally, Daisy Walsh spoke up. "I don't intend to force my lessons on your father. Clearly, there's been some sort of misunderstanding here." Her gaze met Owen's directly and movingly. "I'm very sorry, Mr. Cooper. You seem almost as surprised by all this as I was."

Her gaze lingered on his. Her breath escaped her lips with a soft exhale. Her hands trembled just a bit with emotion. Upon hearing her voice, Owen felt riveted. Before, Daisy Walsh had been nothing but an anonymous female in his bed. But now...

Now she was a woman of flesh and blood and unknown character. For reasons Owen couldn't explain, he found that change fascinating. There was also the fact that, entirely against his will, his mind chose that moment to offer up a delightful scenario involving Daisy Walsh, him and a whole caboodle of time spent together in his bed, time during which she would whisper his name in that melodious voice of hers. Time during which she would urge him— beg *him*—to hold her, kiss her, slowly undress her and reveal all her secrets, one by one...

He blinked. *Why,* he wondered again, had they put such a lissome woman in his *bed?* It was downright evil. No man could be expected to resist such a powerful lure to the imagination.

Nearby, Mrs. Sunley adjusted her bustle, wearing a self-satisfied little grin. She hummed to herself. At that moment, Owen knew. Twice-widowed Viola Sunley undoubtedly recognized a thing or two about masculine nature.

Almost standing on his toes, Élodie gave Owen a worried frown. Puckishly, she grasped his jaw—the way she sometimes did—then forced him to meet her gaze. She gave a very grown-up sigh. "You don't seem happy, Papa. Are you very angry with me?"

"Angry?" Taken aback, Owen frowned again. "With you?"

Élodie swallowed hard. She hung her head. "Because *I* already knew you hadn't entered the raffle, even before you told us so. I knew because..." Another gulp. "Because *I'm* the one who entered your name. Please don't be upset!"

Astonished, Owen stared at her. "You did what?"

"I entered your name in the raffle. I know you didn't want to enter, but... But *I* wanted you to win! So I could maybe listen in on some of your lessons and learn something too. I'm getting older, you know, Papa, and one of these days—"

"You're going to want to embroider something." Owen nodded. He'd known this day would come. Maybe not so soon. But one day.

Élodie's face brightened. "Then you *do* understand!" She hugged him, burying her face in his midsection. "I'm so glad!"

Owen hugged her closer, feeling gutted at the notion that Élodie had felt she needed to behave underhandedly to get the home-keeping tutoring she needed. "You could have asked me."

"I know." Élodie exchanged a look with Mrs. Archer—a puzzlingly devious look. An instant later, her features smoothed into their usual adorable innocence. "But I didn't want you to feel that you had to teach me yourself. I'm *not* desperate to learn six ways to burn toast."

"It's fine if you scrape off the black parts." Gruffly, Owen surveyed the assembled women. "It's not *always* burned."

All of them smiled gamely, not believing him in the least.

Owen turned to Élodie. "This is really what you want?"

His daughter nodded, her gaze a solemn reflection of his own, but in miniature. "It really is."

"Then I'll make sure you get it." Taking Élodie's hand in his, Owen regarded Miss Walsh, doing his best not to imagine what she looked like beneath that coverlet. "Would you be willing to give my raffle prize to my daughter instead?" he asked. "To teach Élodie whatever she needs to know?"

Miss Walsh bit her lips…her sultry, soft-looking lips.

Hellfire. How was he supposed to withstand all this?

"Of course I would." Daisy Walsh nodded. Turning pink cheeked beneath his scrutiny, she cleared her throat. She smiled. "I can assure you, Mr. Cooper, that I'm more than qualified to do so. You don't have to concern yourself with that. I know how to cook, bake, sew, clean, mend, knit, dye, conserve, shop, plant, repair, economize and prepare simple tinctures. I was also top in my class in elementary barbering."

Her gaze settled, meaningfully, on his dark, shoulder-length hair. A certain gleam entered her eyes. Owen swallowed.

He might, it occurred to him, have overstepped with this.

"Well! That settles that, then," Mrs. Archer announced. She gestured at Thomas Walsh and the other women. "Congratulations again, Mr. Cooper. It was a pleasure to meet you, Miss Walsh. Come along, everyone! Let's leave this threesome on their own."

"You're leaving?" Yanked from her daydreams of lopping off Owen's hair, Miss Walsh gaped at the others. "Already?"

"Yes. You'll be fine," Miss O'Neill assured her.

She bustled nearer to give Daisy a hug, then a brisk goodbye. All the other women followed suit. Thomas's farewell was longer lasting, filled as it was with brotherly affection.

Owen watched the two siblings together, saying their goodbyes and making plans to see each other the next day. Thomas and Daisy's fondness for one other was evident. If Miss Walsh could engender those kinds of warm feelings—even from her stiff-seeming, scholarly brother—Owen realized, then she must be a good person. A person Élodie could safely learn from.

And a person *he* could safely board in his household…even taking into account her luscious lips and fascinating voice. There was no reason Miss Walsh's presence had to endanger Owen's plan to be a good man.

As his visitors made their way out, pursued by Élodie's cheerful calls of "Adieu! Adieu!," Owen relaxed a little. He hadn't expected this to happen today. But it had. And it was what his daughter wanted. He could manage it—for Élodie's sake.

At the doorway, Thomas Walsh eyed Owen. "It looks as though you were right, Cooper—at least about the way the raffle drawing would go. You're the last person I expected to win."

"Better me than one of those reprobates who've come into town." Sincerely, Owen offered the newspaperman a handshake. "Don't worry." He nodded toward Miss Walsh. "I'll watch over her."

"You'd better." Walsh nodded, then put on his hat. To Daisy, he promised, "Remember, I'll be only a few blocks away."

With approval, Owen noted Walsh's protectiveness of his sister. Soberly, he nodded to him. As the door shut behind the last of their visitors, Élodie skipped off to her own bedroom to fetch something, leaving Owen alone with Miss Walsh.

"Well, I guess we'd better get started then, hadn't we? I've been idle long enough!" Nimbly, Daisy threw off the coverlet, her manner eager but businesslike. She swiveled, then sat up. Self-consciously, she fluffed his feather pillow to its former loftiness. "I've asked Élodie to bring me one of her dolls to dress," she explained. "That will give the two of us a good starting point for sewing lessons, without proving too overwhelming for an initial project."

As though keen to leave his bedroom and get started, Miss Walsh stood. She pushed herself up from the bed with one hand on the mattress—and the other hand protectively cradling her abdomen. Riveted by that revealing gesture, Owen went still.

In that moment, everything became a thousand times more complicated. Because Owen *recognized* that gesture. He'd seen it in his wife, over and over again. During the months before Élodie had been born, Renée had often laughed over her inability to quit cradling their daughter, even before she'd arrived.

Daisy Walsh was pregnant. And unmarried. And on her own.

And now she was with *him,* at least temporarily.

Chapter Ten

As he and Daisy ventured into his front room, Owen frowned, thinking that perhaps he'd misunderstood. But no—she'd been introduced to everyone as *Miss* Walsh. She wore no wedding ring. She'd mentioned no husband. And surely no husband worth the designation would allow his wife to live in another man's household, however briefly. Would he? Owen's mind whirled with questions—beginning with wondering where the father of *Miss* Walsh's baby was and ending with…wondering where the father of her baby was. What kind of man would leave her alone this way?

As far as Owen knew—as far as Thomas Walsh had explained to everyone in Morrow Creek—his sister had been touring the country for months now, appearing at a series of speaking engagements.

"In the meantime," Miss Walsh went on, oblivious to his jaw-slackening revelation, "I guess we ought to have ourselves a proper introduction, oughtn't we? I'm Daisy Walsh, of course, but I'd be pleased if you would call me Daisy while I'm here."

She extended her hand, her fingers slim and capable.

Owen stared at them, his heart thudding with surprise.

He blinked. "Call me Owen, Daisy." Obligingly, he took her hand. It felt oddly at home in his. "Congratulations to you."

"Congratulations?" Confused, Daisy wrinkled her nose. She smiled. "But *you're* the winner here, Mr.—Owen, not me."

She gazed down at their joined hands, seeming… captivated by that union. With an abrupt motion, she jerked away her hand.

After her hasty withdrawal from their handshake, Owen's grasp felt doubly empty. But that was nonsensical. He didn't need to touch her. He didn't *need* to feel her warmth.

Except he did. Warmth flowed from Daisy Walsh to everyone around her. He'd noticed that about her right away. Like a springtime sun ray, she seemed capable of thawing even the most frozen of hearts… hearts like Owen's. Or like Owen's might have been, he acknowledged, had he not kept such a close grip on it.

"I mean," he clarified, thinking he'd probably been

too abrupt before, "congratulations on your…imminent arrival."

She appeared genuinely baffled. "My what?"

"Your baby," Owen clarified. "You're going to have a baby."

Now Daisy Walsh seemed genuinely gob smacked.

Owen gave a genial wave toward her midsection. In a good-natured imitation of her, he pantomimed cradling his flat belly. "My wife used to do the same thing, before Élodie was born. Any man who's paying attention would recognize that gesture."

She gave a startled laugh. She glanced down, only to find herself, quite automatically, still cradling her middle. Quizzically, Daisy stared at her own hands. "I'm not pregnant, Mr. Walsh."

"Owen," he reminded her. "If we're going to be together—"

"You must be mistaken," Daisy interrupted. Her cheeks turned pink. Her hands fluttered. "I can't possibly be expecting a baby." She gave an awkward laugh. "I don't even have a husband. That's the usual order of things, you know."

"I'm sorry. I didn't mean to upset you." Suddenly, Owen felt as if he'd blundered in on two oversize feet. He dimly recalled this sensation from his newlywed days with Renée. He didn't like it any better now than he had then, especially with a woman who wasn't his wife. "If you don't want me to talk about it—"

On the verge of promising her he wouldn't, Owen hesitated. The plain fact was, Daisy Walsh was unmarried. *And* pregnant. *And,* seemingly, alone. Doubtless, that made her situation a delicate one. He didn't want to scare her away, just when, it seemed, she needed someone to stand by her. "I remember what it was like before Élodie came," he settled on saying. "I felt as though I was waiting on a miracle. And then…there she was. I guess maybe I'm keen to relive those days."

At that, Daisy smiled. "Well, I'd be fibbing if I said I haven't daydreamed about having a family of my own someday," she admitted. "That's why I went to cookery school, in fact—to learn how to be the best possible wife and mother I could be." For a moment, she seemed lost in private concerns. Then she gazed up brightly at him. "That's why I'm so qualified to teach Élodie!"

Plainly, Daisy wanted to steer their conversation toward more practical matters. But Owen couldn't do that. Not yet.

"Will someone be…meeting you here, in Morrow Creek?" He hoped to suggest, subtly, that her baby's father would be welcome there, too. "I don't have much room, but—" Catching Daisy's aghast expression, Owen regrouped. She was probably concerned about propriety. Heaven knew, Renée would have been. "Out here in the West, we don't stand much on ceremony," he reassured Daisy. "Lots of folks come here to start fresh—"

Sometimes with a baby, it seemed. At least in Daisy's case. But as long as she and her baby's father married eventually...

"No. No one will be joining me." Determinedly, Daisy shook her head. "I was traveling with my touring manager, but he's—"

Abruptly, she broke off. A look of dawning comprehension suffused her face. Her cheeks turned a darker shade of pink.

It seemed beyond likely, Owen realized, that this "touring manager" of hers was responsible for getting her pregnant—whether she wanted to admit it or not. Even without saying so, the truth was all over her face. Owen might not have gambled for a while, but he could still read an expression with accuracy.

Daisy, he could read like a book. She was just that open.

"He's moved on," she finished staunchly. "He'll be working with another client soon. Our association is finished."

Another client? An association? That was a hell of a way to refer to it! Owen couldn't help feeling worried—and offended on her behalf, too. He'd never in his life spoken about a woman in such an uncaring way. What kind of man was her baby's father?

The damn knuck had a duty to Daisy now! He had an obligation to protect and care for her and her baby, no matter what. Did she still love the man? Owen sorely wished he could tell. But reading hearts wasn't the same as reading faces.

"I'm not entirely sure what my standing is at the moment," Daisy mused aloud. "With my publisher and my speaking-engagements tour, I mean." She dropped her gaze to her midsection, then hastily lifted it. "I'll send a wire to Conrad to find out."

Conrad. Was that the man who'd abandoned her? Owen disliked him already. He supposed he shouldn't be so quick to judge him. Likely, he should assign some—if not all—the blame for Daisy's situation to her. That's what Renée would have done.

His wife had believed that goodness was the duty of every person, with no excuses made or allowed. But Owen couldn't bring himself to see things that way. His instincts told him Daisy was an innocent. Owen trusted his instincts. If he hadn't, he'd never have survived all those rough-and-tumble years on his own.

"If you write him a message, I'll see that it's sent," Owen promised her. He scarcely knew Daisy Walsh, he reminded himself. He shouldn't involve himself in her private life. But something about Daisy made him want to help her—to watch over her. "Morrow Creek has a telegraph station in town and an adjunct office out by the mountains. Your message will go out quickly."

"Oh. That's good. Thank you." With a fresh smile, Daisy glanced up at him. "Conrad—Mr. Parish, I mean—will be relieved to know I made it here to Morrow Creek," she assured him.

As though he were back at a faro table, assessing players' tells one by one, Owen filed away that name. *Conrad Parish.*

"Was there some doubt about that?" he asked.

"About my arriving here safely? Well…" Daisy gave him a somewhat waggish smile. "A bit. I'm afraid this entire journey has been something of an adventure for me. First, I jumped off the train, then I arrived to that hero's welcome my brother arranged, then I was raffled off to *you,* then I swooned, then I found myself in your bed! All in all, it's been… stimulating."

At that memory, Owen felt himself stir. Gruffly, he cleared his throat. "Yes. Élodie is thrilled about her lessons."

"And I'm thrilled to be giving them. She's a very sweet girl." Daisy glanced down the hallway toward Élodie's bedroom, as though wishing his little girl would emerge and rescue them from their unusual conversation. "You must be so proud. Mrs. Archer and Miss Reardon said you've raised Élodie on your own?"

"Mostly." Uncomfortably, Owen rubbed the back of his neck. He hadn't done nearly enough—certainly not enough to be praised for. "I've done my best. Renée—that's my wife," he clarified for Daisy's benefit, "Renée would have said Élodie needed more."

At that, Daisy seemed appalled. "More than her own father? I can't imagine it!" Warmly, she squeezed his hand. "Anyone can see that as far as Élodie is concerned, you hung the moon."

Owen glanced down at their hands, no longer touching, but still congenially near one another. He hoped Daisy was right about Élodie. He felt wholly unable to say so.

"You must be tired," he said. "Especially in your delicate con—" Spying a telltale wariness in Daisy's face, he thought better of finishing that statement. If she didn't want to admit her pregnancy, he wouldn't press her. Not now. "I'll show you where to clean up. You can use my bedroom while you're here."

Confidently, he strode in that direction. But Daisy didn't follow. Instead, when he turned around, she shot him an empathetic look. "Oh. Your feelings are hurt. I apologize."

"I'm fine." He was. He didn't know what she meant.

"I didn't mean to say anything unkind about your

wife. Honestly, I didn't! Miss O'Neill and the others told me you'd lost her some years ago. You must miss her very much."

"Sometimes." It was the truth. But the original ache he'd felt had faded over the years. Now, he mostly wished Élodie could have had more time with her mother…and he wished his own shortcomings hadn't pushed Renée west where she'd taken fatally ill in the first place. "I can sleep on a pallet. It's no trouble." He gestured. "My bedroom is right this way."

"I know which way it is. Remember?" Daisy's audacious grin served to warm him clean through. It all but invited him to recall seeing her there in his bed, too. Her eyes sparkled at him. "But I do appreciate your gentlemanly behavior."

Likely, Owen thought, that was because she'd experienced so little "gentlemanly behavior" from Conrad Parish—the man who'd moved on to begin another "association" apart from Daisy. But she hadn't seemed overly troubled by that fact. And despite Daisy's precarious situation, which should have cooled him toward her, Owen couldn't help finding her demeanor altogether charming.

He liked her feminine way of walking, too, as she came nearer with the obvious intention of letting him escort her to his bedroom. He liked her fragrance, he liked her nearness…he even liked her bashful habit of examining her high-button shoes.

Just when he'd thought he'd steeled himself to behave in a further "gentlemanly" fashion, Daisy stopped. She put her hand on his arm. His whole body came alive at her touch, making a lie of his good intentions. All he wanted, just then, was to savor her presence. That, and maybe to touch her, too. It occurred to Owen that he might have underestimated how it would affect him to live with a woman again, even if it was only for a short while.

"Thank you for being so kind to me," Daisy said. "You didn't have to be, especially given how surprised you were—"

Was that how Conrad Parish had felt? Owen wondered. *Surprised* by the news of Daisy's baby? Was that why he'd moved on in such an apparently heartless way? And how did Daisy feel about that? She didn't *appear* to be pining for the man…

"—and I promise to do my very best to repay you," Daisy was saying, "by teaching Élodie every last thing she wants to know."

At the end of her sincere speech, Daisy beamed up at him. She gave his forearm an additional squeeze, as though making sure her good intentions were clear to him. But all that was truly clear to Owen was that he was in over his head.

He didn't know how to cope with the conundrum

that was Daisy Walsh. She baffled him in ways he hadn't counted on.

"I might teach *you* a thing or two, too!" Daisy teased.

"I'd be surprised if you could," Owen told her truthfully. "I've done a lot of things in my life, Daisy—things you've probably never even considered doing...most of them bad."

For a moment Daisy appeared wary. Then, "I meant sewing."

Of course. Feeling a fool, Owen headed for his bedroom. He tried to banish the memory of Daisy's curious expression. Undoubtedly she was wondering exactly what he'd done.

He was wondering why he'd all but blurted out the regrets of his past as easily as some people discussed the weather. But there was just something about Daisy...something that encouraged trust. If Owen had believed in romantic twaddle like falling in love in a heartbeat, he might have been concerned. After all, he didn't have time or space or a need for love in his life.

But for now, he decided, he did have time for this. He had time for making sure Daisy was watched over while in his care.

"There's a washbasin on the bureau." He pointed to it. "I'll bring you a fresh pitcher of water and some towels. The mattress isn't fancy," he told her, "but it's comfortable."

"Yes. I remember." She cast him another smile. "Thank you."

Momentarily transfixed anew by the recollection of Daisy in his bed, Owen went still. Damnation, but she'd looked sweet. He'd likely never forget that sight—not as long as he lived.

"Damn Mrs. Sunley and her interfering ways," he muttered. "That old busybody should learn to mind her own damn business."

"Élodie was right," Daisy observed. "You do cuss a lot."

Startled, he glanced at her, then waited for her inevitable reprimand. In his experience, women didn't have much patience for a man's failings—at least good women didn't. Daisy, despite her belly-cradling predicament, seemed to be truly good.

But all she did was laugh. "It makes me feel right at home. You should have heard my father! He could swear a blue streak."

That settled it. He couldn't comprehend her at all.

"When you're ready, we'll go to dinner," Owen said in his gruffest tone, unwilling to soften any further. "The Lorndorff Hotel puts out a good spread. You must be hungry. If you already fainted once today—" *you already provided more proof of your delicate condition* "—you shouldn't wait too long to eat."

"Aren't you sweet, looking after me that way?" Daisy's reward to him was a sunny smile. "But I won't hear of going to a hotel restaurant. I'll cook for you and Élodie right here!"

Owen frowned. "We don't have much to cook with."

"Don't worry. I'm good at making do."

She was good at making him feel befuddled. Standing near her this way, Owen could scarcely summon up a sensible thought.

"You must be tired," he repeated. Then, still flummoxed by the fact that she *hadn't* chided him for swearing, Owen relented. "But only a fool would argue against a home-cooked meal."

"You accept? Good! That's *very* wise of you."

"Me? Wise?" At that, Owen shook his head. "I've got a word of advice for you there, Daisy—don't be fooled. I'm not wise."

Then, before he could blurt out another imprudent word, Owen strode straight out and closed the door, leaving pregnant and unwed Daisy Walsh alone to sort out her predicament…and to wonder, more than likely, what to make of a raffle prizewinner who hadn't wanted to win at all, but who now couldn't seem to bear the thought of losing what he hadn't known he'd needed.

Hellfire. If that wasn't a muddled thought, Owen didn't know what was. It was fortunate that whiskey was off-limits to him these days. Otherwise, who knew what other trouble he might find himself in... especially with a lissome woman nearby.

Chapter Eleven

"And *these* are buttermilk-spice muffins!" Daisy announced in her most jovial and generous tone. "Still warm from the oven."

With a flourish, she set the muffins on the kitchen table, adding them to the other items she'd already arranged there.

"Ooh! They look so tasty!" Élodie exclaimed. She glanced at her father, who sat across the table from her. "And so pretty!"

Happily, Daisy agreed with that assessment. Even given the limitations of Owen Cooper's bachelor-like kitchen, she'd still managed to assemble a veritable spread for dinner: baked beans from a tin—but doctored up with molasses, salt pork and plenty of fresh black pepper—a compote of dried apricots and raisins, hot stewed dandelion greens and muffins with apple butter.

"Where did that wicker basket come from?" Owen

asked, suspicion evident in his voice. "And that…
flowery thing?"

"Flowery thing?" Puzzled, Daisy examined the
table. Élodie had helped her assemble plates and cutlery. She'd had her first lesson in cookery, too—a
tutorial on using the stove safely. Daisy's gaze
landed on the lining of the muffin basket. "You
mean the napkin I used? There were some lovely
linens crammed in the back of the cupboard. They
were clean, so I ironed them. And now…voilà! A
very nice table setting and muffin basket."

Owen gave the cheerfully printed linens a mis-
trustful frown. "Those aren't mine. I don't even recognize them."

"Miss O'Neill gave them to us last Christmas,"
Élodie piped up. "Remember? You said the bright
colors made you feel queasy."

Queasy. Ugh. Unhappily reminded of her own recent bouts of travel sickness, Daisy considered how
she'd felt since arriving in Morrow Creek. She'd
fainted at the train depot, it was true—but she'd
been under enormous strain at the time. Since then,
it occurred to her, she hadn't experienced a single
instance of nausea. Perhaps, despite Owen's suppo-
sitions about her "delicate condition," she really had
nothing to worry about. No sickness, no troubles…
no baby whose father didn't care a whit for Daisy.

But she couldn't think about that now. With an efficacy born of long practice, Daisy turned her mind to something else—to some*one* else: Owen. Even after several hours in his company, she still wasn't tired of gazing at him. The very sight of him filled her with fascination. He was so rugged, so masculine, so very *present* in every movement and gesture and thoughtfully voiced word.

"I *didn't* say that to Miss O'Neill at Christmastime," he was saying now, in his own defense. He cast the vivid floral napkin a dour look. "I don't need silly fripperies, that's all."

He might not "need" them, Daisy knew, but more than likely, he secretly enjoyed them. Who wouldn't? Embellishing a household and caring for the people inside it were her favorite things to do—an expertise she'd gladly share with Owen and his daughter. Even though she'd prepared only one meal for them, she'd enjoyed it. She'd enjoyed having someone to pamper and fuss over.

"Attractive linens enliven the dining experience," Daisy told Owen as she took her seat between him and Élodie. "A pleasant ambience aids in proper digestion and healthfulness."

"So does agreeable conversation," Élodie added, showing off the knowledge she'd gleaned during their lessons so far. "That means you should tell Daisy how nice everything looks, Papa."

With an inexplicably curmudgeonly frown, Owen gazed at his daughter. Then he blinked. "Élodie, did you cut your hair?"

Élodie, caught in the midst of diligently copying the precise manner in which Daisy split and apple-buttered her buttermilk-spice muffin, nodded proudly. Her new forehead fringe bobbed above her eyebrows. "I used the sewing scissors!"

Owen gawked. "You cut your hair yourself?"

Another nod. Élodie cast Daisy an adoring look. "I wanted to look *just* like Daisy. And now I do!"

Owen's thick dark brows drew together. He aimed a censorious glance at Daisy. This time, it was her turn to defend her good name. "I had nothing to do with it!" she said. "When I saw Élodie after I'd settled in, she'd already cut her hair."

"I *told* you Papa wouldn't notice for hours!" Élodie crowed.

"Yes. I guess you were right." Amused by the little girl's perspicacity when it came to her father's observant nature—or lack thereof—Daisy tried, playfully, to push things further. "How long do you suppose it will be before he notices the collection of flowery bric-a-brac I arranged at the stable?"

Owen's chair scraped back. "Flowery *what? Where?*"

Feeling better than she had in days, Daisy laughed.

She reached to give Owen's hand a tug, intending to draw him back to his place at the table…and instead found herself giving him a more lingering touch. Just as she had before, she squeezed Owen's hand, then let her fingers dawdle awhile against his arm.

She shouldn't have done it, Daisy knew. Not then, and not earlier today, either. But something about Owen emboldened her. He made her feel as though she could be herself with him. Owen was blunt but nonjudgmental; he was honorable. With him, there was no need to watch her every word or deed, the way she'd learned to do with Conrad. Before her speaking engagements tour had begun, Daisy recalled, she'd been an ordinary, high-spirited woman. After spending so much time alone with Conrad, though, she'd become a timid, fearful girl, relying too much on her tour manager to help her meet her obligations to Barker & Bowles.

Tonight, for the first time in months, she felt as though her usual womanly self was returning. But perhaps, Daisy decided as she looked at her pale hand nestled contentedly atop Owen's sun-browned wrist, she'd become a little *too* comfortable here.

Owen already assumed she was having a baby out of wedlock—a thought Daisy could scarcely bring herself to consider. Did she truly need to add fuel to the fire by behaving so familiarly?

Reluctantly, she withdrew her hand. "I'm only

teasing. Sit down and eat your dinner, won't you? It's getting cold."

Grumbling, Owen did. For a little while, the only sounds were those of enjoyment as everyone tucked into their meals. The apple butter was passed; coffee was poured and drunk; sighs of enjoyment were released and gratefully savored by Daisy.

Owen had been very kind to her. Élodie was adorable. Daisy liked them both already. And as she listened to Owen talk in his deep, thoughtful voice with Élodie about the merits of knitting versus embroidery, she felt strangely heartened by the two of them, too. Owen had raised Élodie on his own. And little Élodie seemed happy. Didn't that prove that a child could thrive, even if she had only one parent to care for her and love her? If that were true, Daisy mused with a new sense of hopefulness, then maybe she didn't need to be afraid.

Maybe she could admit the possibility that had been niggling in the back of her mind for weeks: that she *was* going to have a baby, and she *could* raise her child without Conrad.

Contemplatively, Daisy glanced at Owen. To her, he seemed brave and astute and resilient…if a little too somber. He seemed to bear the weight of his responsibilities capably and earnestly. He seemed to be a good man—the kind of man who'd take in a stranger on a moment's notice…then make her feel welcome, even going so far as to invite her to live in sin at his house!

Will someone be...meeting you here, in Morrow Creek?

His earlier question still made Daisy's ears burn. Owen had meant Conrad Parish, of course. He'd wondered if Conrad would be scandalously joining her here and helping her raise the baby Owen imagined Daisy was expecting to have.

The notion was unthinkable. Daisy didn't love Conrad. She didn't even miss him. As a point of fact, it had been a relief to comport herself according to her own wishes tonight. It had been *fun* to teach Élodie about sifting the flour twice to ensure airy muffins and about using a heavy cloth to shield her fingers from the hot cast-iron baking pans. Moreover, Daisy's newfound autonomy seemed to have gone straight to her head! Dreamily, she considered what it might be like to touch Owen's hand again—but he, apparently, didn't harbor any such wistful yearnings.

Will someone be...meeting you here, in Morrow Creek?

She had to make it clear to him that she wasn't promised to some other man, least of all to her erstwhile speaking-tour manager! As far as Daisy was concerned, Conrad could just move on to his new assignment with Astair Prestell and leave her be.

Right now, Daisy wanted to envision what it would be like to see Owen look at her with devotion, the way Miss Reardon had looked at Thomas today. She still felt downright enraptured by their attraction to one another. It was inspiring to think that two people could find one another, even in such a remote place as Morrow Creek. Daisy hadn't seen much of the town yet, but she intended to remedy that soon. She liked what she'd seen so far—even if the place *was* reportedly wildly permissive.

Out here in the West, *we don't stand much on ceremony.*

That's what Owen had told her today. As Daisy looked at him now, with his shaggy dark hair, hawk-like nose and caring eyes, she blessed him for saying so. He'd obviously sought to set her mind at ease over her supposed pregnancy. Another person might have turned her away, but not Owen. Owen had, in what appeared to be typically taciturn fashion, tried to reassure her.

Tardily, he blurted, "Everything is very nice, Daisy!"

His voice boomed across the kitchen table, startling her. Daisy jumped, making cutlery clatter. Élodie grinned, obviously proud of her papa for having remembered her earlier decree.

"Well done, Papa! You minded your manners!"

"Don't be sassy. It's not the first time, you know."

"I know." With patent care, Élodie examined Daisy. She adjusted her grasp on her fork, mimicking Daisy's hold. She sat up a little straighter. "But Daisy says encouragement helps us learn new things better. Daisy says everyone likes a kind word."

Owen angled his head. He squinted, seeming to notice his daughter's mimicry of Daisy for the first time. "That's true."

"Daisy is very clever. And talented. And beautiful!"

Discomfited by so much praise, Daisy stood. "I should get busy with washing up. If you'll point me to the water pump—"

"I'll get the water." Brusquely, Owen stood. He eyed her recently vacated ladder-back chair, all but intimidating her back into it. "You should rest. You've done too much already."

"I feel fine!" Undeterred, Daisy strode toward the potbellied stove. She'd spied a tin bucket earlier that would work wonderfully to haul in some wash water. Knowing she was probably still blushing from Élodie's effusive praise, she grabbed the bucket. "I'll just—"

"You'll just let me do it." Owen's broad chest and wide shoulders filled her vision. How had he moved so quickly to intercept her? He was much too big to move so agilely. Yet he obviously had. Without a word, he seized the bucket handle.

Inadvertently, their hands met again. Owen's hand felt warm and callused and capable. Daisy's hand felt…in dire need of more contact. Suffused with a longing for exactly that, she gazed up. "I can do it. I'm perfectly capable," she said.

But her voice trembled on the words. And her breath, oddly enough, seemed to run away before she could catch it. How had she not noticed until now, Daisy wondered, how velvety and intriguing Owen's eyes were? How had she not noticed how soft his lips looked…how arrestingly stubbled his jaw appeared?

Owen's gaze dipped, tellingly, to her midsection. "While you're here," he said staunchly, "I will pump water for you, haul firewood for you, carry anything heavy and make sure you don't overexert yourself in any way. Is that understood?"

Daisy wanted to disagree. She didn't want to be under the thumb of anyone, not when she'd finally freed herself with that first brave step off the train and into her future. But on the other hand, Owen was only trying to safeguard her well-being…

As though sensing her hesitation, Owen lowered his voice. He angled his head nearer to hers. "Please, Daisy." Now his tone sounded intriguingly compelling…private. His fingers stroked hers atop the bucket handle. "I want to do it. Let me help you."

How had he become so charismatic? So…persuasive? In the blink of an eye, Owen had gone from a stableman to a charmer. Fascinated by the change in him, Daisy nonetheless managed to hold her ground. "I'm not as fragile as you think I am, Owen."

"I can see that." His gaze lifted to her face. Remarkably, there seemed to be respect—and compassion—in his eyes. "But I've already done enough I regret. Consider this a favor."

Lulled by his intimate tone, Daisy wavered. "That's the second time you've mentioned your dire past," she said to buy herself time. "Exactly what have you done that's so terrible?"

Owen frowned. His gaze never left hers. "I can hold out longer than you can." He tightened his grasp on the bucket's handle. "Agree to let me do all the strenuous work for you."

"Well, that's hardly fair, is it? I'm not even—"

Pregnant. It stood between them, scandalous and absurd.

Daisy couldn't say it aloud. Not again. Maybe she'd already used up her quantity of self-deception and denial for the day.

"I don't want to be a problem for you," she said instead.

Owen scoffed. "You're far from problematic. Except..."

"Except?" Daisy echoed, reminded of Conrad's

insulting assessment of her. *You won't be my problem to deal with anymore.*

"Except when you bite your lip that way." Owen seemed mesmerized by the unconscious motion she'd made. "It's very…" Roughly, he cleared his throat. "I can't help being distracted."

Imprudently thrilled, Daisy perked up. "Really? By me?"

She still couldn't believe Owen hadn't reprimanded her—for not acceding to his wishes, for not tamping down her arguments…for being herself, with all her foibles and hopes.

His frown did deepen imposingly, though. His eyes gleamed. "This doesn't mean I won't insist on doing all the difficult work for you. Give in, Daisy. I'll have my way eventually."

She believed him. Owen seemed to be the kind of man who got what he wanted, most of the time. But now Daisy had a small sense of her own burgeoning power. Testing it, she shook her head. Then, for good measure, she bit her lower lip again.

Owen glowered…but then he sighed, tellingly, as well.

For a long moment, they stood at an impasse. Obstinacy and attraction flared between them with equal measure. They each gave the bucket an ineffectual, possessive tug. Then a huge, childish sigh burst out. Élodie shoved back her chair.

"Fine!" She flapped her arms with girlish indignation, the movement most likely a dead ringer for a similar gesture Owen made. "If you're both going to argue, *I'll* get the water!"

Élodie took a similar bucket from beside the door. She tromped downstairs to the stable, leaving both adults behind.

For a moment, Daisy wondered about the prudence of being left alone with Owen, especially after they'd shared...whatever had passed between them. She still felt breathless, owing to its galvanizing effects. Gazing up at Owen, she wondered if he felt the same way. She wondered if he knew how effective his charms had been against her, or if he even knew he'd used them at all.

If that's what he'd meant by the *bad* things he'd done...

Well, she guessed *bad* was a matter of perspective.

A second later, Daisy realized she wouldn't find out—at least not today.

"I'd better go help Élodie," Owen told her, then he took the bucket from Daisy's slackened grasp and headed downstairs.

Chapter Twelve

Eventually Daisy could delay no longer. With the dishes washed, the kitchen put to rights and Élodie safely tucked into bed, Daisy took her leave of Owen, then headed to bed herself.

Several minutes later, with Owen's gruff "good night" still ringing in her head, she stood alone in his bedroom. The place was plain but spotless, unassuming but comfortable—a lot like Owen himself, in fact. And there, alone with no lessons or conversations or chores to distract her, Daisy finally allowed herself to contemplate the life-changing statement Owen had made earlier, when he'd seen her cradling her belly.

You're going to have a baby.

Could it be true? In a way Daisy hadn't dared to do until now, she glanced down speculatively at herself. With trembling hands, she smoothed her white, ruffled-hem nightgown—a garment generously lent to her by Miss Reardon—then took a careful look.

Her belly *was* undeniably rounder, she saw. Not by much, but the change was noticeable. At least it was to her.

Evidently it had been noticeable to Conrad, too.

That blue dress makes you look a bit stout, he'd told her. At the time, she'd attributed his observation to the effects of minor overindulgence while on her speaking-engagements tour—and to the fact that such overindulgence had led her to loosen her corsets a tad to compensate. But now, after her encounter with Owen and his startling revelation, Daisy wondered.

She wondered…then retreated instantly from the thought. Granted, she *had* been feeling a bit…different lately. She'd been feeling tired, weepy, and anxious, by turns. But that was easily explained by the pressure she'd been under while traveling across the country on her tour. Wasn't it?

She simply could *not* be having a baby. It wasn't possible.

Or at least, Daisy allowed, it wasn't *probable.* Still cradling her belly, she recalled that she *had,* regrettably, been intimate with Conrad. During those early, impressionable days when she'd been so bedazzled by Conrad and so eager to please him—so keen to retain her job and prove herself worthy of her publisher's esteem—she'd given in to Conrad's flattering attention and allowed him to be with her.

But Conrad had *assured* her that he knew how to "take care of things." He'd promised her that their liaisons were pure hearted…and all but expected, too, while on her speaking tour. He'd sworn, with utmost sincerity, that he cared about her and wanted to help her "grow into womanhood."

Well, Daisy thought with a sad quirk of her lips, it was possible now that she was growing an entirely new person.

Except it wasn't. It wasn't! Daisy had been innocent, but she hadn't been gullible, she reminded herself. She'd kept her heart her own, as much as possible. And that had been a good thing too, since Conrad had hurtfully lost interest in her very quickly. Their last liaison had been weeks ago. *Several* weeks ago, in fact.

Surely, if she were actually pregnant, she would know it?

Owen must be wrong, no matter how certain he'd sounded today.

You're going to have a baby, he'd said…but as much as Daisy wanted to have a family of her own someday, the thought of being pregnant now truly scared her. Already she felt alone in the world. She was miles from home, miles from her friends. She was without any ready means of financial support of her own—except for the money she'd cadged from her last speaking engagement, which still remained in the pocket of Conrad's pilfered overcoat. To make matters worse, she was without even the most fundamental of personal items, too.

Thanks to her impulsive actions, she'd left her touring train without so much as her traveling trunk by her side. As of right now, Daisy possessed exactly one satchel, one dress and set of undergarments, one pair of shoes, one reticule and one copy of the *New Book of Cookery and General Home Keeping: with Recipes and Formulas for All Occasions, Both Informal and Grand.* The generous women of Morrow Creek had volunteered to lend her a wardrobe while she was in town visiting, but that didn't change the fact that Daisy had behaved impetuously.

Certainly she could be forgiven for wanting to see her brother, for wanting to keep her promise to visit him in Morrow Creek. But if Thomas knew how recklessly she'd behaved—

Daisy stopped, coming to an even more alarming realization. When her brother learned about her… secret, he would be *so* disappointed in her. That was simply one more reason it could not be true. It could not be! In search of reassurance, Daisy glanced down at her belly again. Its undeniably rounded curve sent fresh apprehension coursing through her. Thomas was truly kindhearted, but he had his own life to enjoy. If he thought she was having a baby, he would feel compelled to help.

Daisy tried to envision herself breaking the news of her impending motherhood to her brother. The imagined sight of his disappointed face made her feel worse than ever. Thomas would say, quite rightly, that Daisy was in no position to be a mother. He would say she was unprepared to have a baby.

But oh…how she *wanted* one! For the space of a heartbeat, Daisy allowed herself to imagine how differently this situation might have unfolded, were her circumstances different. She pictured herself with a loving husband by her side, with a cooing infant in her arms, with a safe and secure home to enclose and comfort all of them.

That was what she wanted most of all. Having a home and family of her own was her very fondest dream. But now…

Now that dream was gone. No man would want an unwed mother for a wife, Daisy realized. No man would want to play father to another man's child. And since Conrad would be her baby's father… Well, that fact brought complications of its own.

Fretfully, Daisy paced Owen's bedroom. With Conrad as her baby's father, she couldn't deny him the right to be with his child. No matter that she didn't love Conrad. Perhaps she would learn to love him. Perhaps, given the bond of parenting, they would be able to transcend their differences: his distaste for her failings, his dismay at her ineptitude, his dissatisfaction with almost everything she said and did, at least lately—

Abruptly, nausea overwhelmed her. With a startled cry, Daisy bolted for the empty basin on the other side of the bedroom. Apparently, leaving the train hadn't been sufficient to cure her traveling sickness.

Either that, or Owen was right: *she was having a baby.*

What in the world was she going to do?

Chapter Thirteen

In the early-morning brightness of his ramshackle kitchen, Owen grabbed a cloth. He wrapped it securely around the oven's door handle, then opened the heavy cast-iron door. Heat blasted him, almost making his eyebrows curl. He scowled inside, damn near fiercely enough to coerce it into cooking more quickly.

It wouldn't do, he'd decided in the restless hours before dawn, to appear *too* eager for Daisy's approval. Yesterday, she'd all but led him around by the nose, with all her smiles and tender touches. Today, Owen was determined to be tougher.

"Is the toast ready yet, Papa?" Élodie asked.

"Almost, *mon petit*—" On the verge of completing that endearment, Owen felt himself flush. Or maybe it was only the heat from the oven with its rack of toasting bread inside that made him feel overwarm. Probably the fact that Daisy sat across the table from Élodie, close enough to scrutinize every move Owen made, had nothing to do with his reticence. "*Chou*," he finished in a burst of defiant sappiness. "Almost ready."

He hoped his pet name for Élodie would pass by unnoticed. He was instantly disappointed. His daughter turned to Daisy.

"*Mon petit chou* is what Maman used to call me before she passed on," Élodie confided eagerly. "Now Papa calls me that too, to make sure I don't forget her." His daughter wrinkled her nose in—it occurred to Owen—near-perfect imitation of Daisy. "I don't remember Maman too well because I was so little then, but I do like hearing my papa speak French, ever so much!"

"Yes, it's charming." Daisy delivered him an amused look. "I guess a fluency in French is a good thing for a man to have in his arsenal. All the better to impress ladies with."

"Oh, that doesn't matter. Papa could speak gibberish, and the ladies would still swoon. Ladies hereabouts are *awfully* impressed with him!" Élodie kicked the leg of the nearest chair with typical restiveness. She smiled at Daisy. "Here in Morrow Creek, all the ladies go downright spoony when they see him!"

Now Daisy appeared skeptical, gallingly so for

a woman who'd almost flirted with him yesterday. "Hmm. Is that right?"

"Yes! It is!" Élodie alleged with a vigorous nod. "Papa is quite a catch, they say! He's the most marriageable man in Morrow Creek. At least that's what I hear around town these days, when I'm on my way to school or accompanying Mrs. Archer."

"Truly?" Wearing a dubious expression, Daisy put her chin in her hand. "Your father is considered marriageable? Even with those eyebrows? That long hair? Those scowling faces he makes?"

She was teasing him, Owen realized with a sense of astonishment. Daisy was teasing him the same way she'd done when she'd pretended to have adorned his stable with flowery bric-a-brac yesterday. Then, as now, he'd fallen for her ruse, too.

No one in town ever teased him, he realized. They all took Owen exactly as seriously as he did, as seriously as he'd needed them to do, to keep himself on the straight-and-narrow path.

Telling himself he didn't care what Daisy Walsh thought, Owen scowled anew, fighting a ruinous urge to tug at his hair—his perfectly ordinary, shoulder-length dark hair. If Daisy thought she would play Delilah to his Samson, she'd better think again. But he almost had to tie his hands behind his back to avoid smoothing out his purportedly problematic eyebrows.

They were fine. Fine!

Unfortunately, his daughter disagreed.

Woefully, Élodie regarded him. She nodded. "Yes, even with all those problems, everyone still loves Papa. I reckon he'll sweeten up even more, though, with a good lady nearby."

Doubtfully, Daisy examined him. The woman was a downright prankster, it seemed, intent on bedeviling him at every turn.

"Well, if you say so..." she said, seemingly unconvinced.

Their girlish, gossipy tone got under his skin. That was enough, Owen decided. Perfect toast be damned. He needed to end this conversation before things got out of hand.

He opened the oven door again, pulled out the rack of toast, then slammed it on the stove top hard enough to make the burner covers rattle. "Who wants toast?" he demanded to know.

As he'd expected, his easily diverted daughter gleefully proclaimed her fondness for toast. Owen doled out a portion on her plate, then did the same for Daisy. He stood nearby them both, arms crossed, waiting for the breakfasting to commence.

This was what Owen did every morning. Today, he felt unusually conspicuous, though, in his every word and deed. Not many people observed him parenting Élodie. He hoped he was doing everything correctly. He had no way to know for certain.

Élodie smeared on a hearty dollop of apple butter, then took a bite of toast. "Mmm! For once, it's not burned!"

Daisy only regarded her toast through wary eyes. "I'm not sure about this." She gestured toward the bedroom. "After all the…troubles I experienced this morning, maybe I should wait."

"Your 'troubles' are the reason I refused to let *you* cook."

Owen had stepped in to take charge right away, just as he'd done with the water bucket yesterday. He refused to let Daisy overexert herself. That was the least he could do. But Daisy only shook her head, doubtless remembering the brief verbal tussle they'd shared when he'd insisted on making breakfast.

"Besides, it will make you feel better to eat," Owen told her. "As far as this morning goes… That should improve as time goes on, too. I understand it's usually the worst early on."

He gave Élodie a cautious look, wondering if his daughter realized her papa was discussing her new tutor's pregnancy and the morning sickness she'd suffered because of it. Thankfully, his reassurance—as cryptic as it was—seemed to sail over Élodie's head…and to help ease Daisy's fears, too.

Daisy gave him a shaky smile. "Well, that's good

to know. I'm glad *one* of us has experience in these matters, at least." That was as close as she might ever come to acknowledging her delicate condition, Owen guessed. She gazed down the hallway, then sighed with evident dismay. "Although I still think you and Élodie made too much of a fuss over me."

Élodie quit chewing in midcrunch. "You were ill!"

"Of course we 'made a fuss,'" Owen added, mystified by her claim. It made no sense to him. "You needed help. We helped."

"Well… It couldn't have been pleasant for either of you, and I'm sorry for that. I'll try to do better next time, and not disrupt our lessons. I promise, I will." Ruefully, Daisy sipped the ginger tea he'd brewed her. "Although I have to say, this tea is miraculously effective. I feel much better! Thank you."

Owen was happy the tea had made Daisy feel better. She'd been retching like a three-day drunk after a bout with tequila when he'd heard her and hastened down the hall to investigate. Even so, Daisy had still tried to shoo away him and Élodie, claiming that she didn't want to "inconvenience" them. When they'd persisted in helping her, Daisy had apologized over and over again for subjecting them to her bout of nausea.

Owen didn't know what kind of people had been looking after Daisy recently, but he didn't think much of them. Daisy seemed to feel she was a nuisance, just for needing help when she felt ill. Whoever had instilled that callous notion in her head deserved to suffer his or her own bout of nausea—only a hundred times worse. Owen gazed at her, wondering…

Had the father of her baby been that coldhearted man?

Or was he a blameless bystander, like Owen, who only wanted to see her well cared for and happy? Would Daisy tell him if he asked? Now was not the time, with Élodie present, but later…

"Where did you get it?" Daisy surprised him by asking. "The ginger tea, I mean? Perhaps I should purchase my own supply."

Owen hedged, lifting his coffee cup for a mouthful of that bracing brew. He frowned, reluctant to admit that he'd deliberately sneaked over to his neighbors' house yesterday evening—under guise of "seeing to the horses" downstairs at the stable—and borrowed everything he could think of that might be helpful to Daisy. He did have his reputation as a "hard man" to consider, after all. He didn't want to seem too sentimental.

On the other hand, if Daisy wanted more tea to lessen her nausea, then maybe she was close to acknowledging her pregnancy.

"There's no need for you to buy your own ginger tea," he said roughly. "I'll get you as much as you can carry. All I want in exchange is—" He broke off, considering striking a bargain. He was concerned that she hadn't yet touched her toast. She needed to keep up her strength, for her baby's sake and her own.

Daisy's curious gaze met his. Her eyes sparkled. "Is…?"

Is…a kiss, he imagined her saying, and could have kicked himself for having such a base thought as that. He was not here to kiss Daisy, Owen reminded himself. "Is four bites of toast."

The disappointment in the air felt palpable. At least to him. Somehow, he knew that kissing Daisy would feel like a little slice of heaven, right there in ordinary Morrow Creek.

Doubtfully, Daisy gazed at her plate. "Three," she suggested. "Three bites, and you have yourself a deal."

"Nope. That won't work." Élodie shook her head, her wee face filled with hard-won wisdom. "Papa won't bargain anymore. He refuses. Once I tried to wheedle out an extra few minutes of reading before bedtime, and he lectured me about the 'evils of gambling' for at least half an hour! It was *so* boring!"

Daisy eyed him. "You don't gamble? But I thought all Western men were inveterate gamblers, scoundrels and ne'er-do-wells who'd as soon eat their boots as skip a card game."

"You've been misinformed," Owen told her with

a meaningful look at Élodie. "I don't gamble, drink or smoke. Or swear."

His daughter and Daisy both burst out laughing.

"You don't *swear?*" they asked in unified disbelief.

"All right. You've got me there. But just for that show of impertinence, I'm making it five. Five bites."

"That's not fair!" Daisy objected, laughing. "I won't do it." She gave him another contemplative look. "Anyway, if you've done as many 'bad' things as you claim, surely you've gambled a time or two, as well. Not that I mind that—I fancy your wicked past helps make up for my own lack of adventurousness. It must have been terribly exciting!"

"Six bites," Owen said. Even though she'd persisted in bringing up his past—the past he'd left behind him—he couldn't be annoyed at her. He felt far too good right now to quibble.

Besides, if a woman like Daisy—a sweet and moral woman, despite her predicament—liked even the worst parts of him...

Well, maybe there was hope for him after all.

Or maybe he was simply a fool for hoping so. Either way, in Daisy's presence, Owen couldn't seem to stop feeling carefree.

"Go ahead," he urged, intent now on teasing her every bit as much as she'd teased him. "Get started. Six bites."

"Now you're just being silly," Daisy judged, gesturing at her plate. "I doubt there are even six bites of toast here."

"No problem. There's more toast in the rack."

"Oh, is there?"

"Lots more toast. All the toast you can eat."

"Hmm. I see. Well, I guess I'd better go along with you then, before you change your mind and make it six pieces."

"Don't do it, Daisy!" Élodie cried, breaking into their teasing talk. "Please, *please,* don't do it! Not yet!"

At her urgent tone, Owen looked at her. So did Daisy.

"Why not, Élodie?" she asked. "What's the matter?"

"Well, it's just that…" His daughter swallowed. She shifted her gaze to Owen's face, then addressed Daisy again. "The more you refuse to eat your toast, the more Papa smiles. And I haven't ever seen so much of him smiling in all my life. I just…don't want it to end too soon."

At that, Daisy's expression sobered. She glanced at Owen, catching him just as his smile faded. She bit her lip in thought, then nodded at Élodie. "All right, Élodie!" she said with deliberate cheerfulness. "There is no *possible* way I intend to eat six whole bites of toast!" Daisy announced in her most grandiose-sounding voice. "So what do you think of that, Owen?"

The clock ticked loudly, counting off the moments between her facetious challenge and his expected response. Owen frowned.

"Eat it or don't." He refused to be goaded. Bothered by his daughter's plaintiveness, for reasons he couldn't explain, Owen grabbed his hat. He plunked it on, scraping back his ladder-back chair as he stood. "It's no skin off my nose if you retch again. I'll put a bucket near your chair while you tutor Élodie."

Daisy's troubled gaze seemed to follow him. "Owen, I'm sorry. I was only having fun! I didn't mean to upset you."

"Upset? I'm too hard-hearted to get upset. Ask anyone." Hastily, Owen pressed a kiss to the top of Élodie's head. He tousled her hair, then straightened. "I'm going downstairs to the stable to see to the horses. I'll be back directly."

Then he tromped away from them both, down to the refuge of the stable and horses, down to the place where no one expected him to change things…where no one tempted him to abandon all his past efforts, the way Daisy had with a single conversation.

Smiling. He'd been *smiling!* Like a man without a care, like a man without responsibilities or people counting on him. Like a man without a motherless daughter who needed his full attention.

If he wasn't careful, Owen thought as he descended grumpily into the calm, earthy-scented stable, he'd be taking up his scandalous ways all over again. At Daisy's urging, he'd be indulging in every scoundrelly action that crossed his mind. Like kissing her. Like holding her. Like *smiling* as he bantered with her over a cozy breakfast of unburned toast and tea.

It had been nice, he realized as he reached for a pitchfork. It had been *too* nice, probably, for the likes of him.

Hellfire. He must have been crazy to allow a woman in his household again. He was never going to survive it…at least not with his sanity, and his hard-won virtue, entirely intact.

Chapter Fourteen

It took Owen a remarkably long time to return from seeing to the horses. Although Daisy managed to keep her and Élodie busy with washing up after breakfast, beginning their sewing lessons and putting on a pot of soup prepared from the items in Owen's surprisingly well-stocked cupboards, she still felt as though time crawled without Owen. For the tenth time in an hour, she glanced at the clock on the fireplace mantel. She sighed.

At the sound of her exhalation, Élodie glanced up from the seam of the doll-size dress she'd been basting. "What's the matter, Miss Walsh?" she asked. "Are you going to be ill again?"

Daisy shook her head. "No, I'm fine." She mustered a smile for Élodie's sake. "Why would you ask? Do I seem ill to you?"

"No, but you have your hand on your tummy again. See?" The little girl pointed. "You've been doing that all morning. And yesterday too. That's what I do whenever I feel a bellyache coming on. I could make you another cup of tea if you'd like."

"No, thank you, Élodie. That's very kind of you." Daisy smiled at the girl, struck anew by what she'd said about her father earlier. *I haven't ever seen so much of him smiling in all my life. I just don't want it to end too soon.* "I feel fine. Sometimes I…simply like to rest my hand on my tummy."

Because I feel drawn to do so, she thought. *For reasons I can't explain…but which Owen would be happy to account for.*

Could it be possible that she was safeguarding her baby, without even knowing it? That she was irresistibly drawn to coddle and protect a child she hadn't even acknowledged yet?

That's what Owen would have said. It didn't seem like him to indulge in such fanciful notions, but he appeared to believe wholeheartedly in that one. He appeared entirely convinced of Daisy's pregnancy, based on that one significant gesture.

The realization made Daisy wonder… If a ten-year-old girl took such notice of Daisy's new belly-cradling habit, how many others had noticed it and not mentioned it to her? How many others might well come to the same conclusion Owen had?

Daisy froze, abruptly reconsidering her plans to

visit her brother at the *Pioneer Press* offices later for a personal tour. If she was pregnant, she probably shouldn't flaunt her condition, no matter how tolerant Owen insisted the town was.

"Oh. All right." Élodie scrutinized her. She nodded, seeming satisfied by Daisy's admittedly disingenuous answer.

Élodie shifted on her chair, then lay her hand on her own belly in perfect imitation of Daisy's pose. Placidly, the little girl gazed toward the stairs leading to the stable. It was exactly the same position Daisy had found herself in, time and again, while anticipating Owen's return. Struck, Daisy stared at Élodie, unable to hold back a smile at what she saw.

Not only had Élodie copied her hairstyle and demeanor, but she'd also mimicked other aspects of Daisy's appearance. Between breakfast and now, Élodie had tied a hank of green ribbon around her waist, in replication of the sash on Daisy's dress. She'd also—she recalled just then—sighed when Daisy sighed, stitched when Daisy stitched and sipped water when Daisy sipped water.

Experimentally, Daisy gave an enormous yawn. So did Élodie.

Daisy fussed with her forehead fringe. So did Élodie.

Amused, Daisy put down her sewing. She stretched her arms.

Élodie…did not.

Instead, the little girl turned directly to Daisy, her face a study in concentration. "I just thought that maybe you put your hand on your tummy to try to feel the baby inside," she said. "Are you *sure* that's not it? Because that would be wonderful!"

Daisy gazed into Élodie's shining eyes and knew she was lost. She could no more fib to her than she could to herself.

On the other hand, wasn't that exactly what she'd been doing all along? Lying to herself about what was happening?

Wasn't that the real reason she'd risked so much to come to Morrow Creek and see her brother? Because, in her hour of need, she'd wanted to be with Thomas, who loved her?

If it was—or even if it wasn't—Daisy couldn't change that now. Now she was here, with lessons to teach and an obligation to fulfill…and an alarmingly incisive query to answer.

I just thought maybe you put your hand on your tummy to try to feel the baby inside. Are you sure that's not it?

Cautiously, Daisy opened her mouth to deflect Élodie's question. But before she could, the little girl spoke up again.

"Can *I* feel the baby too?" Eagerly, she leaped to

her feet. "I always wanted a baby brother! Only I couldn't tell Papa that, on account of his not having a wife." Élodie's impatient gaze met Daisy's dismayed one. "Please, *please*, can I try to feel your baby too? I promise I'll be very, very careful. I will!"

Caught, Daisy prevaricated. "I don't think so, Élodie."

"Mrs. Archer and Mrs. Sunley will be *flabbergasted* by this!" Gleefully, Élodie circled Daisy's chair. She eyed her belly, her enthusiasm entirely undiminished by Daisy's rebuff. "They thought you were a puny and weak easterner, and that's why you fainted yesterday at the depot. But I *knew* they were wrong! You were just growing yourself a new baby! Of *course* that would make you feel a bit weedy. That would make *anyone* feel weedy."

"No," Daisy insisted. "It was very hot outside yesterday. I'm not used to the Arizona Territory, that's all. And I was surprised by my brother's raffle drawing, too. Not to mention all the crowds, and the band, and the bunting, and the banners—"

"And the baby!" Undoubtedly catching Daisy's ensnared expression, the girl chortled. "I overheard you and Papa talking about that yesterday afternoon. It makes sense that he'd guess about your baby, even if nobody else has." Confidingly, Élodie leaned nearer. "Nobody else has guessed," she assured Daisy, "because Mrs. Archer and the others would have *defi-*

nitely discussed that, if they had. Because everyone likes babies! And it makes sense that Papa would know what to do when you took ill this morning, too, on account of growing your new baby." Élodie danced in place. "See?" she boasted. "Papa didn't think you were puny! He didn't! He's very wise about things, you know."

Dumbly, Daisy shook her head. "Not about this, he's not."

"Oh, yes, he is! About everything." Still seeming downright joyful, Élodie hesitated beside Daisy's chair. Her hand hovered several inches above Daisy's belly in obvious anticipation. "I thought all I was getting Papa was a new wife in that raffle drawing, but now he's getting a baby, too! It's like a miracle!"

I remember what it was like before Élodie came, Owen had told her yesterday, Daisy recalled suddenly. *I felt as though I was waiting on a miracle. And then...there she was.*

Could a miracle really happen twice?

"No. Your father isn't—" *Getting a baby.* "And I'm not—" *Going to be his wife.* Stymied, Daisy broke off. This was disastrous. She regrouped, feeling more and more trapped by this conversation. "I'm...keeping the baby a secret for now." She could scarcely say the words. They brought her far too close to acknowledging her situation. "Please,

Élodie," Daisy begged. "It would mean a great deal to me if you didn't tell anyone."

"I *knew* I'd guess your secret, too!" Élodie crowed. "I'm good at that, just like Papa is." The little girl frowned in evident confusion. "But babies are happy news. Everybody likes babies, Miss Walsh! Why shouldn't I tell anyone about yours?"

"Because… It might interfere with our lessons!" Firmly, Daisy caught hold of Élodie's hand. She gave an affectionate squeeze, nodding at the little girl as she did. "I'm so hoping those lessons go well. You're an excellent student so far."

Easily sidetracked, Élodie grinned. "I am? Really?"

"You are, indeed," Daisy acknowledged, searching for a new activity to occupy her student. "In fact, I think you're ready to try making biscuits for lunch. Would you like to do that?"

Élodie's eyes shone. "Yes, very much so! I like biscuits!"

"All right, then." With her heart still pounding in alarm, Daisy set aside her sewing. She stood. "Let's get started!"

As soon as she finished with that, Daisy decided as she headed for the kitchen with Élodie in tow, she was going to have a word or two with Owen Cooper, and remind him of that aphorism about little pitchers with big ears—and keeping his big, fat, undeniably attractive mouth shut in the future…before Daisy found herself in even more trouble than she was in already.

Chapter Fifteen

Rounding the corner of the nearest empty stall, Owen caught sight of his helper, Gus, who appeared to be hoofing it toward the stable's door with his hat on his head. That was peculiar.

Admittedly, the stable had cleared out considerably over the course of the morning—the degenerates who'd flooded town for the raffle drawing were already pulling foot for new unsavory opportunities—but that didn't mean the workday was over with.

Frowning, Owen whistled for his stableman's attention. "Gus! Where are you off to? The workday's not done yet."

"I got myself an errand to run, boss."

"On whose orders?" Owen asked. "Because I sure as hell didn't send you out for anything. And if a customer needs—"

"Weren't a customer." Huffily, Gus swiveled. He

crossed the stable floor, past the stalls still occupied by their tail-swishing, hay-chomping inhabitants. "And I plumb forgot once today already, so if I'm gonna git this done, I'd better go."

"What you'd better do is tell me what you're up to."

"Why, I'd have thought you'd have known that one already." Gus shrugged, giving him an elaborately guileless look. "Seein' as how you're the boss around here, and all."

Owen frowned. Obviously, he didn't know a damn thing, or he wouldn't have asked about it. Gus knew that. But he appeared to be taking special delight in baiting Owen about it all the same.

What the hell was going on around here? All of a sudden, Owen's carefully constructed life seemed to be careening unstoppably out of his control. He didn't like it. Not one bit.

He waited, knowing that Gus would fold before he did.

Predictably, Gus did. He heaved a sigh. "I'm runnin' an errand for your lady friend upstairs. The one who's teaching Élodie about sewing and whatnot?" His helper pulled a scrap of paper from his overalls. He showed it to Owen. "She asked me to send this wire at the telegraph office for her, on account of her not knowing where it is. She gave me some money for it too."

"You met Daisy?"

A broad smile wreathed Gus's face. It fairly cracked the coating of dusty grime he customarily wore above his bandannaed neck. Shyly, Gus kicked the hay-sprinkled floor. "Shucks, I met her, all right. Last night, while you was over visitin' with the neighbors next door. She's a mighty nice one, too."

"You met Daisy." It wasn't a question this time.

Gus appeared to realize he'd erred somehow. He held up both lanky arms, waving the paper like a white flag. "Hey! Don't git all riled up, boss! She tole me that you tole her to see me if'n you weren't around and she needed anything done for her." Gus waggled his eyebrows. "You know, like help with… things."

Well, Owen had told Daisy that. He'd wanted to make sure she was cared for, no matter what. All the same, he glowered at Gus. He didn't like the way this sounded—or the overexcited manner with which his reliable helper referred to Daisy.

"I meant help with hauling heavy things," Owen specified tersely. "Carrying water. Lugging wood for the stove. *That's all.*" He eyed the folded paper.

He snatched it. "I'll take care of this. And while I've got you here, there's one more thing."

Hesitantly, Gus swallowed. "Yeah, boss? What's that?"

"I'll be away from the stable awhile," Owen said. "Upstairs, mostly, supervising Élodie with her lessons."

He'd just decided it, that moment. Apparently, his helper was almost as surprised as Owen was to learn of his new plan.

Gus snorted with laughter. "Gonna learn to bake, boss?"

Darkly, Owen gazed down at Gus, not the least amused by his wisecracks. "Maybe I am," he said. "Got a problem with that?"

"No!" Gus backed up. "No, sirree, I don't. Not a'tall."

Satisfied, Owen nodded. His helper's joking didn't bother him that much. His new, impulsive decision to spend more time upstairs with his daughter and her pretty tutor did. But he liked the idea of supervising Élodie's lessons. It was the right thing to do. Besides, there was something about knowing that Gus was all keyed up about Daisy that just…niggled at Owen. It niggled powerfully hard.

Vaguely, he wondered if—on some level—he felt he was *competing* with Gus for Daisy's attention.

But Owen dismissed that ludicrous thought almost as quickly as it arose. He was a better man than that. He was also, if Renée's exhortations were to be believed, a scoundrel at heart, now and forevermore.

That meant that if the time ever came for Owen to compete for a woman... Well, he'd win. It was as plain as that.

With all the authority he could muster—and it was a considerable quantity—Owen drew himself up. "Good. I'm glad we understand each other." He gave his man a companionable cuff to the shoulder, happy the matter was settled. "I'll be relying on you to keep an eye on things down here while I'm busy upstairs."

Smartly, his helper saluted. "Will do, boss."

"See that everything runs smoothly, you hear? I won't tolerate any nonsense just because I'm busy." Owen tucked the slip of paper in his vest pocket. He turned to make a properly authoritative exit...and all but collided with Daisy.

She folded her arms. "I need a word with you, Owen."

At the sight of her, Gus gave an uneasy whistle. It wasn't difficult to guess why. From her high-held chin to her crossed arms and tapping foot, Daisy was the very picture of annoyed femininity.

Owen quailed. He couldn't help it. A riled-up woman was something no man wanted to be confronted with, leastwise not while another man stood near. Especially a man who might well be sweet on the same woman whom Owen longed to have for his own.

"Good luck, boss!" Gus yelped. "I've got stalls to muck out." He tipped his hat hastily to Daisy, then hotfooted away.

Relieved for a chance to lighten the mood, Owen hooked his thumb at his helper. "Gus isn't usually so keen to shovel horse pucky. You must be some kind of miracle worker."

Daisy only cocked her head, still at a wrathful simmer.

"Well!" On to innocence next, then. With deliberate naiveté, Owen raised his brows. "Is it lunchtime already? I'm so hungry, I swear I could eat a mouthful of this hay."

He waved his arm at the closest stack. Daisy only narrowed her eyes, plainly not anteing up to the game Owen had in mind.

"You sure do look pretty," he tried next. "Very pretty."

Daisy *humphed*. "There's no use trotting out those dazzling smiles of yours, Owen. I'm not going to be dissuaded."

He was smiling again? Damnation!

That made three…six…seven… Hell, he'd lost count of how many smiles he'd accidentally unleashed over the past few hours. What's worse, just like the last time he'd been caught smiling, he hadn't even realized he was doing it. Deliberately, Owen schooled his expression into one of sober attentiveness.

"I'm not going to be swayed by your looking at me as though I'm some sort of…one-in-a-million miracle, either! So you can quit that, too. Honestly, Owen. I'm standing in a stable wearing yesterday's dress. I can't possibly be all that fascinating."

He was looking at her as though she was fascinating?

Well, that was probably true, Owen allowed. But this situation was rapidly getting worse and worse. Self-consciously, he darted a glance at Gus. His helper was watching his exchange with Daisy with rapt interest. He saw Owen looking, jumped about a foot, then went back to work shoveling at double speed.

"I'm sorry," Owen told Daisy. "I'll try to quit that."

Daisy sighed, shaking her head. Firmly, she recrossed her arms in the other direction. "I can't *believe* you've never remarried. Between your smiling and your spoony looks, women around here must think you're constantly flirting with them."

Owen scratched his head. "Honestly, this has never happened before. The women in town don't think anything of the kind."

"They must! If they feel *half* the things I do when I see you looking at me that way, then—" Abruptly, Daisy broke off. She tried again. "The point I'm making is, you are a handsome and appealing man, Owen, and right now I'm in no position to fight off whatever attraction you might accidentally kindle between us. So if you'd be so kind as to rein in all… that—" she gestured crossly at him, indicating his overall personhood "—I would greatly appreciate it. Especially when I'm trying to have a serious discussion with you. It's very distracting."

Now she knew how he'd felt yesterday, when she'd kept on biting her lip so seductively. Reminded of that, Owen couldn't help grinning. "So you say. But I think you like it."

He certainly had. In an unwise, unstoppable fashion…

"See? There you go again! With that smile of yours!"

Hellfire. She was right. "I'll try harder to stop."

"I'm not sure you can."

Owen wasn't either. Not now, he wasn't. "I can," he swore, hand on his heart. "You don't know how determined I can be."

"That may be true." Speculatively, Daisy looked him up and down. She seemed to become…distracted partway through her survey. Blushing, she jerked her gaze upward. To his mouth.

She stared, dreamily, at him. Owen began to feel warmer. Much warmer. He tugged at his shirt collar, shifting his feet.

No. He couldn't simply *endure* this. It was too much to ask of any man, much less a reformed ne'er-do-well. "Daisy?"

Her still-dreamy gaze drifted upward to his eyes. "Yes?"

"Now you're doing it, too."

She started. Blinked. "No, I'm not!"

"You're looking at me as though *I'm* fascinating, too." Owen cleared his throat. He nodded. "To be clear, you're looking at me the way a woman looks at a man when she wants to be kissed."

She opened her mouth in shock. "I came down here to give you a piece of my mind about talking so freely when Élodie is within earshot! Not to be kissed! By you or…or *anyone*."

Owen felt unconvinced by her protest. He had two good eyes. He knew what he saw and had the experience to interpret it correctly, too. "Furthermore," he added, "I have a problem with the 'anyone' part of that declaration you just made." He shifted his gaze, irritably, toward Gus. "Certain people around here would like nothing more than to be helpful to you. Especially if it gave them a leg up toward earning your affections."

"My 'affections' aren't available!"

Did she mean because she was enamored of her baby's father, Conrad Parish? Or because she wasn't interested in Owen? Or—heaven help him—was sweet on Gus? "Are you sure?" Owen asked.

"Of course I'm sure." Daisy caught the drift of his gaze, glanced at his busily shoveling stable helper, then inexplicably grinned. "You think I'm sweet on Mr. Winston?"

This time, it was Owen's turn to toe the hay-strewn floor. "Could be," he muttered grudgingly. "No accounting for taste."

She chortled. "Well, I guess that's true. But for that to happen, I'd have to move my sights away from you, Mr. Cooper."

Daisy batted her eyelashes at him. Owen would *swear* she did. He swallowed hard, suddenly feeling joyful. Also, unaccountably rattled. A truly good man would not even entertain the thoughts he'd been having. "You've set your sights on me?"

"Got you!" Daisy laughed again. Playfully, she poked him in the chest. "You're not the only one who can flirt. See that?"

Owen saw. He saw that he was in over his head with Daisy, and he'd spent only a couple of days in her company. How much more besotted would he become if given even more time alone with her? He reckoned he'd find out over the next week or so.

"Actually, I'm as surprised about that flirting of

mine as you seem to be," Daisy mused aloud, breaking into his troublesome thoughts. "Lately, I've been just about as retiring as a woman can be. But for some reason, when I'm around *you*..." She eyed him—this time *not* in an overtly enticing way—then shrugged. "I feel quite free to be just as bold and as brazen as I please."

"That's because you know there's nothing you can do that's worse than the things I've done," Owen told her glumly. Already he'd shared more with Daisy than with anyone in Morrow Creek. "Next to my sins, a little feminine flirtation is harmless."

And effective. Damnation, it had been effective. Owen had never before been a sap for a woman— not even Renée. He'd always been too savvy to fall for feminine wiles. Yet...he just had.

"Yes, about that." Daisy perked up, her expression winsome and interested. "You were going to tell me exactly what you'd done that was so bad."

Her pert tone made it sound as though they were discussing the vagaries of the weather. Owen needed to disabuse her of the notion that he was a harmless rascal—the sooner the better.

For reasons he couldn't explain, though, he didn't. Not yet. Soon, he would. But for now... "No, I wasn't."

"You keep mentioning it," Daisy persisted. "You

keep saying how 'bad' you were. You must want to talk about it."

He crossed his arms. "The hell I do!"

"Don't you think I have a right to know?"

That one was easy. "Nope."

"I'll tell you about me," she coaxed, laying her hand on his arm. "I'll tell you anything you want to know."

Lured by that intriguing offer, Owen couldn't resist gazing at her. Damnation, but Daisy looked pretty—and vulnerable, too. The sight of her, so sweet and yet seemingly so alone, put only one query in his head.

"Do you love Conrad Parish?" Owen gestured at her midsection. Roughly, he added, "I'm assuming he's the man you—"

"Yes." Daisy cut him off. Her cheeks reddened. She moved away her hand. "He's the... Well, he's the only one who—"

Who I love, Owen imagined her saying, and didn't want to hear any more. Of course Daisy loved Conrad Parish. What else had he expected? That she'd forgotten her baby's father the minute she met Owen? That she'd want *him* more than the man she'd been with—the man she'd already, apparently, given her heart to?

"You don't have to explain." Unassailably crushed by her response, Owen raised his palm. Discomfort prickled between them. "It's only natural that you'd feel that way about—"

About your baby's father. Remembering that Gus had been listening—and that the only thing Daisy had ever chastised him about was talking unwisely when Élodie could overhear him—Owen stopped. Cautiously, he glanced sideways.

Gus was gone—busy grooming a horse at a distant stall.

A hasty survey of the stable told him Élodie was safely upstairs, providentially out of earshot this time.

"About your baby's father," Owen finished in a low tone. "He should be here with you, helping you. Standing by you."

Daisy gave him an unaccountably wry look. "Conrad stands by himself. That's pretty much it."

At that, Owen frowned. Catching sight of his undoubtedly ferocious and protective expression, Daisy widened her eyes.

"I don't mean to say that Conrad is a bad person!" she insisted. "Or that I would keep him from his… from me." She inhaled deeply. "From *us.*" Probably unknowingly, she stroked her slightly rounded belly. "After all," she mused, "it's possible that the bond of parenting would allow Conrad and me to overcome our differences and be happy together. Eventually."

Then she *did* hope they would reconcile, Owen

realized. Whatever their differences were, Daisy hoped to overcome them.

"I understand," Owen said. "That's all I needed to know."

Daisy peered at him. "I'm not sure you *do* understand. Not given the way you're looking at me." Pensively, she sighed. "I'm not a bad person, Owen. Truly, I'm not! I realize that I'm in an unusual predicament right now, but ordinarily—"

"You're good. I know that."

She laughed. "How can you?"

"The same way you knew to believe me," Owen told her unflinchingly, "when I said I'd done bad things in my life."

Daisy shook her head. "You were exaggerating."

"Was I?" Owen asked. "If you really believed I was telling tales, you wouldn't persist in asking me for details."

Daisy bit her lip. Evidently stymied, she shook her head.

"I don't care what you've done," she insisted stalwartly—and naively. "It's who you are now that matters."

Briefly Owen closed his eyes. "I wish that were true."

"It is true!"

He opened his eyes to the sight of Daisy's determined face, gazing at him with utter certainty. "You don't know me."

"I know you care about Élodie," Daisy disagreed. "I know you are kind to your stabled horses, because I saw you with them earlier. I know you're from the East, because I recognize your accent—as much as you seem to have lost parts of it. I know that you sound meaner than you are." With a gentle touch to his arm, Daisy gave him a squeeze. "I know you should smile more."

With that, she went too far. "I know that you shouldn't deny your baby a father, just because you see faults in Conrad," Owen said. "Sometimes a man deserves a second chance, Daisy."

Looking wounded, Daisy stared at him. Then, she rallied.

"That's interesting, Owen. Are you talking about Conrad?" Her astute expression unnerved him mightily. "Or yourself? Maybe you're the one who's looking for a second chance."

Hellfire. Swearing beneath his breath, Owen looked away. Without knowing it, he'd said far too much. What was it about Daisy that revealed all his most painful parts as though they were nothing more frightening than laundered britches on a line?

"I can't stand here jawing all day. I have work to do."

"Yes." Uncomfortably, Daisy shifted. "So do I."

Owen cleared his throat, unwilling to leave things on such tense terms between them, but unsure how to rectify the situation. He settled on asking, with stiff politeness, "Are things going well? With Élodie's lessons?"

"Very well. Élodie and I made biscuits a while ago."

"Fine." Owen rubbed the back of his neck. From beneath the cover of his overlong hair, he peeked sidelong at Daisy. "I like biscuits."

Unexpectedly, she laughed. "That's what Élodie said!" Somehow, her laughter made the tension between them fall away. "In almost exactly that same tone of wonder and delight, too."

"Like father, like daughter," Owen allowed, smiling too.

"So don't dawdle," Daisy went on in a mock-lecturing tone. "The biscuits are fresh now, but they won't stay that way long."

"I won't dawdle, I promise," Owen told her.

He watched with genuine, puzzling relief as Daisy accepted his assurance with a nod. Lifting her skirts, she turned away.

"And I'll watch what I say around Élodie, too," Owen called after her, belatedly recalling why she'd visited his stable in the first place. "I'll be more careful in the future."

Daisy nodded again. "Thank you. I'd appreciate that."

Feeling somehow at a loss still, Owen searched his mind for the reason. He reached only one conclusion. "Daisy?"

At the foot of the stairs now, she paused. "Yes?"

I'll tell you about my past, if you really want to know.

On the verge of making that impossible promise, Owen stopped. "Save me a few biscuits. I'll be upstairs directly."

As though she'd sensed, somehow, that he'd been on the verge of confiding in her, Daisy frowned. Then she nodded.

"You can count on me!" she promised him.

Then, just as though that were true, Daisy blew him a kiss and headed upstairs...this time, carrying a little piece of Owen's heart with her—just when he'd decided for certain that she needed her baby's father in her life, no matter what.

Chapter Sixteen

It was past lunchtime by the time Owen recalled the note in his pocket. Happily sated with vegetable-barley soup, buttered biscuits with mesquite honey and the promise of more delicious treats to come—courtesy of Daisy and Élodie—he stopped at the water pump, where he'd gone to collect water for Daisy.

He felt ridiculously pleased that, this time, she hadn't argued with him over the need for him to perform that strenuous task. It was good that Daisy let him care for her a little bit. She needed help, and Owen wanted to give it. That was that.

While reaching for the pump handle, Owen heard something crinkle in his shirt pocket. Puzzled, he glanced downward. He retrieved the slip of paper he'd stashed there, then unfolded it, absently scanning those few neatly hand written lines.

To: Mr. Conrad Parish

Horton House Hotel, San Diego, California

I'm sorry. I hope you can forgive me.

Please do not tell Barker & Bowles what I have done.

I will make it right somehow. I promise.

Yours Fondly, Daisy Walsh.

Fondly. Staring at those words, Owen frowned. *Yours fondly.*

He wondered what Daisy possibly had to feel sorry for. He wondered why she wanted forgiveness, when he couldn't imagine her doing a single thing that warranted absolution. He wondered how Daisy meant to make things right and what—exactly—she was so desperate to keep a secret from her publisher, Barker & Bowles.

Most likely, Owen reasoned, she wanted to hide her pregnancy. Most likely, Daisy had decided there were no further denials possible. She'd penned this message to Conrad Parish, to beg his forgiveness and ask for his help.

Looking at that name again, Owen felt his frown deepen.

With all his heart, he hoped Conrad Parish was worthy of Daisy's esteem. He hoped the man wasn't the scurrilous bastard Owen assumed he must be, to have left her on her own. He hoped Daisy knew what she was doing by promising to make things up to him. Owen hoped further, as he looked at her message again, that Daisy would understand why he couldn't possibly send it.

Crumpling the note in his fist, Owen shoved it back into his pocket. He grabbed the pump handle, then gave it a vigorous tug.

Later he'd visit the telegraph office himself, he decided. Later he'd dictate another message in Daisy's name—a more appropriate message. He'd deliver a message that would bring Conrad Parish to Morrow Creek in person to do what was right—to care for Daisy the way she deserved to be cared for.

By the time the man arrived, Owen told himself, Daisy would be grateful to see him. Because in her delicate condition, what she needed most was a good man to love her. And no matter how much Owen might want to be that man, he knew he never could be.

Renée had made that more than clear.

Maybe, he hoped, Conrad Parish could do better.

But only if he knew where to find Daisy. Only if he believed she wanted to see him. Only if he knew for certain about the baby Daisy was carrying…and the complicated future she was facing on her own. Surely, once he knew all that, Conrad Parish would do the right thing and make Daisy his wife.

Then, if Owen were truly lucky, Parish would take Daisy far, far away. He'd take her someplace where

Owen would never have to see her again—someplace where he'd never have to wonder what might have been between them…if only things were different. If only he were better, and had the wisdom to stay that way.

But since Owen knew he couldn't be better—and he didn't have the luxury of time to fool himself about that fact—he had to act now. So that's exactly what he meant to do.

For Daisy's sake.

It was surprising to Daisy how quickly she fell into an enjoyable routine while tutoring Élodie. Each morning, she awakened to the sounds, sights and delicious smells of Owen preparing breakfast—a task he insisted on not relinquishing.

"Mmm!" she exclaimed on one such morning, giving the rumple-haired, sleepy-eyed Owen a fond smile. The sight of him always cheered her. "I think I must be having a positive influence on you. Your toasting skills are improving."

"Nonsense. You're only growing more tolerant," he said.

"I've always been tolerant," Daisy disagreed. "And you've rebuffed my compliments long enough! You must believe me. You *are* improving with your cooking." Encouragingly, Daisy patted his brawny shoulder. "At this rate, you'll be writing your own cookery book, and making my own book obsolete."

"Hardly. My skills scarcely compare with yours." Owen smiled at her—a sight that never failed to delight Élodie—then urged her with a shoulder shrug toward her chair. "Sit. Enjoy."

Obediently, Daisy took her place at the table, a place that unfailingly made her feel at home every morning. Afterward, she and Élodie cleaned up. Next, they typically had sewing lessons together— or, more recently—embroidery tutorials. The little girl had proved to be a very adept learner. Already Élodie had stitched up two dolls' dresses, a tea towel and a pillowcase with a dropped hem. Daisy was proud of the little girl's accomplishments—and proud of her own achievements in tutoring Élodie, as well.

Here no one criticized her methods, the way Conrad had. No one complained or made snide remarks. Given a few days without such treatment, Daisy found herself feeling downright liberated. This was what she'd felt like before—before Conrad, before her speaking engagements tour...before her baby.

Even that situation was becoming easier to cope with. At first it had been difficult—especially on that day in the stable, when Owen had pressed Daisy to confirm that Conrad was her baby's father. Owen had seemed to take the news particularly hard, although Daisy couldn't understand why. *Someone* had to be her baby's father, after all; Owen had plainly guessed who.

Daisy's confirmation of that fact couldn't have surprised him. Yet Owen had seemed almost downhearted. It was very odd.

Now, though, those days had passed. With Owen's support and encouragement—and ginger tea—Daisy made it through her next few bouts of morning sickness more easily. With Owen's reassurances, she gradually dared to speak aloud about her baby. With Owen to listen, she even sometimes indulged in the occasional daydream about her baby—and their future together.

"I think he's a boy," Daisy confided in Owen one afternoon while Élodie was occupied in her bedroom. "That's what Élodie wants—a boy. She's suggested I knit booties for him." At Owen's unusual expression, Daisy hastened to explain. "It won't be too difficult. After all, they'll be *very* small booties."

"That's a good idea. I'm glad you've…accepted things."

"Yes. It's getting easier." Not wanting to go into detail, Daisy smiled brightly at him. "And so are you! You didn't even notice that I carried that heavy Dutch oven by myself just now."

Owen gave a disgruntled sound. He looked gorgeous, even while being his most curmudgeonly self. Unhappily, he glanced at the aforementioned pot, which she'd placed on the stove top.

"I know how to fix that." He strode to the hall, moving with his usual mixture of strength and straightforwardness. "Élodie! Hurry up with your hair brushing. We're going out."

"Out?" Daisy balked. It was one thing to come to terms with her situation while safely ensconced in Owen and Élodie's household. It was another to confront Morrow Creek directly. She'd spent some time with her brother, of course, but Thomas still didn't know about her baby—and she wasn't ready to tell him. "But I have yeast dough rising, and a rug-hooking lesson to finish, and I don't have a single presentable thing to wear—"

"You look very pretty to me," Owen said. "As always."

Torn, Daisy dithered. Through force of habit, she held out her calico skirts, performing a dutiful turn. "Do you think this dress will do? It's borrowed, and it's not a very good fit—"

Blandly, Owen gazed at her. "Are you asking me to wear it?"

Daisy boggled at the very notion. "Of course not. But—"

"Then all that matters is what *you* think of it."

Well. That was true. Chagrined to have allowed

Conrad's long-standing control of her behavior to resurface, Daisy dropped her skirts. Truthfully, she'd only been tossing out ready-made excuses, preparing herself, as always, to deflect unfavorable judgment. But now, she no longer needed to do that. Now she'd struck out on her own. "Well, then...I think it's fine!"

"Good." Owen nodded. "I agree. Let's go."

"In fact, I think it's more than fine!" she elaborated giddily. "It's *very* flattering! This color looks marvelous on me!" With a sideways glance at the reflective surface of the nearest window, Daisy lifted her chin. "My hair looks nice today too."

"All the more reason to show yourself off." Obligingly, Owen crooked his elbow, offering himself as her escort.

At the same time, Élodie emerged from her bedroom. She saw her father's proffered arm, glimpsed Daisy's obvious hesitation, then marched over to them both. With an utter lack of subtlety, Élodie forcibly tucked Daisy's hand where it belonged.

"Your hand goes *here,* Daisy," the little girl explained with an air of helpfulness, "right in the crook of Papa's arm."

"Thank you, Élodie," Owen said, darting a glance at Daisy.

"Yes." Awkwardly, Daisy cleared her throat. She

felt wildly aware of Owen's warmth and strength and closeness. "Thank you."

"You two look a right picture!" Élodie announced with evident satisfaction. She clapped proudly. "I'm very pleased!"

"I blame you," Owen grumbled to Daisy from the corner of his mouth. "You're the one who's taught her to be so forceful."

But Daisy could tell he was only joshing. The twinkle in his eyes gave him away. "There's nothing wrong with a female who knows what she wants. Someday, you'll thank me for that."

With his free hand, Owen touched Daisy's chin, urging her to look directly at him. Startled, Daisy did. She smiled.

"I already thank you," he said sincerely. "Thank you for all you've done for Élodie. And for me." He gazed into her eyes, his thumb still on her chin. He stroked her there—just the merest whisper of a touch that set her senses aflame. "It's high time I showed you a little gratitude for all your hard work."

With that, Daisy found herself whisked outdoors for another adventure, with Owen by her side and Élodie dogging their steps…and her teeny unborn baby kicking up his heels, too.

Chapter Seventeen

"Over here." Owen waved, coming to a stop in the uneven shade of a ponderosa pine. "This looks like a good patch."

Daisy hurried over. Holding an empty bucket, she gazed at the ground with surprise. "Are those wild strawberries?"

Owen nodded, happy to have pleased her. "All you can pick and then some." He gestured. "Hand me your bucket. I'll start."

"I didn't expect to find strawberries in the Arizona Territory." Daisy hunkered down beside him to help. Her skirts flowed in a circle around her, lending her an angelic appeal. "But then, it seems I've found much more than I dreamed of here."

Sensing her gaze fixed meaningfully on him, Owen went on picking strawberries. He didn't dare hope that Daisy meant what it seemed she meant.

"This isn't the desert, or Tucson or Tombstone. Here in the high country, things are different."

"I can see that." Adeptly, Daisy added a handful of tiny, ripe red berries to their shared bucket. She glanced around the hillside where Owen had brought her and Élodie, a short distance from Morrow Creek. Nearby, the town's namesake stream trickled past. It had already lured Élodie to take off her shoes and wade in its shallow, sun-dappled waters. "Thank you for this."

Uncomfortable with her gratitude, Owen shrugged. "This? It's the same kind of chores you'd be doing, except outdoors."

"Joke all you want," Daisy said, her gaze still pinned on him. "That doesn't change the fact that it was kind of you to bring me someplace so beautiful. And so peaceful. Thank you."

She acted as though she didn't deserve it. Perturbed by that realization, Owen frowned. "If you thank me again—"

Daisy startled him by popping a strawberry in his mouth.

Automatically, Owen chewed. The berry tasted sweet and luscious, full of juicy goodness. "I'll go on strike," he said.

"Go ahead," Daisy dared him, full of merriment—and more handfuls of strawberries. She fed him another. "That only means you won't have any strawberry pie. Or strawberry jam. Or strawberry shortcake. Or strawberry tart. Or strawberry—"

This time, Owen was faster. This time, he fed Daisy.

Her eyes widened. She chewed, her eyes briefly closing in apparent ecstasy. Owen began to doubt the wisdom of his actions. Seeing Daisy in the throes of pleasure was dangerous, indeed. It only made him imagine her in other, more carnal, situations.

"Fool," she burst out. "*Strawberry* fool," she went on, doubtless continuing her sham threats from earlier. "It's a mixture of stewed fruit, folded into whipped cream, then—"

"I know what a fool is," Owen interrupted. *It's me. It's me, because I can't stop wanting to be near you.* "Believe me."

Daisy didn't seem to hear the warning in his voice. Wearing the same dreamy-eyed look she'd had in his stable days ago, she leaned nearer. She'd stopped picking strawberries, Owen noticed abstractedly. Instead, she'd apparently decided to stare at him.

At his mouth, to be precise. Damnation.

She wanted to kiss him, he realized. God help him, he wanted that too. He wanted to kiss Daisy until neither of them knew what day it was—and neither of them cared a whit.

Owen refused to take advantage of Daisy that way. Desperate and determined, he blurted, "You asked me to tell you what I've done that's so bad? Fine. I'll tell you right now."

Surprised, Daisy leaned back. She blinked. "All right."

Good. The truth was already working to protect her. Knowing that what he was about to tell Daisy would likely erect a permanent barrier between them, Owen nodded. "You were right about me," he began. "I *did* do some gambling. Lots of gambling."

"Oh." Appearing relieved, Daisy smiled. "See? That's not so bad! Owen, I don't know what you were so worried about."

Was that compassion in her eyes? He didn't deserve it.

"Including riverboat gambling," Owen told her. "The kind of gambling that fleeces gullible travelers looking for adventure."

"Gullible?" *Like me,* she seemed to think…at least to Owen's mind. Her gaze turned wary. "I see. Is that all?"

"No. I had unwise affairs with women too. A few of them married," Owen admitted. "They were *unhappily* married, but I still shouldn't have done it. I shouldn't have taken advantage."

Daisy seemed to sense what he meant. "I'm not married."

That wasn't the point. She would be married—and deserved to be—once Conrad came. And, Owen realized with dismay, he still hadn't banished the wistful look from Daisy's eyes. What kind of hellacious admissions would it take to make her see the truth about him? Whatever they were, he vowed to make them. For her.

Ruthlessly, Owen pushed onward. "I did some stealing when I was younger. Some fighting, too. I had the occasional tussle with the law. Most of the time, I wasn't gainfully employed. I spent money rashly and widely." He glanced sideways, making sure Élodie couldn't overhear him. She was still happily playing in the creek. He gazed at the sky, trying to recall his other transgressions. Renée's voice came to him, reminding him of them all. "In my youth, I was an awful layabout," Owen confessed to Daisy. "All I wanted to do was visit gambling halls, drink myself into oblivion and make mischief with my friends—preferably all at the same time." Owen quirked his lips, remembering. "All of them were equal miscreants, I promise."

"Oh. I see." Daisy pondered that, appearing to consider his revelations. She nodded. "Yes, that does sound pretty bad."

Despite his purposeful ruination of his own reputation—at least in Daisy's eyes—Owen felt crestfallen. But he couldn't allow Daisy to believe he was a better man than he deserved. He nodded in acknowledgment, not yet finished with cataloguing his indiscretions. "It *was* bad. I've worked faro tables for easy money, pickpocketed crowds in Baltimore, had affairs—"

"You already mentioned that one."

"—with more women than I should have, all in the name of enjoying myself as much as possible." Still feeling ashamed of that behavior, Owen looked away. "Some of those women, I probably broke their hearts," he admitted roughly. "That's what I'm most sorry for. If I could take it back, I would."

"I'll bet those women wouldn't want it that way." Daisy brushed her fingers over the glossy green leaves of the strawberry plants, her expression full of quixotic dreaminess. "I'll bet they still treasure whatever time you had together."

Well, at least he'd never gotten one of those women with child, Owen thought in his own defense. At least he'd never left one of his former paramours to fend for herself, in Daisy's dire circumstances. Certainly, he'd never abandoned someone he'd cared for—no matter how little time they'd shared together. He'd never purposely hurt anyone, Owen knew. Whatever injured feelings he might have caused had been the result of immaturity and misunderstandings, rather than deliberate unkindness.

He was still doing his best to atone for that immaturity too, even after all these years…and all of Renée's urgings.

"That's a romantic view," Owen said, "but it's wrong. I made a lot of mistakes, Daisy. I'm still paying for them."

Silently, Daisy gazed at him. She appeared to be taking in everything he'd said…everything he was. For one cowardly moment, Owen wished he hadn't had to disillusion her. He wished he truly was the easily forgiven man Daisy seemed to believe he was. But the truth was far harsher than that. Owen could never have the forgiveness he longed for, because Renée was gone.

Renée hadn't lived to see Owen redeemed. That meant he could never be forgiven…not for any of his youthful mistakes.

Finally Daisy spoke. "You've done good things too, Owen. You've established a thriving stable business. You've earned the respect of your friends and neighbors in Morrow Creek. You've raised Élodie all by yourself." Tenderly, she took his hand. "You've taken in a worried young woman and made her happy."

Owen shook his head. He couldn't believe it.

"You're a good man," Daisy insisted. "I can see it. Élodie can see it. Everyone in town can see it!" With apparent frustration, she squeezed his hand. "Do you think I would have consented to stay with just any man who won that raffle?"

She had him there. "No," Owen admitted grudgingly.

"See?"

"Just 'any man' might not have made such good toast."

At that, Daisy laughed. The sound of her laughter made Owen's whole body feel looser. Could Daisy be right? Could she, as an outsider in Morrow Creek, see things that he could not?

Could Daisy see that he *wasn't* beyond redemption?

Filled with foolhardy hope, Owen boasted, "I know how much you love my toast. It's the best in four counties, at least."

"At least," Daisy agreed. "And just for the record, I think Élodie was pulling my leg before. Because you've smiled at me *far* too much for me to believe it's an infrequent occurrence."

Soberly Owen shook his head. He didn't want to remember what his daughter had said over breakfast. He didn't want to admit that it was true. But since he was a *former* scoundrel, he said, "Élodie believes it. She believes she never sees me smile."

And I don't know if it's true or not. He hoped not.

"Well." For a long moment, Daisy merely looked at him. Then she said, "If that was true once, it's not true anymore."

Owen shook his head. "You're too kind, Daisy. I hope—"

I hope you're happy...with Conrad, he intended to say.

Instead, his daughter saved him from making another foolish misstep. From the creek bank, Élodie waved to him and Daisy.

"Oh, come quick!" Élodie yelled, fresh-faced and possessed of muddy skirts. "I think I found a frog! You've got to see it!"

Daisy went on looking at him expectantly, obviously waiting for him to tell her what he hoped for. But Owen only shrugged.

"We can't miss a frog." He held out his hand for Daisy to grasp, lifted them both to a standing position, then called out to his little girl, "We're on our way, Élodie! We'll be right there." With tardy concern, Owen glanced at Daisy. "Will you be all right? Be very careful on the rocks. Don't slip."

"I'll be fine," Daisy assured him. She waved to Élodie. She tugged Owen's hand—this time, apparently, determined to lead him. "I'm not the least bit worried, as long as we're together."

For one reckless moment, Owen agreed. Then, before his good sense could return, he led Daisy to the creek, where—exactly as reported—they found a frog. And maybe, Owen couldn't help hoping, he and Daisy had found a whole lot more, besides...

Chapter Eighteen

Seated snugly in Owen Cooper's bachelor living quarters, Thomas Walsh gazed at his sister in warm bemusement. When he'd made plans to meet her there, on her seventh day in Morrow Creek, he'd never expected to stumble upon such a scene of domestic bliss. If he hadn't known better, he'd have sworn that Daisy, Élodie and the laconic Owen Cooper were a proper family.

"I've never seen you appear so content!" Marveling at her, Thomas accepted a cup of the lemonade she offered him. "Not even when we were younger, back home in New York City. It seems that tutoring students in the arts of home economics and cookery suits you. Either that," Thomas elaborated with a grin, "or Mr. Cooper has already worked his *magnificent* charm on you."

At his joke—for Thomas could imagine no man less conventionally charming than tough, unsociable

Owen Cooper—a peculiar silence fell in the room. Daisy glanced at Owen. The stableman scowled fearsomely at Thomas. Then Élodie grinned.

"I think it must be the second one you mentioned, Mr. Walsh," Élodie piped up. "Because Papa *is* ever so charming!"

At her girlish avowal, Daisy seemed to find her voice.

"Yes, he is that, isn't he, Élodie? Here, Thomas. Have a jumble to go with your lemonade," she urged him. Appearing flustered, she aimed the plate in his direction. "Élodie and I baked them just this morning, especially for your visit."

Gratefully, Thomas accepted a cookie. The sweets smelled delicious. They tickled his senses with spices, molasses and dried fruit, proving Daisy's expertise—and his own wisdom in promoting her skills via his newspaper editorials and raffle.

"Thank you, Daisy. These certainly do look wonderful!" Miss Reardon said as she, too, accepted a cookie. "Look at that! You've even arranged the plate so prettily, with a doily."

"I crochet them," Daisy explained. "I'd be pleased to show you how to do it. The pattern is a snap of the fingers."

"Oh, yes, please," Miss Reardon said. "That would be nice."

Thomas smiled at her, delighted that his sister and

Mellie were getting along so well. Mellie had agreed to accompany him when he'd slipped away from the *Pioneer Press* offices today. On their way to the Coopers', he and Mellie had encountered Miss O'Neill too, her arms laden with her customary weekly delivery—two bundles of clean laundry, a set of stiffly starched linens and several jars of her personal specialty: spiced apple butter.

With a natural hostess's skill, Daisy made the rounds of their assembled company, chatting and offering jumbles. For a few moments, the only sounds heard were moans of gustatory pleasure, including his own. It was, Thomas thought, quite *bold* to be making such sounds in mixed company, but he couldn't help himself. His sister and Élodie's cookies were just that good.

"Mmm. These are scrumptious, Daisy! And Élodie," he said.

"Thank you! Papa helped us bake them!" the girl enthused. She directed a broad, proud grin at her father. "He stoned the raisins himself. Then he pounded the nuts with a hammer."

"With…a hammer?" Thomas blinked. "Truly?"

Owen stiffened. "It seemed expedient," he growled.

The ladies seemed to consider this revelation, doubtless imagining the stableman clobbering the stuffing out of a pile of nutmeats. Protectively, Thomas moved nearer to Miss Reardon.

"Yes, I had to admire Owen's...unorthodox approach. It worked a trick, I must say. Lickety-split, too." Staunchly, Daisy took her place beside Owen, as though to defend him. "Besides, I'm learning that things are done a bit differently out west."

"Yes, they are." Owen nodded, seeming—to Thomas's relief—far less inclined to pound anything else for a while. The stableman gazed up at Daisy. "But your good results can't be denied. I've never tasted a more delectable sweet in my life."

At his praise, Daisy beamed, her cheeks a delicate pink.

Even more strangely, Owen almost...smiled back at her.

But that couldn't be, Thomas mused, trading a puzzled glance with Miss Reardon. Everyone knew that taciturn Owen Cooper did not smile. He did not laugh. He did not suffer fools gladly, and he did not—ordinarily—entertain guests in his home.

Evidently, Daisy had changed some, if not all, of those things. After all, there were four of them currently visiting, if Daisy were included among them. That meant that lonesome Owen Cooper *was* entertaining guests in his home. Not only that, but the man was currently mooning at Daisy, too. The two of them appeared more like cooing lovebirds than tutor and host, Thomas realized. At this rate, Owen

Cooper would be attending sociable events on a voluntary basis. But that was laughable. Wasn't it?

Everyone knew Owen Cooper would rather pluck out his own toenails with blacksmith's tongs than attend a soiree. He'd muttered something to that effect not two months ago, in fact.

"I hope you're not finding our customs *too* strange for your liking, Miss Walsh," Miss Reardon said, bringing Thomas back to the conversation at hand. "Sometimes our methods aren't ideal, but that's what happens when you're forced to make do. My own family originated from the East, you know. It's been a challenge, at times, to orient ourselves to the territory."

"Actually, I like it here, more than I expected," Daisy said. "If not for…other matters, I could happily settle here."

Alerted by her odd tone, Thomas wondered what matters she spoke of. As far as he knew, his sister had been eager to leave New York City for other experiences. That's what she'd written in her letters to him, at least. "You mean if not for your ongoing speaking-engagements tour?" he asked. That must be it. "But that's easily settled! When your tour is finished, you can come back to Morrow Creek to write your next cookery book."

"Yes, do!" Miss Reardon agreed. "That's a lovely idea!"

Smiling, she and Thomas glanced at Miss O'Neill,

expecting her to agree. Instead, the laundress gazed at Owen Cooper, her expression dreamy and her soap-roughened hands slack in her lap.

Miss Reardon noticed Miss O'Neill's expression too. "Isn't that right, Abbey?" she prompted her friend. "Wouldn't it be nice if Miss Walsh came back to Morrow Creek sometime soon?"

Miss O'Neill blinked. She frowned. "Indeed. *So* nice."

Daisy seemed to notice Miss O'Neill's distractedness, too. She glanced from Abbey to Owen, then back again. She frowned.

Peculiarly, Daisy glanced down at herself next, seeming displeased. Perhaps that was because she was wearing one of the dresses Miss Reardon had lent her, Thomas decided. Doubtless the garment had looked lovelier when worn by its original owner.

In fact, on Daisy, that dress appeared downright snug, Thomas saw, especially in the midsection. As though conscious of that fact, Daisy rubbed her palm over her belly. She sighed.

But then, perhaps he was biased in Miss Reardon's favor, Thomas thought with another smile at his companion. If only he knew how to dazzle Miss Reardon with wit, or charm her with masculine allure. But if there were anyone more hopeless than himself in such matters, Thomas didn't know who it might be.

Even Owen Cooper, for all his intimidating and unsociable ways, had the skill to set the ladies aflutter. Thomas had seen it himself, although he still couldn't fathom the reason for it.

Perhaps one had to be a woman to discern the stableman's apparent magic, though. Because Miss O'Neill went directly back to her spoony expression, right on cue. As though in living proof of Cooper's magnetism, she gazed quite sappily at him—much to Daisy's continued and obvious displeasure. Could his sister, it occurred to Thomas, possibly be *jealous* of Abbey O'Neill?

With new curiosity, Thomas examined the interplay between Daisy and Cooper. The two of them *did* appear uniquely attuned to one another, he observed. When Daisy wanted to set down her plate of jumbles, Cooper seemed to realize her dilemma and moved immediately to relieve her of her burden. Daisy, upon receiving his help, smiled in girlish appreciation. Then, Thomas would be blasted if Owen Cooper didn't smile at Daisy *again*.

As though doing so came quite naturally to her, Daisy turned next to Élodie. She fussed with one of the little girl's braids, adjusted the ribbon that tied it with maternal care, then tickled Élodie beneath her chin. The two females, young and old, traded smiles. Mutual fondness was evident in their gazes.

Thomas gawked, scarcely able to believe his eyes.

Was this merely a display of Daisy's homemaking aplomb? Or had something more...*monumental* occurred while she'd been boarding with the Coopers? For his money, Thomas believed it was the latter.

What had he unleashed with his raffle now? He understood the power of the press, but this was... ridiculous.

"Well, I'd say you're a natural fit here in Morrow Creek, Daisy." Deftly, Miss Reardon steered their conversation in a new direction. "And at Mr. Cooper's home, of course. I don't think any of us have seen this place appear cozier or more welcoming. You've definitely given it a much-needed woman's touch."

"Thank you, Mellie! That's so kind of you." Daisy smiled. Casually, she dropped her hand to Owen's shoulder. She gave him an affectionate squeeze. "I've been fortunate, though. I can't take all the credit. Owen has given me free rein to do whatever I want with his home while I'm here, so I don't have to limit myself to cooking and speaking, the way I usually do. I can decorate and sew and add little homey touches here and there—"

Daisy went on speaking, describing some embroidery she'd done and spinning a funny yarn about a strawberry pie she'd prepared that had especially pleased Owen Cooper, but Thomas couldn't listen. All he could see, suddenly, was his sister's innocent hand resting so familiarly on the stableman's shoulder. All he could discern was the besotted way she looked at him. All he could hear was…

Owen Cooper *laughing* over Daisy's humorous tale.

At that incredible sound, everyone stilled. They gawked.

Everyone, that is, except Daisy. She seemed to accept Cooper's until-now-unheard laughter as an ordinary occurrence.

Flummoxed, Thomas gaped at Miss Reardon. She frowned back at him, seeming as taken aback as he was. Even Miss O'Neill snapped from her reverie at the stableman's rousing chuckle.

"Well," she announced in a stilted tone, "all I can say is, Owen must be *thrilled* to have your expertise for his very own, Daisy! And to think—it's all because of that *raffle drawing.*"

Miss O'Neill punctuated those last words by glaring daggers at Miss Reardon. She even tossed a dissatisfied look in Élodie's direction. Thomas didn't know what was going on, but it seemed plain that something remained unsaid between them—something to do with his recent and exceptionally successful raffle drawing.

"I hope you weren't longing to win the drawing," Thomas said, offering the likeliest commiseration he could think of. "I think we'd all agree that you don't need any lessons, Abbey."

"I certainly don't!" Miss O'Neill raised her chin. "Why, my laundry delivery and prizewinning apple butter prove that."

She gestured at the jars she'd brought with her, which were currently arrayed in a row on the table. Together with Thomas, everyone else looked at those jars, too. Miss Reardon did so politely. Owen did so blandly. Little Élodie did so hungrily.

And Daisy? Well, Daisy gazed at those jars of apple butter as though she wished they would explode and leave Miss O'Neill splattered with sticky sugariness and unsightly bits of apple.

Thomas had never known his sister to be even remotely unkind. Plainly, something had arisen between her and Abbey.

"Yes, thank you for those," she told Miss O'Neill. "I'm not sure where we'll put all of them, though. The pantry is already chockablock with apple butter. It's quite remarkable, in fact."

Miss O'Neill preened. "Well, I *do* like to keep Owen happy."

"Yes." Warily, Daisy eyed her. "So I've gathered."

"After all," Miss O'Neill continued, "he's been on his own for so long now. He needs looking after in the worst way."

"Well. Then it's fortunate I'm here now," Daisy

returned ever so sweetly, "so I can make sure Owen has what he needs."

"Oh, but…aren't you here to tutor Élodie?"

"Yes, I am. Of course. And we're having a wonderful time together too, but…" Daisy appeared stymied. She glanced to Owen for help, saw that the man of the house was oblivious to the drama being played out beneath his nose, then tried again. "But of course I want to make sure Owen is satisfied, too."

"It's so admirable you think you can accomplish that," Miss O'Neill said in an arch tone. "After all, you told us yourself how strange you find it here in the West. And you'll be leaving soon too, won't you? So whatever contentment you and Owen find together… Well, it can't possibly endure for long, can it?"

"Abbey," Miss Reardon interrupted tightly. "That's enough."

"But it's no *secret*," Miss O'Neill said. "Is it? It's no *secret* to any of us. No matter how pleased Daisy and Owen might appear with each other right now, it simply can't continue."

"Well," Daisy tried gamely, "I *do* have another book planned—sort of a cookery book and memoir combined. If I return to Morrow Creek to write it, as Thomas suggested, then maybe…"

She trailed off, as though hoping Owen Cooper would add his approval to the idea of her returning to town. But for once, the lummox of a stableman seemed not to recognize his cue.

"Then everything will be wonderful!" Thomas said in a vigorous tone, doing his best to bring closure to his sister's quarrel with Miss O'Neill. "And none of us would dare argue otherwise. Daisy, I know how difficult it can be to make the adjustment to Western living. *I* certainly struggled with it. But I assure you, if *I* can do it, anyone can do it—especially you."

As his reward for speaking out, Miss Reardon smiled at him. Ridiculously infatuated by her, Thomas smiled back. He ought to capitalize on this moment, it occurred to him. He ought to make the most of Miss Reardon's sudden burst of esteem. But how?

Before he could conceive of a way, Daisy spoke up.

"Thank you, Thomas. I'm happy you think so. But if you only knew—" She broke off, traded a puzzlingly enigmatic glance with Owen, then resumed. "If you only knew the challenges I'm faced with, you might not feel quite so confident about my abilities."

"To the contrary. There's nothing you can't do, Daisy!" Thomas offered her a brotherly grin. He gestured at the inviting home she'd created for the Coopers. "Why, if Mother and Father could see you now, just imagine how proud they'd be!"

To his horror, Daisy's eyes filled with tears.

She sniffled, patted her skirts, then turned away.

"I—I'm so sorry!" Daisy cried. "I seem to have… something in my eye. Everyone, please continue enjoying the cookies!"

Futilely, she went on searching for something. Seated at her side, again divining what she needed, Owen Cooper pulled out a handkerchief. He glowered ferociously at Thomas—who couldn't help shrinking back in response—then moved nearer to Daisy.

With his back to his assembled guests, Owen gave Daisy his handkerchief. He muttered a few kind-sounding words. Élodie moved, too. Hurriedly and fiercely, she hugged Daisy's middle.

"Don't worry!" the little girl said. "This will pass before you know it, just like all the other crying jags you've had."

There'd been others? Thomas wondered. Concerned, he scowled at Owen Cooper. If the stableman had dared to hurt his sister…

Well, he'd earn himself a piece of Thomas's mind, at least. And maybe a bout of fisticuffs, too, just to set the lesson.

Filled with indignation and protectiveness, Thomas rose. He balled his fists, then marched over to confront Cooper.

"Have you been making my sister cry?" he demanded. "Because I heard Élodie just then, and if you have, I'll have you know—"

"No, you fool. *You* made your sister cry." Owen's formidable visage loomed into view, a head taller than Thomas's and twice as daunting. "And now you're making it worse."

As corroboration, he nodded toward Daisy. She sniffled again, her face a piteous, scrunched-up, blotchy ball of misery.

"I don't know how and I don't know why," Cooper intoned in a scary voice, "but if you don't make it stop, I swear to God I will make you regret ever opening your mouth."

Thomas quavered. Owen *did* care about his sister, he realized in a burst of awestruck realization. He cared enough to threaten Thomas with bodily injury if he accidentally hurt her.

"See there? You two *do* have something in common after all!" Brightly, Miss Reardon bustled over. Bravely, she inserted herself between the two men, arms outstretched. Efficiently, she wormed Daisy away from Owen's protective presence and Thomas's anxious hovering. "You both care about Daisy, and you're both willing to threaten bloody murder if you don't get your way." She put one arm around Daisy. "Isn't that *dear,* Abbey?"

Miss O'Neill harrumphed. "It must be awful having *two* men fighting over you. Poor, poor Miss Walsh. How *do* you bear up?"

"Pettiness isn't becoming, Abbey," Miss Reardon said in a brisk tone. She guided Daisy away. "Come along, now. Let's see if we can fix you up. How about a good washup and a chat?"

Streaky-cheeked, Daisy nodded. "That sounds nice."

"Yes, it does." A turn. "Are you coming, Abbey?"

"No, I think I'll put away all this apple butter for Owen."

"I truly think we could use your help," Miss Reardon said.

"You'll be fine," Miss O'Neill insisted breezily. "And after all, Miss Walsh *did* seem downright befuddled at the notion of making room in the pantry. So I'll help in that way. Go on!"

Appearing left with no choice, Miss Reardon gallantly whisked Daisy away to the bedroom. Thomas felt simply bedazzled.

"Isn't Miss Reardon *breathtaking?*" he asked. "Did you see the way she swept to the rescue just then? So graciously? So munificently? So *beautifully?* My word, Cooper! I'm just—"

Still searching for an apt word, Thomas turned to Owen. Upon seeing his undoubtedly silly grin, the stableman scowled.

"There's something you need to know about your

sister," Cooper said. He turned to Miss O'Neill. "Can you mind Élodie for a few minutes? Walsh and I need to visit the stable together."

"Certainly, Owen!" she trilled. "Anything for you!"

Acknowledging her helpfulness with a nod, Cooper gave his curious-looking daughter a pat on the head. Then he addressed Thomas again. In a dark voice, he said, "Come with me."

"But I—" Feebly, Thomas gestured. "The stable isn't my—"

"I'm talking. You're listening," Cooper said. "Come on."

Chapter Nineteen

By the time Miss Walsh and Miss Reardon had been in Papa's bedroom for ten minutes, Élodie was nearly out of her skull with boredom. At first, she tried to entertain herself by helping Miss O'Neill put away all those jars of spiced apple butter. Élodie liked apple butter; she wanted to make sure it was within her easy reach the next time Papa made toast for breakfast.

But quickly enough, that task grew dull. Partly because it was a chore—Élodie was no fool; she recognized labor when she saw it—and partly because Miss O'Neill, as friendly as she might be, was one of those grown people who did not know how to speak with children. Not even with Élodie, whom she'd known for years.

"Well, Élodie!" Miss O'Neill said gaily, the moment Papa and Mr. Walsh headed downstairs. "It looks as though it's just you and me now. Er, how are things at the schoolhouse?"

"Fine. It's summertime now, so we're not having lessons."

"Oh. But you'll have them soon, I hope? Shortly after the Independence Day town picnic is over with, I suppose?"

"Yes, I suppose so. Mrs. McCabe did lend me a book to read until school starts up again. It's a very good story, about rabbits who lose their warren. In the illustrations, they're all wearing trousers and little jackets, which is absolutely—"

"Mmm. That sounds excellent." Skirts swaying, Miss O'Neill strode to the cupboard. Hands on hips, she examined its contents. Within plain view, row upon row of apple butter could be seen. There was apple butter sufficient to feed an army of grizzly bears, should any come calling. Or to feed a contingent of trouser-wearing rabbits, Élodie mused, which reminded her...

"—*so* funny to see," she continued, "and they learn—"

"*How* can there be so much apple butter left over?" Miss O'Neill demanded to know, her tone deeply dismayed. "Surely your father enjoys my apple butter a little bit...doesn't he?"

Miss O'Neill's plaintiveness roused Élodie's sense of sympathy. Although she felt disappointed that

Miss O'Neill was obviously not listening to her story about the hilarious rabbits, she didn't want to be rude. Or see Miss O'Neill sad.

"We eat as much apple butter as we can," Élodie explained. "I even put it on griddle cakes, but Papa prefers maple syrup."

Miss O'Neill narrowed her gaze. "Oh, he *does,* does he?"

"Um. Only some of the time, he does!" Élodie blurted. Then, feeling unaccountably uncomfortable, she skedaddled for the relative safety of her bedroom. "I'll be back in a minute!"

"Take your time," Miss O'Neill muttered, not caring.

And that's how Élodie came to be—very accidentally—within earshot when, about four games of jacks later, Miss Reardon slipped out of Papa's bedroom and came to speak in the kitchen with Miss O'Neill. Voices low, they'd conversed hurriedly.

"Abbey, we have to abandon the plan," Miss Reardon insisted, coming straight to the point. "You don't have to worry—I'll tell Matilda and Viola myself. I know these aren't the results we'd hoped for. Not exactly. But wasn't the goal all along to make sure that Owen Cooper didn't wind up a lonely old man, without any hope—or help with Élodie?"

Hearing her name, Élodie perked up. Carefully, she sidled to the very edge of her bedroom doorway, still listening. She was interested in the plan—the raffle-drawing plan to find Papa a wife. Especially now that it might gain him a baby, too.

"Of course it was!" Miss O'Neill hissed. "Of course that was the plan. I helped devise it, remember?" The apple-butter jars scraped across the cupboard shelf, clanging against each other. "But he wasn't *supposed* to find happiness with her."

At that venomous tone, Élodie cringed. Cautiously she glanced toward the closed door of Papa's room. She hoped that, whatever Miss Walsh was doing in there, she couldn't hear this.

"What difference does it make whom he's found happiness with, as long as he's found it?" Miss Reardon coaxed in that soothing voice of hers. Élodie liked the sound of it. "As long as he's happy? We were all worried about how reclusive Mr. Cooper had become—how lonely. And truly, Abbey—when was the last time you heard him laugh that way? Joyfully? Out loud?"

Élodie knew the answer to that one. *Never.*

The apple butter jars clanged again. A sigh was heard.

"Never," Miss O'Neill admitted, echoing what Élodie knew to be true. There was a pause. Another sigh. "But…why *her?*"

"If you'd give her a fair chance, you might learn

that for yourself," Miss Reardon said. "Daisy is a very lovely person."

"No. This only means that we're on the right course," Miss O'Neill disagreed. "This only means that Owen is properly softened up, all the better to appreciate the *right* woman."

"Abbey…" Quiet fell on the kitchen. Then, in an even gentler tone, Miss Reardon said, "You might have to admit it—"

She kept talking, but her voice suddenly faded too low for Élodie to hear. Frowning in concentration, she stepped into the hall. Her foot touched a loose floorboard, making it creak.

The door to Papa's bedroom opened. Miss Walsh stepped out, as though drawn by that creaky floorboard. Her hair was freshly dressed, her forehead fringe was beautifully golden and her face was all scrubbed and pink. She glanced at Élodie, then gave her a kind and inquisitive smile as though wanting to help.

That was Miss Walsh, Élodie reckoned just then. She wanted to help and she wanted to *love*. And Miss O'Neill, no matter what else she said, only wanted to *win*—to win Papa for her very own.

Miss O'Neill looked at Papa the way Élodie looked at her apple butter, hungrily and greedily. But Miss Walsh only looked at Papa the way Élodie herself did...with care and admiration and a whole passel of love. That made all the difference.

"The right woman might not be you," Miss Reardon went on, her voice clearer now. "We've given this a fair try, and—"

"And we're not done trying yet!" Miss O'Neill insisted. "I know I can make Owen fall in love with me. I just need time!"

That was it. Élodie couldn't stand it. She rushed into the kitchen, sticking out her chest fearlessly, the way Papa did.

"He won't ever love you!" Élodie declared fiercely. "He won't." Triumphantly she eyed the surprised women. "So you might as well give up. Because Papa already told me—he won't *ever* love anybody ever again! Not the way he loved my *maman!*"

Élodie could tell by their expressions that they were astounded. They couldn't even argue. They didn't so much as try.

That's how Élodie knew she'd won.

Well, she'd told off Miss O'Neill but good. And maybe it wasn't proper or polite to do so, but it was truthful, and that mattered more. That's what Papa always told her. Proudly Élodie glanced over her shoulder, wanting to share her victory with Miss Walsh. After all, it was partly her victory too. Because it didn't take a summer of book learning or a grown woman's bustled gown to realize that Miss Walsh was head over feet for Papa.

But then Élodie caught sight of Miss Walsh's stricken face, and she realized something she *hadn't* reckoned on until now. As she looked at Miss Walsh, Élodie recalled that, no, Papa could not love Miss O'Neill because he'd already sworn not to.

The trouble with that was, it meant Papa couldn't love Miss Walsh, either, no matter how much she might love him herself.

And now, thanks to Élodie's big mouth, Miss Walsh knew it.

Everyone knew it.

Feeling in a true pickle, Élodie scrambled. "I didn't mean *you,* Miss Walsh!" she cried. "You're different! You know—"

"I think I'll go see if I can find Mr. Winston downstairs," Miss Walsh said quietly, "and find out if he's delivered the message I gave him." She offered Élodie a smile. "I'll be right back."

"You know how to talk to little girls!" Élodie wound up saying, her voice small and meek, as Miss Walsh slipped by her…then disappeared down to the stable without a single glance backward. "That's got to count for something!"

But all it counted for right now, it seemed, were two compassionate looks from the ladies left behind, as Misses Reardon and O'Neill both came forward to comfort Élodie.

Élodie didn't know what to do next. But she did know one thing: if she wanted a baby brother of her own—and if she wanted a wife for Papa—she'd better act quickly. She'd better make Papa forget his vow about Maman…and come to love Miss Walsh just as ardently as she seemed, at least to Élodie's eyes, to love him already.

But how? And would she have enough time to act?

"You never told us about your father's vow," Miss Reardon said, her gaze kind and concerned. "You should have mentioned that, Élodie. It might have made a difference in our plans."

"It might have *ended* our plans, you mean!" Miss O'Neill shook her head, seeming thoroughly put out. "A man who's still in love with his departed wife is no man at all. Leastwise, he's no good to a woman who's living and wants to go on enjoying it."

"Papa is *too* good!" Élodie vowed. "You take that back."

But all the ladies did was give Élodie a little hug and go on staring at the stairway. "I wish she hadn't had to hear it that way," Miss Reardon said. "That must have been difficult."

Miss O'Neill harrumphed. "She's only known him a few days!"

"Sometimes it doesn't matter how long you've

known someone. Sometimes all that matters is how you feel about them. And that can come clear in an instant." Miss Reardon gave Miss O'Neill a sad smile. "I'm sorry, Abbey, but it's true."

Miss O'Neill sniffed in disagreement, but Élodie brightened. All that mattered *was* how people felt. And these days, her papa felt like smiling and laughing. Élodie had to make sure these happy days continued. No matter what it took!

Chapter Twenty

Hurrying down the stairs into the stable below, Daisy lifted her skirts, doing her best not to think about what Élodie had said. But no matter how fiercely she concentrated on each step she took, those innocently spoken words still haunted her.

Papa already told me—he won't ever love anybody, ever again! Not the way he loved my maman!

Could Élodie be right? Daisy wondered. Could Owen really have sworn off love? It was true that he and Daisy hadn't known one another for long. So she was probably being foolish even to imagine that Owen might have feelings for her. And yet…

And yet, Daisy dearly hoped that he might. She hoped that she wasn't the only one who felt compelled to stare, to linger, to wait in anticipation every day for that first "Good morning!" they shared—the greeting that made every day feel brighter. Against all reason, Daisy felt an ease with Owen that she'd never encountered before. She felt an eagerness to be with him that defied all experience. But if Élodie was right…

If Élodie was right, then Daisy might well be making a silly spectacle of herself. If Élodie was right, then Daisy might well be as obvious and pitiful in displaying her feelings as Miss O'Neill was, with her love-struck looks and overzealous gifts of spiced apple butter…delivered by the wagonload.

Not that Daisy felt particularly sorry for the woman, she realized as she reached the stairway's midpoint and clutched the railing to safely slow her hasty descent. If truth be told, Daisy felt decidedly uncharitable toward Abbey O'Neill all of a sudden. In fact, she hoped Miss O'Neill sprouted a few chin hairs and possibly a wart or two before she next encountered Owen—all the better to render her as unappealing as possible.

Not that it would matter, if Owen truly had sworn off love.

Or that it would matter, if Daisy continued traveling down this unkind and unflattering path. Berating herself for her ungenerous thoughts, she lifted her chin, then kept going.

Doubtless, Conrad would have said that Daisy *deserved* to have her romantic hopes dashed. He would have reminded her that, had Owen been offered a chance to choose, he would likely have chosen Miss

O'Neill, who was statuesque and titian haired and handily accustomed to life in the West—all things, Conrad would have rightly pointed out, that Daisy herself was not. Conrad would have tried to save Daisy from her own unwise hopefulness.

Because the truth was, Owen Cooper did not want to love anyone, ever again...least of all pregnant Daisy Walsh. No quantity of wistfulness or delectable jumble cookies would change that.

But no matter how stringently Daisy tried to remind herself of that fact, nothing could stop her heartbeat from quickening as she stepped onto the stable floor. Nothing could stop her breath from catching as she glimpsed Owen, far down the nearest aisle, speaking earnestly with Thomas. And nothing could stop her smile from blooming, unstoppably and nakedly, as Owen spotted Daisy there, too, and offered her a nod hello.

She'd come here to talk with Gus Winston, she reminded herself staunchly. She'd come here to ask about her telegraph wire to Conrad and to find out if there'd been any reply. And indeed, she did catch sight of Owen's faithful helper, currying a mare near the stable's doors. So Daisy could have accomplished her original mission. But almost of their own accord, her feet carried her away from Mr. Winston and down the aisle to Owen.

Regardless of what her mind thought of the matters at hand, Daisy realized, her feet had other ideas. And they intended to carry out the selfsame rebellion she'd begun by boarding that westbound train to Morrow Creek just a few short days ago.

As she approached, Thomas blanched. Her brother gave her a startled look, seemed to grow increasingly uncomfortable, then said something to Owen. For his part, Owen glared at Thomas in a forbidding fashion. He nodded, issued a warning that Daisy couldn't quite make out, then pointed toward the stable's exit.

Without delay, Thomas scurried in that direction. He didn't even pause to offer Daisy a tip of his hat— or to collect Miss Reardon, who'd accompanied him today along with Miss O'Neill.

"That's strange," Daisy said upon reaching Owen. She watched as her brother rushed through the doorway onto the street. "Thomas didn't even wait to say goodbye to me!"

"He feels torn up about hurting you before." Owen turned his face to hers, his gaze probing hers—probably searching for signs of another imminent crying jag. Not finding any, he went on. "He probably doesn't want to risk making you cry."

"Did you threaten to hammer him like a nut if he did?"

Her joke made Owen narrow his eyes. "Something like that."

"You shouldn't have." Still mortified by her out-burst, Daisy looked away, toward a nearby horse. The beast nickered, nosing for Owen's broad shoul-der. "Thomas didn't mean any harm."

"It doesn't matter what he meant. It matters what he did," Owen said. "And what he did is hurt you. He made you cry."

Owen looked as though he'd like to make Thomas cry. Most likely, he could do it, too. Daisy had never met a man more solidly built, more full of strength and vigor, than Owen was. But to her relief, Owen used his strength to protect and help and nurture. She only had to look at Élodie to realize that.

Which was all the more reason why Daisy couldn't fathom Owen's insistence on regretting his scan-dalous past. While it was true that he'd done some awful things in his youth, those days were behind him now. Owen had atoned for his sins many times over.

Still differing with him on the matter of her broth-er's intentions, Daisy shook her head. "Thomas only made me cry because he reminded me of the truth," she insisted. "And the truth is, my parents would *not* be proud to see me as I am right now. They would be…horrified and disappointed." Again, she felt tears well in her eyes. Mightily, she struggled to go on, her voice squeaking with emotion. "Just the way

I am disappointed in myself. So it's not Thomas's fault. It's mine."

"You're defending him."

Daisy blinked. She sucked in a deep breath, her mind awhirl with embarrassment and confusion and dashed hopes. "What?"

"You're defending your brother and blaming yourself." Owen crossed his arms as though the notion displeased him mightily. His frown—so seldom seen these days—deepened. "You do that often, you know. When Élodie's knitted scarf unraveled, you blamed yourself for not teaching her purling better. When Élodie's Scotch barley soup burned, you charged yourself with inattentiveness at the stove top. When Élodie's perfumed tincture wound up smelling like a wet skunk, you promised her it was your fault for not checking the ingredients more carefully."

Towering over her in the stable's earthy peacefulness, Owen shook his head. His demeanor, ordinarily so hard and unaffected—unless he was teasing Élodie—seemed to soften. The longer he looked at Daisy, the softer it became. "You should stop it."

"But my purling lessons were incomplete," Daisy stated. "I didn't watch over the cookstove adequately." *I was looking at you,* she remembered, *wondering how it would feel to have your arms close around me in a hug...imagining how it would feel to*

have your mouth lower to mine, in a kiss so sweet...
She shook herself. "I didn't check the tincture ingredients sufficiently. Obviously, I didn't, or everything would have been fine." Exasperated, Daisy gazed up at Owen. "Élodie is a child. She can't be expected to do everything perfectly."

"But you can?"

How had they begun talking about this? "If I'm at fault, yes!" Daisy said. "It's the same thing Conrad always told me—I must be especially vigilant to guard against my flaws so I can eradicate them. So I can pluck them like garden weeds and—"

"I don't think I like Conrad," Owen interrupted.

At his stony, belligerent expression—so like Élodie's, when confronted for the first time with unfamiliar foods and difficult stitches—Daisy laughed. "You don't even know him!"

"You've told me all about him over the past few days."

"Only bits and pieces." She hadn't wanted to delve too deeply into her time with Conrad. She'd been too busy enjoying herself for that. She'd been too busy decorating for Owen, entertaining and surprising Owen and Élodie, making sure they had little things to enjoy, from tasty treats to plump pillows to shined shoes and even an off-the-cuff harmonica recital. "Not enough for you to truly understand Conrad or my life with him."

Owen didn't seem to appreciate her allusion to the time she'd spent on her speaking-engagements tour with Conrad.

"I don't like anyone who criticizes you."

"Even when that criticism is deserved? Because I can assure you, it's not Conrad's fault he had such a wealth of flaws in me to choose from." Daisy smiled, trying to make a jest of it. "I'm—"

"I don't see any flaws," Owen interrupted her. "I don't."

"*Your* flaw is interrupting people," Daisy said. Obviously, his statement was too nonsensical to be taken seriously. "I would say *you* should stop *that,*" she added in imitation of him.

But Owen appeared undeterred. Still gazing at her, still making her heartbeat quicken just by existing in the same space, he moved closer. Transfixed by the sudden and quite unexpected look of…well, *fondness,* in his eyes, Daisy couldn't move.

Heaven help her, at Owen's look of caring, a part of her dared to dream about what might happen between them. A part of her, at Owen's increasing nearness, dared to hope that what Élodie had said earlier wasn't true. Owen *could* love again.

"I don't see any flaws," Owen repeated. He raised his hand to tuck a wisp of stray hair from her cheek. His fingers lingered there, warm and callused and careful. "I don't. I'm very close to you, Daisy. I'm getting closer all the time, and I don't see a damn thing I wouldn't call wonderful about you."

"You—" Trapped against the gate of the nearest empty stall, Daisy stared up at him. "You're swearing again. Scoundrel."

Briefly, Owen closed his eyes. He appeared to be battling something, but Daisy couldn't imagine what. He sighed, then stroked his fingers over her cheek again, almost cradling her.

"You shouldn't call me that," he warned. "You don't know how scoundrelly I'd like to be right now, here, next to you."

And *he* couldn't know how much Daisy wanted to close her eyes, the better to savor the feeling of his fingertips against her skin. But then she would have missed the sight of him, gazing so fixedly at her. So she just went on looking at him.

"You're so remarkable to look at." She couldn't help sighing, even as Owen cracked a smile—an endearingly bashful smile, suited for a lover. "You are. You're handsome and kind and whip smart, too. But when it comes to me, you aren't looking closely enough. I have plenty of flaws, and it's only right to admit it." She swallowed hard, hoping to regain her rapidly fading sense of perspective. "The fact of the matter is, you've only known me a short while, whereas Conrad—who's a bona fide expert—

has known me for months now. So clearly, he's the one—"

"Clearly he's the one who's a fool for letting you go." Owen's voice grew deeper. Rougher. More fraught with…needfulness? He raised his other hand to her cheek, framing her face in his grasp. Intently, he said, "I don't intend to make the same mistake. I don't intend to let you go."

"Well," she quipped, "I'm staying at least a week longer."

"That's not what I mean. There's a reason I was talking with your brother just now, and it's got to do with you."

"I know. You already told me. You wanted to scare Thomas into being sweet as pie to me." Daisy said those words dreamily, thinking as she did that Owen's protectiveness had endeared him to her in a way that not much else could have. Even if he *was* wrong about Conrad…wrong about her supposed wonderfulness, too. "That's very thoughtful of you, Owen, and I'm sure that my brother was duly chastened. But I'm not worried about Thomas."

He frowned. "What are you worried about?"

"You. That Élodie is right, and you'll never love again." He appeared stricken. She forged on. "That you'll remember who we are—" Daisy broke off, gently patting her expanding belly "—who *I* am, and decide you're better off without me. Most of all,

I'm worried that I'll spend all this time near you, dreaming of what might happen, and never find the courage I really need."

Owen appeared befuddled by at least half the things she'd said. Dispiritedly, he lowered his hands from her face—all the better to gaze at her pregnant belly. "Courage for what? If you're worried about the baby, Daisy, you should know that I—"

She laughed. She couldn't help it. "Of course I'm worried about—" Daisy stopped. Then, strengthened by Owen's kind regard, she hastened onward. "Of course I'm worried about the baby."

Owen's eyes flickered. Obviously, he'd realized how difficult it was for her to acknowledge the truth about her situation and all she faced in the months and years ahead…possibly alone. But rather than tell her what he thought, all Owen did was listen. He listened…and went on looking at her belly.

"But that's not all I'll need courage for." Daisy smiled. "I'll need courage to go back upstairs and face everyone after bawling in their faces today. I'll need courage to apologize to Miss O'Neill for slandering her innocent apple butter—"

"*Please,* no more apple butter!" Owen cried, palms out.

They both laughed. "But right now, I'm thinking of the courage I'll need to do this, with you, right now," Daisy said.

Then she grasped the nearest stable post for balance, drew in a deep breath, lifted herself on tiptoe…and kissed Owen.

Chapter Twenty-One

Daisy kissed Owen with all the newfound, leafy-green, just-beginning-to-flower love she'd been carrying in her heart since the day she'd met him. She kissed him with gratitude and awe and fledgling passion. She kissed him with tenderness and poetry. She kissed him—and Daisy devoutly hoped it was true—the way a woman kissed a man whom she could not get enough of kissing. And when she'd finished kissing Owen, she lifted her head…

And then she kissed him again. Because when it came to Owen Cooper, one shy, tentative touch of the lips simply wasn't enough. It was possible, Daisy reminded herself, that this kiss had to last her a life-time—that this kiss, and the memory of it, would be all she'd have to sustain herself with later…when she was alone with her fatherless child, or unhappily wed to Conrad.

She had to make it good. She did. So she gave the

effort—amateurish as it was—everything she had. And when she'd finished kissing Owen for the second time, when she'd finally opened her eyes again, Daisy knew something she hadn't first reckoned on.

Once or even twice would not be enough. Not with Owen.

"So!" she said blindly and brightly. "Thank you for that! I appreciate your cooperation, Owen." Nervously, Daisy chuckled. "You don't know how much it means to me to experience a proper kiss. I realize that must have been a shock and an imposition—"

He gawked at her, frowning *again* for some reason.

"—but I find, once again, that with *you* I feel quite open to be myself. To indulge every whim. It's quite liberating, actually, because ordinarily I'm very concerned with propriety—"

"You're wrong," Owen said, his voice gravelly and sure.

"Wrong?" she blinked, as baffled as he'd been. "Wrong how?"

"That wasn't a proper kiss," Owen told her. Then he pulled her against him, lowered his mouth to hers and showed Daisy exactly how shortsighted she'd been in the arena of kissing.

This was a kiss to remember, Daisy realized as Owen's mouth moved against hers. *This* was a kiss she would never forget. How could she forget the warm touch of Owen's lips? The teasing flutter of his breath? The husky groan he gave as, tightening his hands in her hair, he kissed her even more deeply? Thrilled by that sound—thrilled by the overall experience—Daisy curled her toes against the stable floor and just held on. In her arms, Owen felt strong and wonderful and *right,* and as unexpected as it was to feel him nudge open her mouth, to feel him sweep his tongue against hers, to feel their hearts and minds and breath come together in a way that was so shockingly intimate…as unexpected as all those things were, Daisy simply felt she could not have enough of any of them. Owen wanted her. He wanted *her.*

In that moment, she thought she might be capable of flying.

Joyfulness filled her—that and another sensation, one that raced along her limbs and suffused her body with warmth and made her struggle to catch her breath as Owen kissed her again and again and again. Backed against the gate of the nearest stall, Daisy wound her fingers in Owen's lapels. She longed to caress him fully, to spread her palms over his broad shoulders and wide chest, to press herself against him from knees to chin in just as brazen a fashion as any woman could have done. But then…

But then it occurred to Daisy that if she did any of those bold things, Owen would undoubtedly believe the worst of her. Already, he probably believed her a wanton hussy, flinging herself at him—in public, no less!—and making him kiss her.

Of course, Owen *was* kissing her back. He *did* seem fully engaged in the process, as his hands swept from her face to her shoulders and then lower, skimming her waist, too. So maybe he would not think too poorly of her behavior. But then Daisy felt herself utter a tiny moan, a sound wrung from her by Owen's next kiss, and she couldn't stand it any longer. She wrenched back.

"You must think I'm awful!" she blurted. "I'm so sorry."

"You're wonderful," Owen insisted, grinning. His smile, so bedazzling, never failed to make her heart race—and this time, that poor organ was veritably galloping already. *"Wonderful."*

"I swear, I don't ordinarily hurl myself at men. I—"

"I didn't think you did." Quite naturally, Owen's hands came to rest on her middle. He stroked his thumbs carefully over her belly, as though caressing her *and* her baby—as though caring about her *and* her baby, both at the same time. "But I'm glad you did today." His smile broadened to a rascally degree. "Please," Owen said gallantly, "feel free to continue. I'm at your mercy."

She scoffed at that. "You? At *my* mercy? I can't imagine."

"You don't have to imagine." His gaze lifted to hers. "Just kiss me again, and you'll see. I'm helpless to resist you."

His challenge emboldened her. Still, Daisy hesitated. "You're very kind to say so, but I don't think I'm good at—"

"You're *wonderful,*" he repeated. "It's true."

Tempted but uncertain, Daisy watched Owen's hands, still cradling her. If she hadn't suspected otherwise, she'd have believed that Owen had *tremendous* love to share. He certainly seemed willing to lavish affection on her and on a child who wasn't his own. Surely that was an unusual quality in a man.

"If you're thinking I can kiss wonderfully because I'm…experienced in that area, you're wrong," it occurred to her to explain, belatedly and hurriedly. "I've scarcely kissed anyone at all! Conrad didn't care to kiss—" in fact, he hadn't seen the point of it; he'd claimed to view kissing as "a waste of time" for any "decisive man" "—and I never wanted to change his mind about that. The few times that we…" Embarrassed, Daisy paused. "Well, that we were together, in that way—"

Appearing concerned, Owen waited. The only

sign that he might be bothered by the subject she'd broached was the balled-up condition of his fists. All the same, he managed to be there for her—to be unmoving and unjudging. Doubtless, he sensed she still struggled with what had occurred between her and Conrad. Owen wouldn't have been himself—caring and perceptive and loyal—if he hadn't. Grateful for his quiet forbearance, Daisy went on.

"I hated it!" she confessed, before she could lose her nerve. "I didn't feel…a *part* of it. I almost didn't feel as if it were really happening to me. Doesn't that sound strange?" Feeling ashamed, yet determined to be honest with Owen, she said, "Even now, when it's months in the past, I can't make myself believe it happened. Yet I have proof that it *did* happen. I have proof so obvious, even I can't deny it any longer."

In an effort to make light of her situation, Daisy smiled. She cradled her belly, feeling unexpectedly heartened by the gesture. "The truth is, I let myself be forced into something that was regrettably wrong. I let myself be fooled, lured by my dreams for the future and my hope that someone—anyone!—would love me. So when someone truly did seem to love me—"

"You are eminently lovable, Daisy. You are," Owen insisted with his usual fidelity. "Anyone would love you."

Except me, she imagined him saying. *I'll never*

love anyone the way I loved my wife...the way I loved Élodie's mother.

The realization made Daisy feel even sadder just then. Who would love *her* child's mother? Most likely, no one at all. After everything she'd done, Daisy could hardly expect anyone to love her truly, least of all a decent man whom she'd want to be with.

Faced with that awful truth, she made herself go on talking about Conrad. Now that she'd begun, she needed to finish. Also, more than anyone else, Owen had a right to know everything that had brought her here. He was the one who, with matter-of-fact acceptance and, at times, with almost paternal enthusiasm, had helped her accept what had once seemed unimaginable.

A baby. *Her* baby. Borne alone, but no less beloved.

"When someone truly did seem to love me," she said again, "I didn't consider whether I loved him in return. That almost didn't matter. Not then. Things were moving so quickly." Daisy swallowed hard, suddenly swamped by memories she longed to forget—memories of everything that had happened with Conrad, before he'd grown so cold with her. "I wanted to keep up with it all. I wanted to belong, to be right, to step carefully and not make any mistakes at all. So I just closed my eyes—"

She broke off, instinctively shying away from the memories. There were too many of them, most of them bleak. Conrad on top of her. Conrad invading her. Conrad holding her in place so she couldn't move away. Afterward, he'd always blamed Daisy for having ignited his "coarser instincts." He'd always left her as quickly as he could. It was true that Conrad had desired her, Daisy realized, but he hadn't wanted to. It was no wonder, then, that he'd found so many faults in her—more every day.

Unfortunately, that didn't mean some of them weren't real.

"I just closed my eyes," Daisy repeated, "and went along. I didn't think. And then it was over. And now… I'm alone."

"You're not alone." Appearing surpassingly saddened by the fact that she'd say so, Owen shook his head. His gaze searched hers, full of compassion and…respect? "You'll never be alone."

"Not now!" Daisy laughed, again rubbing her belly. "Not anymore! I quite like that idea, actually. This little person will be with me always, mine to love and cherish." She sighed. "I know I've been behaving peculiarly about the baby, Owen. But it was all so much to take in, at first. It still is."

Soberly, Owen nodded. He remained silent, brow furrowed.

"But the more I learn to accept my baby, the more

at peace I feel." Gently, Daisy touched Owen's chest. She flattened her palm over his heart, feeling unduly reassured by that steady *thump thump* beneath her hand. "I owe that peace to you, for being so insistent—for not judging me or shaming me or pressuring me. If you had been anyone else…I don't know if I could have managed. So, thank you."

Gruffly, Owen cleared his throat. He nodded.

"I know I don't deserve it," she added, "but I truly—"

"Stop. Just…stop." Roughly, Owen muttered a swearword. He raked his hand through his hair. He stared at Daisy in apparent frustration, then lowered his hand to hers. With that same *thump thump* for accompaniment, he laced their fingers together over his heart. "I didn't mean that you'll never be alone because you'll have your baby with you, Daisy. I meant that you'll never be alone because, if you wanted, you would always have me."

In surprise, Daisy gazed up at him. After all the things she'd just confessed, she couldn't imagine… this.

"Not for kissing," Owen insisted. "Not for possessing or promising or cooking or cleaning. But just for *help,* if you needed it. Just for being there, for you. I know I don't have much to offer—not enough by far. But I—" He swore again, still looking pained. "Damnation. Just when I need my hellfired scoundrelly ways, they've up and deserted me! I can tell by your face that you don't know what I mean. I'm not good with words. Not anymore. Renée used to say I could talk the blue out of the sky if I tried, but it's obvious now that I've lost all that."

"Does this mean," Daisy asked in a small voice, "that you don't want to kiss me anymore? Because you just said—"

"Kissing? *Kissing* is what you remember from all that?"

"It's what you mentioned first," Daisy pointed out, quite reasonably, she thought, under the circumstances. "So, does it?"

He shook his head. "I loved kissing you. You're fortunate I stopped." He glanced around. "If we weren't in this stable—"

"Does it mean," she went on before he could elaborate more naughtily, "that all you want from me is cooking and cleaning?"

"No! It doesn't mean that." Another curse word. "See? I can't explain myself. I'm trying to be honorable, Daisy!" He gazed at her. *I'm trying not to be like Conrad,* she fancied she glimpsed in his mulish expression. "I like your cooking—and I like those jumble cookies—but I like *you* more. Much more."

"I like you, too," she admitted shyly. "Ever so much."

For a moment, all they did was look at each

other—almost as though they'd reached a new accord…and a new hope, too. But as relieved as Daisy was by that fact, some problems still loomed. The tiny space dividing them might as easily have been a gulf of several miles. She couldn't fathom how to cross it—how to travel from their flawed and broken pasts to a whole new future.

All she knew was that she wanted to try. And in that moment, just for an instant, Daisy dared to dream that Owen did too. That if she asked him to, he would stay there by her side.

After all, she'd already told him all the worst things about herself. She'd practically thrown her flaws and foibles in his face, where he couldn't refuse to see them—where he couldn't close his eyes to the truth, the way Daisy had been doing for so long now. And, to her amazement, even after hearing all that, Owen hadn't turned away from her. He hadn't so much as made a moue of disgust or shown an eyelash flicker of disapproval.

Couldn't that mean there was hope for them?

"That's why it kills me to know how Conrad Parish treated you," Owen said, breaking into her thoughts. "Love doesn't have to be that way. I guess…your man didn't realize that."

"My man?" Startled, Daisy blinked. She had never, in a million years, thought to consider Conrad *hers*. Nor had she wanted to. Feeling immeasurably lightened by her talk with Owen, she finally cast off all thoughts of her tour manager. "In case you hadn't noticed," she said, "the only man I'm thinking about is the man I'm looking at right now...with both eyes open."

She'd had enough of going through her life with her eyes closed, afraid to speak out and fearful of making a mistake.

From here on, Daisy promised herself, she would stay alert. She would keep her eyes open and see things as they really were.

"He's a mighty fine man, too," she elaborated teasingly, still gazing at Owen. "He's strong and kind and handsome—"

"You already said that one."

"—and if he doesn't kiss me again soon, I can't imagine—"

Swiftly, Owen *did* kiss her. Ardently yet tenderly, he pulled her into his arms once more. He gazed down at her, truly *seeing* her in a way Daisy didn't think he had before. Then, just when she feared he would change his mind, Owen brought his mouth to hers. His kiss was sweet, fraught with emotion and promise and, she fancied further, filled with the beginnings of love.

"See?" she said when their kiss was finished, feeling flushed and tingly and oddly optimistic. "Your wife, Renée, was right about you. I think you *could* still talk the blue from the sky—and make it happy to have fallen away, besides." Daisy stepped a little closer. This time, she dared to put both hands on Owen's shoulders, just as though they belonged there. "You might be a scoundrel, but you're—" *mine* "—an admirable one."

"Renée would not have agreed with you about *that*. She would have said there's no such thing as an admirable scoundrel."

"Well." Daisy shrugged, not caring. "I'm right, so there's no point arguing about it. You know how stubborn I can be."

"Aw, Daisy." Seeming almost as affected by their coming together as she was, Owen gazed at her. He stroked his thumb over her cheek, then sighed. "If only I could be that certain."

"You can be. I've just decreed it."

"But," Owen began, typically obstinate, "my past is—"

"In the past!" Daisy declared. She needed to make him understand. "It's over with. You can leave it behind, just the way I've done…only without a daredevil's train ride and a coat full of contraband earnings." She grinned, feeling herself turn downright carefree. "Besides, how could I hold against you all the things you've done?" Boldly, she hugged him. "They're exactly the things that have made you the man you are today."

"That's the trouble. You deserve more," Owen alleged. "I'm going to make sure you get it, Daisy. I promise, I am. All the things I don't have… I'll make damn certain they're yours."

If he meant to improve himself, she couldn't comprehend how. "Will that include a lifetime supply of cussing?"

"I'm not joking!" But Owen laughed, all the same. He looked at her, then shook his head. He laughed in a way that made Daisy's heart turn over with reckless glee. "I mean what I say," Owen said as he sobered, squeezing her hand in his. "I'm going to give you everything I can. Everything you need. Everything."

"But all I want is you," Daisy told him. There was no point holding back now. "Can you promise to give me that?"

In answer, Owen shook his head with—she assumed—vexation at her doggedness. Well, maybe she was being a mite bossy. Hoping to improve her rapidly devolving manners, she softened her tone.

"Will you *please* give me you?" Daisy tried. *"Please?"*

At that, Owen groaned. A heartbeat later, she was in his arms again, being thoroughly kissed. Giddily, Daisy clapped her arms around him. She kissed him back, triumphantly and joyously, feeling that she'd finally made a sound decision at last.

Trusting Owen was right. It *felt* right. It *was* right.

* * *

It wasn't until later that night, lying snugly and solitarily in Owen's bed, remembering the exhilarating events of the day, that Daisy realized something she'd overlooked. Something important.

Owen *hadn't* promised to give her himself, it occurred to her. But he'd done it anyway. Hadn't he? Yes. He'd kissed her. In his kiss, he'd shown her his caring. And wasn't that just as good as a promise? Better even, owing to its forthrightness?

Assuring herself that it was, Daisy rolled over.

Then she realized something else: she was doing it again. She was closing her eyes. She was managing her life based solely on her own assumptions. What she needed were facts—and there was only one way to get those. With her time in Morrow Creek so limited, she couldn't afford to dally, either.

Slipping out of bed, Daisy adjusted her borrowed lacy nightgown. She smoothed down her hair. She took a deep breath.

She plodded into the kitchen. She found Owen on his pallet in the semidarkness, his arms cradling his head as he gazed upward into the night. His face was somber, his hair tousled.

"Daisy! What's wrong?" He sat up, all readiness and flexing muscles. Instantly alert, he looked at her. "Are you all right?"

"No." Heart pounding, she shook her head. "I need you."

"I'm right here." He frowned. "Did you have a bad dream?"

"No. I mean…" She stepped nearer. "I need you."

"Need me? For what?" Appearing confused, Owen rose. He took her hand, certain about *her*. "Just name it, and it's yours."

"Fine." Another deep breath. Her knees knocked. She hoped he'd understand what she was asking for. "Please, Owen," Daisy said. "Will you *please* give me you? Truly, this time?"

Then, she knew, if he couldn't be with her later, at least she'd have known love once. At least she'd have felt it…once.

And just when Daisy began to feel certain that Owen would refuse, just when she began composing a dithering apology in her head, Owen squeezed her hand. His fingers, she noticed, seemed to be trembling. Could a big, strong man like Owen truly be so affected? By her? By them? By the two of them, together?

Evidently—amazingly—he was. He swallowed hard, then nodded.

"I already said I'd give you anything," Owen told her. "But I'll be damned if I thought you'd ever be asking for *me*."

His humbleness was endearing. His smile... was wicked.

So was Daisy's, she discerned, when she gave his hand a pull, urging them both toward the bedroom. "Only you. Just you."

Forever, she added silently, wishing it could be true.

"Then for tonight," Owen said, "that's what you'll have."

He scooped her off her feet, into his arms. Whooping with surprise, Daisy felt herself being kissed into quietness.

"Shh," Owen said, holding her securely. "Mind Élodie."

"I will!" Daisy whispered. "I'm so sorry!"

But she wasn't sorry for this. She wasn't sorry for being with Owen. She wasn't sorry for being held by him. She wasn't sorry—but she was surprised—to feel tears spring to her eyes, unstoppably, from the moment when Owen carried her over his bedroom threshold...as tenderly as he would have a bride on her wedding night. It was as close as Daisy would likely come to enjoying one of those, she knew. Its sweetness made her sigh.

"Thank you," she said. "Thank you for being you, Owen."

"If it's brought me you, then that's all I could ever want," he told her with raw honesty. In the dimness, his eyes looked grave and warm. "I aim to do my best to show you that."

Owen shouldered the door closed behind them. He gazed down at Daisy with open affection, then set her on her feet.

"There." Scandalously, his grin flashed, wider than ever before. Just for an instant, Daisy caught sight of the fun-loving scoundrel he kept hidden away beneath his workaday cares. "I hope you weren't planning on sleeping much," Owen said in a devilish tone, sliding his fingers seductively along her arm, "because this could take a long, long while between us."

"I wish it could go on forever," Daisy said honestly.

And even though she knew it *couldn't* go on forever between them—even though Owen, for all his kindnesses, knew she'd be leaving soon and had never asked her to stay—all he did was nod.

Then, gently, Owen pulled Daisy into his arms and proceeded to dissolve the miles between them…kiss by kiss, smile by smile, caress by lingering caress, until there was nothing left but togetherness—and a love that, in the dreaminess of the moonlight, felt just as real to Daisy as real could ever be.

Chapter Twenty-Two

If Owen had needed any more proof that he was still a scoundrel at heart, all he had to do was roll over in his wide, rope-sprung bed, open his eyes... and look with wonder at the woman who had shared that bed with him for the past few nights.

Daisy. Even watching her sleep, Owen felt awestruck by her. She was beautiful and kind and good—and she wanted to be with him. With *him.* Was there anything more wondrous than that?

Owen didn't think so. Not that that excused his behavior; he knew it did not. When Daisy had come to him, he should have refused her. He should have—with his greater experience and knowledge of the things that went on between men and women—recognized that Daisy had most likely been lonely. He should have offered to keep her company—chastely and responsibly.

But Owen hadn't done that. Instead, when his rascally nature had come to the fore—just as Renée had always warned him it would—he had instantly given in. Like the most love-struck and lustiest of grooms, he'd carried Daisy across the threshold of his bedroom without a single qualm. Then he'd loved her, as well as he could, with a vigor and a reverence that amazed him.

In his lifetime, Owen had seen many things. But he'd never seen a sight like the one Daisy had presented, as she'd stood before him, wearing only her lacy nightgown, and implored him.

Will you please *give me you?* she'd asked.

To put it plainly, Owen had been unable to say no.

He didn't regret it, either. He couldn't. Propping his head on his pillow now, gazing at Daisy in the morning sunshine, he couldn't regret a single one of the nights they'd spent together. He'd loved them all. He'd loved holding Daisy in his arms and showing her how close true closeness could be. He'd loved kissing her, laughing with her, opening himself gratefully to her in the darkness that had cradled them both. He'd loved hearing her sigh, seeing her smile, knowing he'd pleased her.

He *had* pleased her, too. Owen couldn't help feeling proud of that. And happy, too. To judge by all that Daisy had told him, she'd never known real love before—not with that selfish dolt Conrad Parish. Not with any man. And maybe it was wrong for

Owen to do what he'd been doing—to love her without right or lasting responsibility or even a spoken
promise between them. But Daisy had wanted his
love. Owen had wanted to give it. And even more
than that, he'd wanted Daisy to know what it meant
to be fully loved and properly cared for. At least for
a while.

She sure as hell hadn't been getting any of that
love or caring from Conrad Parish. All she'd seemed
to have gotten from Parish were heartache and confusion and criticism—and a baby. So before Owen
delivered Daisy back to that man, he meant to love
her completely and well. He meant to make sure
Daisy was as all-fired happy as she could be, for as
long as possible.

And that's how Owen knew he was still a scoundrel at heart. Worse, that's how he knew he'd never
be redeemed. Not now. Because he'd done his utmost
to please Daisy—even with no right to do so—and
now, days later, he still wasn't a bit sorry.

In fact, he was *glad.* Lying there next to her, snug
and warm and replete, Owen felt fiercely glad—and
overwhelmingly protective, too. When—*if*—Conrad
Parish turned up in Morrow Creek to claim Daisy,
Owen told himself as he trailed his fingertips along
Daisy's arm, savoring the sleepy blush in her cheeks
and the delightful pink pout of her mouth, he'd bet-

ter treat her kindly and fairly. He'd better be *perfect* at being with Daisy. Otherwise, Owen would…

Well, he would die inside. He knew that.

But he wouldn't be able to stop it. Because Conrad Parish was the father of Daisy's baby, and she seemed to care for him. Against all reason, Daisy seemed to want to make excuses for that sorry knuck—to believe the twaddle he'd spewed at her and to blame herself for the problems they'd had… problems which, as she'd enumerated them, had included a dearth of kissing, a deficit of cuddling and a sorry lack of mutual regard.

Over the past few days—and nights—Owen had done his best to make up for those awful shortfalls. He'd done all he could to provide Daisy with a lifetime's worth of feeling beloved…even though he'd had to cram those feelings into just a few days.

He didn't know if he'd succeeded. After all, even a scoundrel could not rightly decipher all women, all the time. Owen felt reasonably certain he'd done a good job. All the same, one thing still nagged at him. One thing still echoed in his mind, voiced in Daisy's most melancholic tone and possessed of the power to make Owen stop where he stood.

That Élodie is right, Daisy had said, before kissing him senseless, *and you'll never love anyone, ever again.*

Owen didn't know where Daisy—and Élodie—

had gotten that idea. He couldn't remember telling Élodie that. He couldn't imagine under what circumstances his daughter would have shared such a notion with Daisy, either. It bothered Owen mightily. It bothered him in ways he couldn't describe. He'd been stricken when he'd first heard Daisy say those words, in the midst of her rambling chatter in his stable days ago, and Owen was still struck now.

Would he love anyone again? Was he capable of it?

Or had his scoundrelly ways doomed him to be alone forever?

Uncomfortable with those questions, Owen shoved them from his mind. Right now, all that mattered was the moment at hand and the woman by his side. Right now, he could pretend Daisy was his and always would be. Right now, he could lose himself in her—in the two of them, together—and take them both to a place where questions didn't matter. All that mattered was closeness.

With new thoughtfulness, Owen went on stroking Daisy's arm. But this time, he broadened his reach. This time, he added soft kisses to his touching, and whispered words of caring to his nearness. And by the time Daisy's eyes fluttered open—by the time she gave him a drowsy, besotted "Good morning"—Owen knew that everything good was already within his grasp. All he had to do was hold on…and try not to think about tomorrow.

Could he love again? He already had, Owen decided. *He was now.* The tenderness he felt for Daisy filled his heart nearly to overflowing. If that wasn't love, he didn't know what was. And if Daisy couldn't feel that—if she couldn't decipher it and believe it— then mere words wouldn't help that. But everything he *did* might. So, with new passion and devotion, Owen committed himself to making certain Daisy understood where they stood.

"Good morning," he whispered back with a devilish smile. He levered himself over her, dedicated with all his heart and mind and soul to making sure she was happy, right now. "I hope you're feeling well rested," Owen said, "because I'm hoping for a number of lessons from you before you get started with Élodie."

"Lessons?" Adorably, Daisy blinked. "What lessons?"

"I want to learn to memorize the look on your face when I do this." Gently, Owen kissed her. He slid his body over hers, enjoying the sensuous pleasures of nakedness, warmth and closeness. He stroked her again, more boldly. "I want to learn how to make you sigh and smile and wriggle… Yes, just like that." He smiled, loving the way Daisy wrapped her arms around him. "I want to learn all about you, Miss Walsh. Every part."

She blushed even more prettily, if that were possible.

"I can't imagine you've missed any parts of me!" she declared, seeming simultaneously bashful and thrilled. "You've been more than thorough, Mr. Cooper, I promise you."

"Then does that mean—" he gave her another, more lingering kiss "—that I get an A in my lessons already?"

"Hmm. I can't rightly say yet." Her smile touched him, blessing him with its openheartedness and beauty. "Perhaps you should..." Another sigh. "Keep on doing what you're doing," Daisy managed to say in a breathy voice, "and we'll see."

"Yes, ma'am." With a new attention to the task at hand, Owen pulled back the sheets—the inexplicably scratchy sheets, which Miss O'Neill had taken to delivering as though they were covered in prickly pear spines, and Daisy had taken to rewashing on her own to properly soften them. Then Owen slid lower, scandalously lower, all the better—he hoped—to make Daisy sigh with pleasure. He kissed her, intimately and enjoyably. "I just decided," Owen told her. "I might need all day at this task."

"All day?" With a smile in her voice, Daisy wriggled again, getting closer to him. "Are you sure?

Perhaps you're not doing this properly, Mr. Cooper, and that's why you need all day."

"Perhaps," Owen agreed with a companionable nod. He gave her a leisurely kiss. "Or perhaps I'm hoping that, with enough practice, you'll finally be pleased enough to never leave me."

For a moment, Daisy stilled. Her gaze met his, full of seriousness and hope. "You don't need...to do *that* for that."

In that instant, Owen would have sworn he glimpsed love in her eyes. Love for *him*. He felt shaken to the core—happily so.

"But if you'd like to continue," Daisy went on in a shy, impish tone, "then I certainly won't stop you!"

"Whatever you want," Owen said. It was his oft-repeated promise to her...one he'd done his utmost to fulfill.

He lowered his head again, lovingly giving Daisy everything he had—everything he could—and wishing only that it could be more. That *he* could be more. Because if Owen were honest, his own shortcomings were all that came between him and the future he wanted with Daisy. Well, that—and the damnable feelings she seemed to have for that ruinous scalawag Conrad Parish. If Owen could have swept away those things, if he could have changed them somehow... But he couldn't, and that was that.

So for now, Owen loved Daisy with his entire heart

and his able, willing body. For now, he hoped against hope that she could discern the love he gave to her... and welcome it, besides. No matter that her love was more than he deserved in return. It was all that he wanted, and Owen prayed that would be enough.

Chapter Twenty-Three

Dreamily, Daisy strolled along the raised wooden sidewalk bordering Morrow Creek's Main Street, hand in hand with Élodie. In her opposite hand, Daisy carried a wicker basket filled partway—so far—with sewing supplies and a few dry goods. She and her little helper, Élodie, were on their way to the millinery shop to purchase a new bonnet for Élodie to wear to the town's gala Independence Day town picnic next month.

Everywhere she looked, though, Daisy glimpsed Owen. In every face, every smile, every gesture, she pictured the man she loved, the man she'd spent the past eventful days with, lolling in bed like hedonists and laughing over the smallest things.

When she'd gone to Owen that night, Daisy had wanted to experience love. She'd wanted to know caring—*real* caring.

Now, thanks to Owen, she did.

She knew a great many other things, too, Daisy reckoned, feeling a silly smile burst onto her face. She knew that Owen was ticklish, but only if playfully and properly touched. She knew that he loved to be with her...that she loved to be with him. She knew that her capacity for pleasure had never before been tested in the ways it had been tested of late—scandalously so. And she knew, beyond a doubt, that she'd done the right thing by being with Owen—by deepening their attraction the way she'd done with that one fateful late-night visit to him.

At the time, Daisy had feared Owen would find her too forward. She'd worried that he would reject her; that he'd consider her hoydenish and lacking. Instead, Owen seemed to find her more fascinating by the day, Daisy thought—at least if their ongoing togetherness was anything to go by. In fact, she reckoned, as she strolled down the street past Mr. Hofer's mercantile and the dressmaker's shop, she wouldn't have been at all surprised to find Owen offering a more lasting commitment.

He *must* love her, Daisy thought. Even if he hadn't yet said the words. Why else would Owen lavish such attention on her? Such caring? Doubtless, he had many tender feelings for her.

And she, in her turn, had *very* tender feelings for him.

Of course, she hadn't yet told him that, Daisy

realized. She hadn't told him that she loved him…
not even when she'd realized it herself, a few nights
ago, when Owen had first held his ear to her swell-
ing belly, delivered her a broad smile, then introduced himself to her baby in the most charming and
gallant manner possible. He'd spent several minutes
on the task too. He'd carried on a downright endearing talk with her unborn child, making funny faces
and gesturing broadly to explain his finer points,
and Daisy had gone smitten all over.

In all the years she had to live, she didn't think
she would soon forget the sight of big, burly Owen
Cooper speaking to her belly that way. He'd made
sure her new baby understood what things were like
in the Arizona Territory. He'd stressed how wonderful a mama was waiting there for him (since Owen
was convinced, like Élodie, that her baby was a boy).
He'd even told a few stories about Élodie and him,
and all the wonderful times they were having with
Daisy teaching them homemaking expertise.

Those moments had been magical for Daisy. She
knew she'd fallen in love with Owen completely
then—so much so that she began to regret her telegraph message to Conrad. At the time she'd sent it,
she'd been concerned about her position with Barker
& Bowles. She'd been desperate to make sure that
she could resume her speaking tour—that she could

go on with her life, unchanged as before, when she left Morrow Creek.

But now Daisy knew better. Her life would never be the same…and it would be all the richer for it. She was still fearful about the future. But with Owen's help, and Thomas's help—and the help of the other good people of Morrow Creek, several more of whom she'd met over the past days—Daisy knew she would manage somehow. She had to.

There would be difficult times ahead, of course. But Daisy didn't need Conrad to help her steer through them. Not anymore.

Now, she had the strength of a woman who'd found her place—and that place lay squarely within a ramshackle Western town, where she'd arrived to an unexpected hero's welcome and would—if heaven granted her most secret wishes—never have cause to leave.

Thinking that she should send Conrad another message, one simply asking him to forward her trunks and possessions, and to provide her with the names of his superiors at Barker & Bowles, so she could properly resign her speaking-engagements tour, Daisy tugged Élodie toward the opposite side of the street.

"Look!" Daisy said. "Isn't that the telegraph office over yonder? I should go send a wire to my friend in San Diego."

"All right." Happily, Élodie skipped along by her side. She smiled up at Daisy. "Hey! You said 'over yonder'! Did you hear that? I think you're becoming a real Western woman, Miss Walsh!"

"Your papa would be proud." Daisy hesitated to allow a wagon to pass by. Its occupants waved in a friendly fashion.

"Yes, he would!" Élodie allowed. "Of course, it's likely because of *him* that you're becoming so westernized. You know, on account of your both sleeping in the same bed now. I suppose a little bit of Papa's westernness is rubbing off on you!"

"Maybe. If so, I reckon that's a good thing."

"I reckon it is. Mrs. Archer will be pleased for certain!"

At that, Daisy quirked a smile. On the morning after the first night she'd spent with Owen, Élodie had tromped into the bedroom to have Daisy fashion her braids for the day—and had been positively unfazed to find her papa in bed with Daisy.

The little girl seemed to have accepted her father's coming together with her tutor without a single qualm. If anything, Élodie was a downright booster for the notion. Élodie seemed captivated by the possibility of Daisy and Owen being in love.

"Just to be on the safe side," Daisy said in an undertone to Élodie, still holding her hand, "let's not share that bit of news with Mrs. Archer. All right? When your papa is ready—"

"He'll tell everyone. I know. But that probably won't take long," Élodie assured her. "Not only does Papa smile more and laugh more these days, he talks at double the rate, too!"

Smiling, hand in hand, Daisy and Élodie continued to the telegraph office. Along the way, they met several of Élodie's neighbors, some of Daisy's newfound friends and a few residents who'd read about Daisy in the *Pioneer Press* and wanted to chat with her, or to extract her promise to autograph their copies of the *New Book of Cookery and General Home Keeping: with Recipes and Formulas for All Occasions, Both Informal and Grand.*

Cheerfully, Daisy agreed. She wasn't sure what her future held, but she was sure that she enjoyed the life she had in Morrow Creek. Here, the townspeople gazed upon her approvingly. They seemed to believe she was capably fit to care for Élodie. Both of those things, combined with Owen's caring, gave Daisy hope. They encouraged her to believe that she *could* manage everything on her own—even without Conrad's constant guidance.

Filled with overall chirpiness, Daisy filed a second wire to Conrad. She inquired about any replies to her first message, but there'd been nothing re-

ceived that was addressed to her. Maybe, she realized, Conrad truly had washed his hands of her.

With that task complete, Daisy again took Élodie's
hand. They headed for the millinery shop. "All right.
A bonnet next!"

Finding that bonnet was a treat. Delighting in the
experience, Daisy watched Élodie try on one hat
after another.

"You're really very good with her, you know," said
Mrs. Fowler, the milliner. "It's been a long while
since little Élodie had a mama to look up to and to
shop for bonnets with."

"Oh, thank you," Daisy demurred, "but I'm not
her mother."

"Pshaw. I know *that*." Mrs. Fowler crossed her
arms, all but cooing at the sight of Élodie in a ruffled gingham sunbonnet. "All I mean is, you seem
the mothering type to me, Miss Walsh, beyond a
single doubt." The milliner winked. "And the mar-
rying type, too. I reckon Mr. Cooper is one lucky
man. I won't be a bit surprised to hear wedding bells
ring, before long."

Despite her private vow not to lose her head,
Daisy couldn't help feeling delighted. If even a local
woman—someone who knew Élodie and Owen—
believed that Daisy had a future with them in
Morrow Creek, then it *must* be true! Aside which,
it was heartening to realize that, here in the West,

the social strictures seemed not to be fixed *quite* so tightly against the kind of informal arrangement she and Owen shared.

"Well...*maybe*," Daisy hedged. "I certainly hope so."

Mrs. Fowler smiled kindly. "Perhaps Mr. Cooper is waiting for the Independence Day town picnic to propose. You are planning to attend, aren't you? It's the must-do event of the year."

"Only the annual Halloween gala comes close," put in another woman, who'd been shopping nearby. "We all enjoy it so."

"I'm sure I'd love to attend," Daisy assured them.

"Papa doesn't like parties," Élodie informed them dourly.

"Not *most* parties, you mean." Daisy cast a self-conscious glance at the two grown women nearby. "Right, Élodie? But surely, when it comes to something like the Independence Day festivities, your papa will change his mind and come along."

"He won't. Leastwise, I doubt it. Independence Day is always busy at the stable, so Papa usually stays there. He can't pass up a chance to add to his *petit chou's* nest egg, he says." Pursing her lips in the looking glass, Élodie tried on another bonnet. She discarded it. She tried another. "I always attend the Independence Day town picnic with Mrs. Archer."

All the women lapsed into silence. Daisy could

read their expressions like a book. *Poor child,* they seemed to be thinking. *Poor Miss Walsh for pinning her hopes on curmudgeonly Owen Cooper, who doesn't enjoy sociable get-togethers of any kind.*

"Miss Reardon told me about your father's…reluctance to socialize," Daisy admitted to Élodie. "I thought he'd changed."

I thought I'd cured him of that unsociability, Daisy couldn't help thinking, with loving-kindness and good cheer.

Now, looking at Élodie's doubtful little face, Daisy realized she hadn't done any such thing. In fact, she might well have reinforced Owen's reclusive tendencies by allowing him to sequester them both at home…in his lovely bed, together.

"Well, I guess I can change *that* easily enough, can't I?" Daisy announced to the millinery shop at large—and to Élodie, in particular. "Most likely, all your father needs is for me to ask him properly to accompany me someplace. Then, after that—"

"Won't work." Élodie adjusted her bonnet. "No matter how nicely you ask him, Papa is about as likely to attend a shindig like the Independence Day town picnic as I am to eat this hat!"

Daisy grinned. "In that case… Get out your knife and fork, Élodie! Because I aim to take your papa on an outing!"

And from that moment on, it became Daisy's personal mission to do exactly that—sooner rather than later, besides.

Chapter Twenty-Four

Daisy made her first attempt to lure Owen into greater sociability later that day. She began quite matter-of-factly, while she was teaching Élodie how to put up rhubarb jam.

"I saw Thomas today, down at the *Pioneer Press* offices," Daisy began, stirring away at the sugary, pink boiling liquid in her pot. "He mentioned that there's a reading of poetry at the Morrow Creek library every single Wednesday. Isn't that nice?"

Seated at the table, Owen gave a noncommittal sound.

"Today is Wednesday," Daisy added—usefully, she thought.

This time, Owen nodded. But he seemed more interested in assisting her with the jam than in hearing any poems read. "Your arm must be getting tired by now. Let me help you stir."

Gratefully, Daisy surrendered her wooden spoon to

Owen's capable grasp. Warrior-like, he approached the stove. He began to stir the molten jam, appearing both determined and wary.

By his side, an apron-wearing Élodie stood on a makeshift stepstool. The little girl peered curiously at the pot, then at her father. "Careful, Papa! It's very hot. If it splatters, it will burn you." She pointed. "It's lucky you have long sleeves."

"I promise I'll be vigilant," Owen told her, smiling.

"Several folks in town are attending," Daisy remarked.

Owen kept stirring. "Attending what?"

"The Wednesday-night poetry reading. Thomas is escorting Miss Reardon. Mrs. Sunley and Mrs. Archer usually come along also, with their families joining them. It's a popular event."

Another noncommittal sound. More manly stirring.

"It sounds enjoyable." Feeling exasperated, Daisy pushed onward, all the way to brashness. "Would you like to attend?"

Owen raised his eyebrows. As though the notion was patently ridiculous, he made a face, then shook his head. "No."

"Not even with me?" Daisy urged. "I'd really like—"

"Is this supposed to foam up so high?" Cautiously,

Owen took a step back. He wielded his spoon like a hammer, ready to subdue the rhubarb mixture by force, if necessary. "Daisy?"

"Just skim away the foam as it rises." Daisy gestured to demonstrate the maneuver, pointing to a bowl she'd set nearby, just for that purpose. She refocused on her invitation. "In the meantime, *do* let's go to the poetry reading! I haven't been to a social event in ages—not one in which *I* wasn't the featured speaker, at least." Still glimpsing no sign of Owen softening, Daisy tried her never-fail maneuver. "Please, Owen? *Please?*"

For an instant, he hesitated. He almost seemed ready to acquiesce. Then Owen glanced at Élodie. He gazed at Daisy.

"Take Élodie," he suggested. "It will be…broadening."

With a sigh, Daisy decided to do precisely that. She might have underestimated Owen's resistance to joining in Morrow Creek's social scene, but she was nothing if not determined.

She *would* convince Owen to accompany her to an event, and eventually, to the Independence Day town picnic, too. All she needed was the right strategy. Seen in that light, every attempt she made brought her one step closer to success.

"All right," Daisy agreed. "I *will* take Élodie!"

Then, with a kiss for Owen to thank him for

his help, Daisy collected Élodie, got them both gussied up and headed out.

Daisy's second attempt to lure Owen into greater sociability arose, quite serendipitously, the next morning.

Again, she stood at the stove—this time, making buckwheat griddle cakes for breakfast. Again, Owen offered to help her. But from there, the situation diverged. Because this time, Élodie was not yet awake. This time, Daisy and Owen were alone. And this time, Daisy had decided to wear one of the borrowed dresses that Owen loved seeing her in the most. It couldn't hurt…

"Mmm." Standing behind her as she cooked, he wrapped his arms around her waist. He kissed the back of her neck in a way that made Daisy feel all goose pimply. "How did you manage to sneak away from me?" he asked. "I didn't hear you get up."

"Oh, I was sure to be quiet." Airily, Daisy waved her spatula. "I thought you might want some extra sleep."

"I want to wake up next to you," Owen said drowsily. His hands slipped lower, cradling her belly. His pelvis pushed titillatingly against her backside. "Every morning, I do."

Gently, he swept aside a tendril of hair from her neck. Softly, he kissed her again. His stubble rasped faintly against her skin, inciting a bout of delicious sensations from her neck to her knees. Balancing herself with one hand on the dry-goods table, Daisy tried to concentrate on her griddle cakes. But those paltry, doughy circles did not have the power to entirely divert her attention from Owen's ongoing seduction.

"Come back to bed," he murmured. His thumbs stroked over her middle; his breath teased her earlobe. "It's early yet."

Daisy gestured. "But I already built a fire for the stove."

"You *did* start a fire," Owen agreed in a husky voice, "but it's got nothing to do with this old stove top." He turned her in his arms, then took the spatula from her grasp. "Please, Daisy."

His *please* finally snapped her to attention. Belatedly reminded of her resolve to draw Owen into the town's social whirl, Daisy straightened. She gave Owen a kiss, then took back her spatula. With a businesslike air, she flipped her griddle cakes.

"I would love to," Daisy said with mock dismay, "only, at the poetry reading last night, one of Thomas's friends from town invited me on a sightseeing excursion today. So I really oughtn't dally this morning."

"What do Thomas's highbrow friends have to do with you? Or with sightseeing?" Appearing displeased, Owen gestured at her—at the very tiny amount of space between them. "Or with us?"

"Well…" Daisy struck a thoughtful pose. "This particular wooded area is supposed to be lovely this time of year, and the invitation was so very nicely offered. I couldn't refuse! After all, we *did* already have the experience of the poetry reading in common."

"This 'friend' of Thomas's," Owen said. "Who is she?"

"Who is *he,* you mean?" With an innocent arch of her brows, Daisy peeked at a griddle cake to check its underside. It wasn't yet fully cooked—just like her strategy with regard to Owen. "I believe Mr. Copeland runs a lumber mill just outside of town."

Now Owen seemed relieved. "Aha. Marcus Copeland's wife, Molly, must have hog-tied him into attending that reading."

Drat Owen's knowing everyone in town! It was plumb inconvenient. Sensing her advantage slipping away, Daisy batted her eyelashes at Owen. "So… Would you like to attend, too?"

He checked a griddle cake. "Attend what?"

"The sightseeing outing today."

Again, Owen gazed at her as though she were mad. "Daisy… I don't attend social functions here in town. I thought you knew that. I thought *every-one* knew that—your new friends included."

Feeling more than exasperated, Daisy sighed. "Why not, Owen?"

"I don't mind if you take Élodie, though," he continued.

"Why?" Daisy pressed, not willing to be dissuaded this time by talk of Élodie. "*Why* won't you go with me? It's important to me, Owen. And it would be good for you to get out."

For a heartbeat, he almost seemed persuaded—most likely by her mention of how important the issue was to her. But then Owen shook his head. "I have work to do. I have responsibilities. I can't gallivant off to have *fun* whenever the urge strikes me."

"You mean because of Élodie? Because if she's there, too—"

"Isn't it enough," Owen interrupted, "that I've given over so much already?" For the first time, he seemed perturbed. He gestured between them with more annoyance than seductiveness. "Isn't it enough that I have you here, tempting me, every damn day? You don't know how difficult it is. You can't know."

"Well. I'm sorry I've made things 'difficult' for you."

"Aw. Don't be hurt, Daisy." Beguilingly, Owen stroked her back—her rigid, poker-straight back. "I don't mean… I never mean to hurt you. Not ever. But the fact is, I've already done my share of carousing. I've already indulged in a lifetime's worth of bad behavior. From here on, what I need to do is—"

"Repent? Hide yourself away? Atone for your sins?" Daisy shook her head, remembering all he'd told her about his wife, Renée. How the two of them had met, incongruously, outside a gambling house in Baltimore. How Renée had condemned Owen's drinking and "immature ways." How she'd insisted they emigrate west…all the better to force Owen to change. "You already have! Hiding yourself away here won't make you a better man."

"Then I guess we're stuck. Because I can't see another way." Sadly, Owen stared at the floor, even as the griddle cakes began to smoke. "The more I go out, the more reckless I become—the more irresponsible and unwise and unfit to care for Élodie."

Daisy gaped at him, astonished to hear such a daft notion.

"Did Renée tell you that?" At his sad, confirming nod, Daisy shook her head, dearly longing to pour some sense into him. She couldn't believe anyone could be so unkind to Owen. He certainly didn't deserve it. He didn't now and he couldn't have then, either. "Your wife isn't here!" Daisy insisted. "She doesn't know the man you've become. She never will."

She doesn't deserve your never-ending love,

either, Daisy thought in a reckless burst of rebellion. *I do. I do!*

"Even if she could see me, she wouldn't believe it," Owen confessed. "I gambled right up till the day Renée died." He gave a rueful quirk of his lips, remembering. "I did quit though, straightaway, as soon as I realized Élodie needed me. Bit by bit, things got better. In the end, Renée's efforts to reform me…" He shook his head. "Well, they were a good idea."

"Renée didn't reform you," Daisy insisted. "*You* did. You just said yourself that you gambled all during your marriage. You told me before—you were drinking then, too."

Again, Owen raised his eyebrow in that *you're mad* fashion. Daisy was becoming heartily sick of that doubtful expression of his. But her own discomfort paled beside the need to make sure Owen knew the whole truth about himself…and trusted in it.

"Well," he acknowledged reluctantly, "I did like a smile of whiskey or two, now and again—even on the long road out west. Renée didn't like it. She was a teetotaler, of course. And she wasn't afraid to lambaste me with her views, that's for certain."

Clearly, that meant Owen had not ended his scoundrelly behavior until *after* Renée had passed on, Daisy thought.

"But I haven't had a drop since I came to Morrow Creek. Renée took ill, I put down the bottle…and I never picked it up again." He almost smiled. "Renée would have been astounded."

"See? *You* made yourself the good man you are today." Daisy moved nearer, her gaze pleading with him to believe her. "*You* did that. You get the credit and the reward. All of it."

"The reward?"

Daisy couldn't help smiling at him. "Élodie, silly! She's a wonderful little girl. She loves you to pieces, Owen."

As if on cue, Élodie emerged. She padded into the kitchen on bare feet, with her hair even more tousled than Owen's was. As though guided by love, she headed straight for her father.

"I *do* love you, Papa, ever so much." She gave him a sleepy hug. Then she sniffed the air. "But I think you're burning the breakfast. Griddle cakes aren't like toast, you know. There's not enough apple butter in the whole world to make a burned pancake taste good." With that message delivered, Élodie hugged Daisy, too. "But I reckon they'll probably taste better than my hat!"

She grinned—likely because Daisy had not yet convinced Owen to attend a social event, and Élodie knew it. But Daisy couldn't admit that to Owen. As she hugged Élodie good-morning, Daisy's gaze met his. He appeared perplexed, and rightly so. With a sheepish smile, Daisy gave him a shrug—a shrug that said…

Little girls…who knows what they mean sometimes?

As Élodie wandered off to practice her embroidery on the sampler she'd begun under Daisy's guidance, Daisy scooped the griddle cakes onto a plate. She ladled in another batch.

"All I mean is," she told Owen, safely out of Élodie's earshot now, "you've had enough of someone tearing you down." She, more than anyone, knew what that felt like. "You need someone who will see you as the man you are *now,* today, with Élodie. And me."

"It wouldn't matter," Owen disagreed. "It's not enough."

I'm not enough, Daisy heard…and it broke her heart.

"How can it *not* be enough?" She gestured. "Just look!"

With reluctance and perceptible skepticism, Owen did. He followed Daisy's pointing arm…all the way to Élodie. For a moment, all he did was drink in the sight of his daughter.

"You think… I'm doing a good job raising Élodie?"

At that hoarsely voiced question, Owen nearly broke down.

Filled with compassion, filled with the need to

comfort him, Daisy nodded. "Yes," she said solemnly. "Of course I do! You're wonderful with your daughter. I've always thought so."

"Always?" Owen's gaze returned to Élodie. Gruffly, he cleared his throat. "But I can't love her the way a mother can. She's lost that." His voice broke. "I can never give it back."

"No." Tenderly, Daisy caught his hand, feeling overwhelmed with caring for him. "But you can give her something else. You can give her the love no one else can…the love of a father."

Owen's hand tightened on hers. Stiffly, he nodded.

"I never thought of it that way," he said. Appearing suspiciously red around the eyes but otherwise bellicose, he frowned at her griddle cakes. "Tarnation! Those are burned too!"

Taken aback by his sudden roughness, Daisy could only stare. Then she realized: no one had told Owen that before. No one had told him he was doing well. All he'd heard from his wife had been criticism and abuse. Evidently, he'd needed more.

Big, strong, foul-mouthed, ornery Owen Cooper needed more.

He needed *her,* Daisy realized. He needed her to love him.

And that was all the more reason she wanted to stay with him. It was all the more reason she wanted to stand by, trading hidden grins with Élodie, as

Owen took charge of the buckwheat griddle cakes himself. It was all the more reason, Daisy thought as she wrapped her arms around Owen in a tremendous hug, that she was not intending to give up on getting him to socialize.

She might have lost this round, Daisy told herself, but as long as Owen needed her, she would be there for him. And one of the things he needed her for, she thought, was making sure he came all the way out of his self-imposed exile and joined in life in Morrow Creek…the way his daughter and his friends—and now, Daisy too—profoundly wanted him to do.

Muttering darkly, Owen served up a plate of griddle cakes. He doused them in twice the usual quantity of maple syrup, seemed to find himself at a loss to know why, then called Élodie to the table. "Breakfast time! Come eat your burned food."

Cheerfully, Élodie scampered in to take her place. Daisy tucked away her latest smile. Then she, too, took her place.

Owen smacked down another plate of griddle cakes. They did not look as burned or as inedible as he made out. "Here. Eat."

"Thank you." Daisy lifted her gaze to his. For the first time, she glimpsed real hopefulness in Owen's eyes. It was tentative—and covered by blustery maleness—but it was there.

With his hands on his hips, Owen surveyed them.

He nodded. Then, apparently satisfied that all was well, he took his leave.

"I'm going down to check on the horses," he announced. But all he did was stand there, watching in apparent consternation as his daughter forked up bites of griddle cake. He glanced from his little girl to Daisy. He sighed. "Don't dawdle, now."

"I won't!" Élodie assured him. "See you in a minute, Papa!"

"Fine. Good." Roughly, Owen looked around, still seeming at loose ends. "All right. I'm going to the stable. You two…eat!"

"We'll be right here," Daisy promised. "Waiting for you."

At that, Owen appeared almost ready to bawl. Instead, he snatched up a mended bridle from nearby, then stomped away. The whole way down the stairwell, Daisy could hear him muttering.

When he'd gone, Élodie looked at her. "Papa's silly."

"But he's also magnificent," Daisy told her. "Isn't he?"

They both traded grins. Then Daisy got busy eating her griddle cakes. After all, she was eating for two now. Besides, she would need her strength later, for that sightseeing outing. If she couldn't persuade Owen to come along, she'd try again another time, with another social event. The important thing was, for once *she'd* helped Owen.

She felt beyond proud of that fact. Proud and grateful. It seemed to Daisy, just then, that she and Owen were like peas in a pod, the two of them, both needing an extra-big dose of love.

It was fortunate they'd found one another, she realized, so they could give each other that extra-big helping of love. They were lucky in that way. As Daisy finished her first griddle cake and started in on the second, she couldn't conceive of a single thing she enjoyed more than being with Owen and Élodie.

It was almost like having a family of her very own—the family she'd always dreamed of. Now, for the first time, Daisy's dream family seemed tantalizingly within reach...with no dreams necessary. If that wasn't a miracle, Daisy didn't know what was.

Chapter Twenty-Five

For Daisy's *third* attempt to lure Owen into greater sociability, she decided to stop fiddling around with half measures. With new optimism, she gathered up the supplies she would need, set Élodie to the task of knitting a few rows on the scarf she'd started, then skipped downstairs to the stable.

In her hand, Daisy held a poster advertising the Morrow Creek Independence Day town picnic, which had been printed on her brother's press at the newspaper office just that morning. In her heart, she carried a lightness that buoyed every step she took. On her face, she boasted a glowing smile—one full of anticipation and every reasonable expectation of victory.

This time, Daisy knew, she *would* convince Owen to accompany her to a social event. And not just any social event, either.

The annual Independence Day town picnic was,

according to Miss Reardon and Mrs. Sunley, the largest and most well-attended event of the entire year in Morrow Creek—and it was Daisy's targeted event for her latest invitation, too.

Once Owen faced such an event as *that,* she reasoned, his fears of descending into debauchery the moment he left his home or his stable would dissipate. Owen would see that it was his own good character—not his rules against socializing—that had granted him the life he enjoyed now. He might also see, Daisy hoped—if she were truly lucky and Mrs. Fowler, the milliner, were truly prescient—that the town picnic was the perfect venue for a marriage proposal. A marriage proposal to her!

With that exciting notion in mind, Daisy all but flew down the final steps leading to the stable. At the bottom, she nearly tripped…over some luggage, she saw to her puzzlement.

At the stairway landing sat two traveling trunks. They appeared rather worse for wear, thanks to their journeys. They also appeared familiar. Amid the scrapes and dings were two engraved tags that Daisy recognized. They bore her initials.

This was *her* luggage. These were *her* things. And if she'd entertained any lingering confusion on the matter, the sight of several copies of her *New Book of Cookery and General Home Keeping: with Recipes and Formulas for All Occasions, Both Informal and*

Grand, perched higgledy-piggledy on top of the nearest trunk, would have set her straight in a hurry.

But how—and why—were her belongings *here*, in Owen's stable?

She'd only sent her telegraph wire to Conrad two days ago. She didn't think her luggage and cookery books could have traveled all the way from San Diego to Morrow Creek in two days' time. Besides, she'd gotten settled so snugly in town! She'd almost begun to believe that her speaking-engagements tour belonged in another lifetime—and so did Conrad Parker, who was undoubtedly busy, even now, escorting the eminent Astair Prestell from place to place.

Gazing down at her newly recovered possessions, Daisy frowned. She couldn't help feeling these things belonged not only to another lifetime, but to another woman. The woman she'd been while touring across the country with Conrad at her side was gone now. In her place stood a stronger woman. A braver woman. A woman who dared to love…and be loved in return.

A woman who, by her own admission, was having a baby!

Those changes in herself hadn't come easily. But they'd come. And now, examining her luggage in bafflement, Daisy put one hand on her belly. She cradled her unborn baby, the way she now loved to do, and wondered again how this had come to pass.

On the precipice of discovering that for herself, Daisy glanced down the stable's aisles. In the stalls nearby, horses shifted and blew. Undoubtedly, they wished she were Owen, with his ever-full pockets of oats and his friendly equine pats. There was no sign of Gus; Owen's affable helper appeared to be away at the moment. In fact, there was no sign of *Owen* himself.

Well. First she'd find him. Then she'd invite him to the Independence Day town picnic. Then she'd inquire about her things. Undoubtedly, Owen had put them here. Or maybe Gus had.

With a final bolstering glance at her poster, Daisy headed down the nearest aisle. Only horses were there, safely in their stalls—but this time, muted by the sounds of restless hooves and wagon wheels outside, Daisy caught the sound of something else.

Voices. Male voices. Voices raised…in anger?

Concerned, she walked faster. One of those voices belonged to Owen, she realized. It sounded gruff but measured. The other voice, while male, sounded higher pitched and full of annoyance.

"You don't understand" came the second voice. "I simply cannot have this…*scandal* come to light! Not now. Not ever."

In an instant, Daisy recognized that voice. *Conrad.*

Conrad was *here*. But why here? Why now? And why, Daisy wondered further, had Owen not already come upstairs to fetch her? The two men didn't have a single thing in common, aside from her. She couldn't imagine they would embark on a friendly conversation just to pass the time. Apart from which, this particular conversation sounded contentious, not friendly.

"Daisy cares about you," Owen said. "You can't abandon—"

"Daisy 'cares' about everyone!" Conrad interrupted in a spiteful tone. "Friends, family, strangers—Daisy loves them all, right from the get-go. And they love her." Conrad made that sound like a bad thing. "But you can't expect me to *marry* that girl just because her 'friendliness' got out of hand."

Shocked, Daisy stopped. Did Conrad really mean... Was he really suggesting...that she'd been utterly indiscriminate? That she was some kind of hussy, to be spoken about so cruelly?

Newly troubled, Daisy ducked into an empty stall. With her heart beating wildly, she angled her head, the better to hear what came next. An instant later she almost wished she hadn't.

On the heels of a stern rebuke from Owen, Conrad laughed. Daisy couldn't hear what, exactly, had prompted his amusement.

"Was I supposed to *refuse* when she threw herself at me?"

Upon hearing that blatant lie, Daisy gasped. But Conrad only chuckled again. "You must not get out of this town much," he said, "if you believe any man wouldn't have done what I did."

"What you 'did' is get Daisy with child," Owen insisted. "It's your responsibility to take care of her and the baby."

Conrad scoffed. Even though Daisy couldn't see him from her position in the stall—and, she hoped, they couldn't see her, as she overheard this awful conversation—she could easily imagine Conrad's expression. It would be contemptuous. Arrogant. Mean.

It would be the kind of expression that had always made Daisy feel sick with the need to please Conrad, at whatever cost. But Owen, apparently, felt no such compunction toward him.

"You'd better think twice before you say anything else," he warned Conrad in a forbidding tone. "Because if you slander Daisy again—whether in my hearing or not—I swear to God I'll—"

"You'll what?" Conrad gibed. "You'll try to scare me? Be—"

A loud thump shuddered through the stable. Next came a hoarse cry. The walls vibrated hard, all the way to the stall where Daisy crouched, horrified and alone and disbelieving.

"What will I do?" Owen asked roughly. The wall shook again. There was another outcry. "I'll make you regret being born."

Daisy believed him. Evidently so did Conrad. Whatever the rest of his snide comment had been, he must have swallowed it.

"You're…choking me," Conrad burbled instead.

"I don't care what it costs me," Owen told him. The stable walls trembled. "I'll make you pay for what you did to Daisy."

"I—" A gagging cough. "Can't breathe. You… brute!"

"No matter what happens here," Owen went on, his voice full of certainty—and a menace that suddenly made Daisy believe every dangerous moment of his scoundrel's life, "no matter where you go and who you see after you leave here today, you *will* talk about Daisy with respect. Or I'll know the reason. Understand?"

Another gurgle came from Conrad. Dumbfounded and concerned, Daisy peeked around the corner. As she'd guessed, Owen had pinned her speaking-engagements tour manager fully against the wall. One mighty fist held Conrad in place; the other clenched and unclenched repeatedly by his side, clearly aching to hit something…or someone. With frightening intensity, Owen glared at Conrad. Then, after the man dumbly nodded, Owen released him.

Conrad tugged his shirt collar. Wearing a nervous, weaselly smile, he cast a wary glance at Owen. "All right. That's fine. I understand." He held up both palms. "You want me to pay? I can pay," he assured Owen with a vigorous nod. "I can pay *dearly,* if you want. All we need to do is come to an agreement."

Owen only glowered at him, still curling his hands at his sides. He appeared ready and willing to thrash Conrad senseless if he said anything else that displeased him. Daisy had never seen Owen appear more intimidating…or more protective of her.

"As I said before," Conrad stammered on, pausing to lick his lips, "I can't have this scandal become public! Not now. I've just begun a new speaking-engagements tour with Astair Prestell. It's very lucrative. It will be extremely profitable, too, once I've skimmed off some of the pr—" Conrad broke off. He seemed to think better of confiding more details. "But all that will vanish if word reaches my supervisors about Daisy."

"I'd be happy to wire Barker & Bowles myself. Today."

"No! No." With another oily smile, Conrad patted Owen's shoulder. At Owen's murderous expression, he hastily quit. But he still seemed shaken to realize that Owen knew his employers. "There's no need for that! What I mean is, you're a man of the world. Anyone can see that. And *I'm* a man of the world. Between the two of us, surely we can work out…an understanding?"

Owen crossed his arms, glaring at him suspiciously.

"Daisy's already here with you," Conrad said, his tone full of coaxing. "She likes it here, you said so! So who am I to alter that? All she needs is a little help to see her through."

He fumbled with something in his suit-coat pocket. Owen tensed. So did Daisy. Breath held, she leaned forward to see.

"Money?" Owen's disgusted tone mirrored Daisy's reaction.

"Not *just* money," Conrad alleged. He patted the wad of bills he'd set on an overturned barrel. "Money for Daisy's future." He cast a speculative glance toward Owen. "Enough money so the man who helps her with that future can have some too."

His meaning was plain. Conrad was trying to *bribe* Owen.

But that would never work, Daisy knew. Owen was far too faithful to her. He was far too honorable. He was far too redeemed—as she'd so often told him—to take up his scoundrelly ways again. It wasn't possible he'd be tempted. Not by this.

On the other hand, he *did* want to amass enough

savings for his daughter, Daisy recalled uneasily. That's why—aside from his concerns for staying away from trouble—Owen worked so hard at the stable. He wanted a big nest egg, as Élodie had explained a few days ago, for his *petit chou*...to assure her a good future.

Owen looked at the cash. "That's not much." Amazingly, he named a figure—an estimate of the quantity on the barrel. Daisy could tell, by Conrad's astounded expression, that his guess was accurate. "I'd need more than that," Owen specified darkly. "After all, I'd be taking a woman *and* a baby off your hands."

Daisy felt instantly dizzy. Light-headed and queasy, she cradled her belly. She leaned against the stable wall, willing herself not to have heard what she thought she'd heard.

Owen...haggling to be paid properly for caring about her.

More uneasy laughter came from Conrad. "I see! You're a man who drives a hard bargain! I respect that about you. I do."

Owen only growled. Daisy couldn't look at him. Her gaze was already full, brimming with tears— and the memory of Owen's face as he'd estimated his payoff. His gambler's acumen had truly come through for him, Daisy reckoned. So had his thieving past. She'd never forget his rough, raspy voice as he'd pushed for a bigger bribe—the better to see him through his days with her.

After all, I'd be taking a woman and a baby off your hands.

The echo of that horrible statement seemed to reverberate from the stable walls, blotting out the place's customary peacefulness. This was where she'd first kissed Owen, Daisy thought in a burst of disbelief. This was where she'd laughed with him while making the rounds to feed and water Élodie's favorite horses.

This was where Owen had shattered her heart to pieces.

Another thump on the barrel. "There! That's my final offer. Take it or leave it," Conrad blustered. "I'll forget I ever knew Daisy. You'll claim her bastard as your own. We'll both go our separate ways." A pause came next. "Do we have a deal?"

Chapter Twenty-Six

Owen frowned. Reeling with the need to bash that smug look from Conrad Parish's odious face, he clenched his fists again.

His whole body quivered, eager to deliver as many punishing blows as he could. So infuriated that he could scarcely see, Owen blinked. He made himself focus on the money on the barrel.

He could probably get more. Maybe he should try—for Daisy's sake. Owen had already raised the ante once. That would help Daisy for certain. Parish was desperate, conniving and about as trustworthy as a bucket of rats. Owen didn't believe he would keep his word not to slander Daisy. Until Owen could be sure…

Damnation. He could never be sure. That was the hell of it.

"You won't say another word about Daisy," Owen specified.

"Never." Parish touched his breastbone. "On my honor."

At that, Owen almost laughed. Conrad Parish had no honor. His talk about Daisy—and his willingness to betray her—proved that much. But he wanted the repellent man gone. He wanted him gone before Daisy wandered downstairs and discovered him there.

He wanted him gone. Period. So, coldly, Owen accepted Parish's handshake. "Yes." He bit out the words. "We have a deal."

"Hurrah!" Laughing, Parish waved his arms. "Well. Now that *that* little chore is settled, why don't we talk about—"

"Get out," Owen said. "I never want to see you again."

"Hold on!" Parish protested. "There's no need to be rude." He gave Owen a devious look. "In fact, why don't you stop by the Lorndorff Hotel later to-night. I'm hosting a party there with Astair Prestell. It would only be fair if you'd join us for a game of faro. Give me a chance to recoup my recent investment?"

Investment? He called abandoning Daisy and her baby a damn *investment?* Owen had never heard anything more heartless.

"Get out." Blinded by rage, he made a fist. "Now."

"No! Wait!" came another voice. "Not so fast. *Please.*"

At the sound of that femininely voiced *please,* Owen froze.

Daisy was here. *Daisy.* If she'd heard what Conrad Parish had said about her... Protectively, Owen turned toward her. The sight of her stricken, tear-streaked face left him little doubt.

She *had* heard Conrad Parish. The man had hurt her—again.

Newly enraged at the realization, Owen tensed his entire body, ready to defend her. This was not the scenario he'd envisioned when he'd sent for Parish. This was not the outcome he'd expected when he'd gambled on wiring Parish that Daisy was expecting. This was a million times worse.

It was better, Owen told himself dismally, that Daisy knew the truth now. It was better that she understood her baby's father was a scurrilous, unfeeling bastard before she wasted even more time caring about him. But none of that made it any easier for Owen to take in Daisy's wounded expression, her tearful eyes...her proudly held chin.

"Ah! Daisy." Parish gave a mocking bow. His gaze swept over her. It lingered, with contempt, on her middle, then rose to her face with sham courtesy. "You're looking...robust these days! Morrow Creek certainly does agree with you."

"Yes. It does." Daisy cast a tremulous glance at Owen. She closed her eyes. Then, after drawing in a wobbly breath, she opened her eyes again, fixing her attention on Parish. "I assume you're responsible for bringing my luggage and books?"

"Well." Another smirk. "*I* certainly had no use for them."

"Of course not." Daisy inclined her head. "Thank you."

Owen shifted, frustrated with their polite exchange. Had Daisy not understood what a dog Parish was? Had she *not* heard?

Owen tried to catch her eye. Daisy was having none of it.

"Before you leave, Conrad," she told her speaking-tour manager instead, "I'll be needing something from you, too."

"Oh?" The man sent an amused glance toward Owen. Belatedly, Parish seemed to realize Owen was *not* his ally in belittling Daisy. He sobered. "What might that be?" Parish hooked his thumb toward the stable's doors. "I was just on my way out—"

"An apology," Daisy said. "You owe me an apology."

At that, Parish couldn't contain his mirth. "An *apology?*"

"Yes. An apology for bullying me all these months," Daisy said relentlessly. "An apology for hurting me. An apology for—"

"Look at you, making demands!" Parish interrupted nastily. "Do you expect me to apologize for your bastard baby, too?"

Owen could scarcely breathe, he was so surprised by the depths of Parish's meanness. But Daisy only shook her head.

"My baby is a gift and a blessing," she said with her head high, "and nothing will make me believe otherwise. So, no. Don't apologize for that. But *do* apologize for all the rest—and for making me believe I wasn't any good at cooking and baking and home keeping, despite my credentials and experience and—"

"Well, Barker & Bowles *did* create several opportunities—"

"It's got nothing to do with Barker & Bowles." Daisy crossed her arms, appearing, Owen thought then, quite magnificent in her certainty. "It's got to do with *me*. I didn't know that before, but I know it now—thanks to being here. You lied, Conrad!" Daisy told him, her voice trembling with emotion. "You lied over and over again. You made me believe I'd simply gotten lucky, lucky to be chosen, lucky to be published by Barker & Bowles, lucky to be touring and speaking. But the truth is—"

"I don't have to listen to this!" Parish cast a disgusted glance at Owen. "Our business is done. I'm—"

Listening, Owen was about to demand. *Then apologizing.*

But Daisy beat him to it. "The truth is," she continued doggedly, "I'm *very* good at cooking and baking and homemaking, Conrad. I'm good at speaking about all those things, too! I'm *excellent* at them. And it's about time you told me so."

Appearing momentarily speechless, Parish frowned.

Daisy, for her part, merely waited, appearing surprisingly formidable. Owen wasn't sure where she'd found the courage to confront Parish this way, but he was glad she had. For her sake.

"Very well." Parish spoke quickly. Peevishly. "You're eminently qualified, Daisy. You truly are. Barker & Bowles know it, and so do I." He inhaled, looking pained. "I'm sorry."

"Thank you." Daisy's hands shook. "That's all I wanted."

Parish darted her a skeptical glance. "That's all?"

"Well, that…" Daisy skewered him with a fierce look. "And all the money you skimmed from my speaking-engagement fees, too. You owe me, Conrad. You took much more than your fair share."

Stunned, Owen stared at her. He'd suspected something was amiss when Parish had quit discussing his current tour duties so abruptly. But it hadn't occurred to him that Parish might have stolen outright from Daisy. The man just got worse and worse.

She was well shot of him, Owen thought. From here on, Daisy had Owen to take care of her. And her brother, Thomas. And she had Élodie—along with most of the townspeople—to love her, too.

She didn't need Conrad Parish to approve of her or help her. Evidently, Daisy had decided the same thing for herself.

Parish swallowed hard. "The rest of my money is in my room at the Lorndorff Hotel. I didn't expect to need more than—"

His gaze shifted tellingly to the cash on the barrel.

At the sight of it, Owen wanted to cringe. It was horrible to see it there—blatant proof of Parish's disregard for Daisy.

"—that to see me through the afternoon." Uncomfortably, Parish tugged his shirt collar again. "I'll give you the money—"

"Along with a full accounting," Daisy specified, seeming to draw strength from her success so far. "I know you kept a ledger. It should be easy enough for you to square up with me."

"'Square up'?" Parish snickered. "You sound like a yokel."

Owen growled, frankly at the end of his patience with the man. His utterance, however primitive, got Parish's attention.

"You're lucky you have Mr. Cooper, here," he told Daisy in a slightly more amiable tone. "He might be a bit…uncivilized, but he *did* get me here. That was more than you could have done."

At that, Daisy's composure wobbled, just a bit.

"I knew you were expecting, of course." Parish gave an airy wave. "Any man would have. You were thick in the middle. You were vomiting constantly." He ticked off those two items on his fingers, then reached the third. "You were annoyingly weepy—"

Owen stepped forward, making another threatening sound.

"No." Daisy held up her palm. "I want to hear this."

"All the signs were there," Parish said blithely. "So when you jumped off my train to come here—" his scornful gaze indicted the stable, everyone in it and the neighborly town beyond "—I was glad to be rid of you. And now I'm glad to be leaving you."

Appearing buffeted by his words, Daisy teetered. Visibly upset, she patted her skirts in place. Then she lifted her head.

Her eyes glittered with unshed tears. But when she spoke again, her voice was steady. "Yes. And I'm glad you'll be gone."

For a moment they only stared at one another— Parish with unconcealed malevolence; Daisy with sorrowful resignation.

She broke the silence first. "I'll visit your hotel later to collect my fees. Thank you for your apology. You can leave."

Parish smirked, obviously having no intention of

complying with Daisy's request. Owen felt increasingly fed up.

"Goodbye, Conrad," Daisy said more firmly, holding her head high. "Please leave me alone and don't ever come back."

Parish opened his mouth. He stared at Daisy. He frowned. Then, as though suddenly seeing the woman he'd abandoned and betrayed through new— and ashamed—eyes, Parish hung his head.

That was purely fitting, Owen knew. He'd be ashamed too, if Daisy were as disappointed and hurt by something he'd done.

Seeming downright cowed by Daisy's certainty, Parish nodded. Perhaps he'd finally glimpsed the truth, Owen thought—that Daisy was a better person than he could ever hope to be.

"I won't bother you again," Conrad said. "Good luck, Daisy." Then he scurried away, suit coat flapping, leaving the stable with as much dignity as, Owen surmised, he did anything.

Which was no dignity at all. Heartily glad to see the knuck pull foot, Owen released a pent-up breath. He turned to Daisy, feeling the tension whoosh from his shoulders instantly. For her sake—for all she'd just accomplished—Owen felt elated.

"First," he said, "you were remarkable! I'm truly impressed by the way you stood up to Parish." Fondly, Owen grinned. "I don't think he knew what hit him! He flopped like a carp, then folded like a gambler with a bad hand. Good for you, Daisy."

Oddly enough, she didn't look at Owen. She only gazed out the open stable doors, watching Conrad Parish disappear.

Slowly, Daisy turned. "'First,' you said? What's second?"

Her tone sounded...peculiarly distant. Wondering at that, Owen frowned. But he wanted this ugly endeavor finished, once and for all. So he scooped up the wad of bills from the barrel. He reached for Daisy's hand. Tenderly, he squeezed her fingers.

"This is second. And final. I'd hoped it wouldn't come to this. But since it has..." Owen pressed the bundle of money into Daisy's palm. Solemnly he closed her fingers around the whole sum. "For you," he said. "Now you'll never have to worry again. You'll never have to struggle. You'll never have to depend on a lying, cowardly bastard—on a scoundrel of a man like—"

"Like you?" Daisy asked.

Stricken, Owen stared at her. "No. Like Parish."

Maybe she was joking, he thought. Maybe she was overwrought, strained and distressed by the events of the day.

Daisy frowned down at the cash. To his bafflement, she did not accept it. "But aren't you forgetting something?"

"I don't think so." Why didn't she take the money?

Daisy pushed the whole bundle back at him. With conviction, she said, "You're forgetting to take your share. Take it."

"My share?" Owen frowned, not sure what she meant.

"In fact," she said, sounding increasingly upset as she pushed away the money, "take it all! I don't want any of it."

"But I got this money for *you*," Owen said, still mystified by her reaction. This was the most valuable assurance he could have offered her. Didn't she understand that? He hadn't *wanted* to resort to bargaining with Parish. He still felt sullied by the effort. "I got this money for you and the baby."

"Truly?" Daisy jerked up her chin again. "And if I hadn't come downstairs to the stable at just that moment? If I hadn't overheard you making your awful deal? What then, Owen? Hmm?" With more tears in her eyes, she jabbed his chest. "Would you have upped the ante once more? Would you have made an even bigger bet against me, like a true gambler? Or would you have sold me out for even less scratch, just to feel a part of the game again?"

"What are you talking about?"

"I have to give you credit," Daisy went on, her voice cracking. "You're almost charming enough to sell me on your innocence. If I didn't know you, I might actually believe you."

That was low. And markedly confusing. Giving up for now on peaceably giving her the money, Owen pocketed the lot of it for safekeeping. Gutted by the accusing look on Daisy's face, he reached for her. "What do you think was happening here?"

"Well. I'd say that's fairly obvious, isn't it?"

"No." Owen reached for her. She jerked away. "Tell me."

"You met me—alone and vulnerable," Daisy said, her voice quivering with emotion. "You knew yourself—a born gambler and thief, eager for some fast takings. So you wired Conrad—"

"To come fetch you! To be with you!" Stonily, Owen stared at her, hardly able to believe Daisy would throw his past in his face this way. "I thought that you loved him," he choked out, "so—"

"So you took me to your bed? How did that fit into your grand scheme, Owen?" Daisy's plaintive gaze collided with his...then swiveled away sadly. "I never loved Conrad. I loved—"

You, he longed to hear. *I loved you.*

But instead, Daisy went silent. Caught beneath all the accusations she'd made, Owen stared at her. Helplessly, he still wished she would love him. Truthfully, he knew she did not.

"You wired Conrad," Daisy finished in a frightfully bleak voice, "and you struck a deal with him. *This* deal. You traded me—and my baby!—for a bundle of money. And now, since I stumbled upon your wretched agreement, you feel compelled to share some of that money with me. Which I suppose must count as honor among thieves, or some such, but I'll confess... I fail to see it."

She failed to see *him,* too. Deeply hurt by Daisy's interpretation of today's events, Owen fisted his hands. The money in his pocket felt like a dead weight. Foolishly, he'd thought Daisy would understand him. He'd thought she would be pleased. He'd tried to give her security—tangible protection for an uncertain world. He'd tried to make sure that Daisy—like Élodie, someday—would never have to rely on an undependable man for her safety...the way Renée had, to her ultimate detriment.

But Daisy didn't see that. All she saw was him.

A born gambler, in her words. *A thief.*

Daisy didn't believe he'd changed. And even though Owen could not, in that moment, imagine why she'd ever pretended she had, all he could do was look at her. "You truly believe that?"

Daisy gazed at him sadly. "Give me a reason not to."

"How can I?" Owen spread his hands. "You've already made up your mind. You've already decided the worst of me." He cracked a humorless smile.

"You were prepared to make excuse after excuse for that scum, Conrad Parish. And yet, when it comes to *me*—"

"I never loved *him!* You're the one I was fool enough to—"

Love, Owen prayed again, desperately wishing she'd say the words. Maybe they could blot out everything else she'd said.

"Trust," Daisy finished brokenly. "I trusted you, Owen!"

Owen stood solitarily, soaking up her pain. "I could say the same thing," he said in a low voice. "I trusted you, too."

They stood there, trapped in their mutual disillusionment, both of them unhappy...but not yet willing to walk away.

Staring at Daisy, remembering everything he'd shared with her over the past joy-filled days, Owen frowned. All this time, he'd believed she'd had feelings for Conrad Parish. He'd believed he oughtn't make promises to her—promises that might unfairly take her away from her baby's father. And now, just when Owen had realized Daisy did *not* have feelings for Parish...

He likewise realized she did not have feelings for him.

Just the way Daisy could get along without her

former manager in her life, it appeared she could manage without Owen, too.

And he *wanted* her to do that. He wanted her to be safe and happy and well. But that didn't make it any easier to see her now, gazing at him through tear-filled eyes, looking at him, it occurred to Owen, almost the way she'd looked at Conrad Parish, in the end. At the memory of that, Owen felt a similar shame.

Daisy was good and kind and loving. And he'd hurt her.

She'd delivered a few raw blows of her own—that was true. Owen's heart still ached with the accusations she'd made. But he was a strong, tough man. He could withstand the pain. Daisy…

Daisy, he feared, could not.

"Just tell me!" she said, breaking into his thoughts. "Just tell me, right now. Tell me you love me…" Her voice broke on the words. She tried again. "Tell me you love me, Owen, and I'll forgive you. Tell me you love me, and I'll believe you. Just—"

"I can't." Anguished, he stared at her. That she would even offer to forgive him—while she still believed him so grievously wrong—proved he should not accept her offer. After everything, Daisy deserved better than that, better than *him*. "I can't," Owen repeated. "I'm sorry."

Her grief-stricken expression met his. Owen knew,

in that moment, that the pain in her eyes would haunt him forever.

But then she rallied.

"You don't understand," Daisy scrambled to say, hopeful to the end. "If you can say that you love me, right now… It's easy, Owen. Please. *Please,* just say you love me, so I can—"

But Owen could not. Now more than ever, he could not. And no measure of desperately voiced pleas would ever change that.

Daisy had only just freed herself from a reprehensible man who'd used and abused her. She'd only just learned to stand up, to be brave, to demand to be treated fairly. Owen couldn't take that from her. Not now. Not ever. Besides, was he really any better a man than Conrad Parish? Grimly, he shook his head.

"I can't tell you that." Owen gazed at her stonily, willing himself not to feel…anything. "I can't. I'm sorry."

"'Sorry'?" Daisy gaped at him. "You're 'sorry' you don't love me? Or 'sorry' you don't even care enough to lie about it?"

Owen tried to respond. But Daisy overrode him.

"*You,* a renowned rascal and a charmer," she blurted, "who can talk the blue from the sky… *You* can't give me a simple, heartfelt *lie?* Not even when I'm begging for it?" She shook her head. "Maybe you're right. Maybe you're not a scoundrel anymore.

Because I don't feel at all seduced by this experience. I don't feel… Well, I don't feel anything except alone. And unwanted."

"Daisy." Swearing under his breath, Owen stepped nearer. She was anything but alone—anything but unwanted. Filled with remorse, he caught hold of her shoulders, wanting to pull her close—to comfort her. At the last moment, he stopped himself. Indulging his own feelings would only hurt her—would only prove his own damnable selfishness. "Please don't do this. Don't—"

"Don't beg you to love me?" Daisy closed her eyes, tears flowing freely down her face. "Fine. I won't. I'm sorry, too."

Gently, Owen stroked his thumbs over her shoulders. At least she'd let him touch her this time, he thought. He felt absurdly heartened by that fact. Maybe that meant Daisy was softening toward him. Maybe that meant she would forgive him, they would talk more, and then things would go back to the way they'd been, with her and him and Élodie, together.

"Sorry for what?" Owen urged her to say. "Tell me. Just—"

"I'm sorry," Daisy said, "that I've stayed here so long already." With a mighty sniffle, Daisy lifted her head. She inhaled deeply. She squared her shoulders. "It was a mistake, plain and simple. But I've learned a few things lately. Some of them I've learned from you. And one of those things—"

She broke off, her chin wobbling with a pent-up sob. She inhaled again, her breath shuddering through her small frame.

"One of those things," Daisy repeated, "is that I'm strong enough to stand up for myself. I'm strong enough to face what needs to be faced—to go on doing what needs to be done."

Thinking that she was referring to her situation with her baby—to the way she'd denied her pregnancy at first—Owen nodded.

"I'm strong enough to say goodbye, Owen," Daisy said. She sounded almost startled by the realization. Startled and sad. "So that's what I'm doing. I'm saying goodbye. To you."

Again, Daisy hesitated. She looked up into his face, almost as though searching for something—almost as though waiting for him to…to do what? To stop her? Owen could not. Leaving him was likely the best thing for her. Daisy was vulnerable and sweet. Her very vulnerability and sweetness had drawn him to her, in fact. But they'd also made it doubly likely that he would let her down in the end… that he'd hurt her, like this.

Eventually, after several drawn-out moments, Daisy seemed to realize Owen was not going to stop her. With a gentle and regret-filled gesture, she raised her hand.

She touched his face, then gazed directly at him.

The only man I'm thinking about, he suddenly remembered her saying to him, *is the man I'm looking at right now...with both eyes open.* Reminded of that, Owen bit back a disgraceful sob.

He wanted to be that man for her. He was doomed not to be.

"Goodbye, Owen. Tell Élodie—" Daisy broke off again. This time, she did cry in earnest. Struggling mightily, she managed to finish. "Tell Élodie I'm sorry. Tell her I'll never forget her."

Setting his jaw, Owen nodded. "I will," he rasped.

Feeling torn to pieces, he watched as Daisy lowered her hand again. As she stepped away from him. As she smiled, weakly.

"I'll never forget you, either," she told him.

And then Daisy was gone...lost to him forever, just the way Owen should have known she would be all along.

Chapter Twenty-Seven

With an impossible task ahead of him, Owen climbed the stairs from the stable to his living quarters. After Daisy had gone, it had taken him a while to stir himself. For a long time, he'd stood silently in the shadows of his stable. He'd held himself still and he'd kept himself planted, just in case Daisy had changed her mind and come back.

Eventually, he'd had to admit the truth: she was gone.

That meant Owen had to go on…somehow. So he picked himself up and headed for the stairs, stopping twice along the way: once, distractedly, to collect a fallen poster for the annual Morrow Creek Independence Day town picnic, and once, with deep misgivings, to tuck Conrad Parish's money into Daisy's luggage, where she would eventually find it and use it. Now, with that done, Owen straightened his spine and kept on moving.

In his hand, he still held the printed poster. It had to have been Daisy's, discarded in shock when she'd glimpsed Conrad Parish. In his heart, Owen carried a misery and a hopelessness that dogged every step he took. On his face, he could manage no better than an expression of stoicism, stark and unhelpful.

Élodie deserved a smile, Owen knew. She deserved to be reassured that all would be well, even with Daisy gone and the two of them alone again. But Owen simply couldn't manage it.

The way he felt right now, he might never smile again.

At the top of the stairs, he landed with a heavy tread.

"Aha! You're finally back!" Élodie chirped, undoubtedly mistaking him for Daisy. "It took you *so* long! What did Papa—" She broke off. She glanced in his direction at last. "—say?"

Even as she finished voicing that question, Élodie frowned. Devilishly perceptive, even at her young age, she seemed to sense that all was not right. Her frown grew. Cursing that ability of hers to read him like a book, Owen shook his head.

Élodie's gaze dropped to the poster in his hand. "That's Miss Walsh's poster. Why doesn't Miss Walsh have her poster?"

"I'm sorry, Élodie." Owen opened his hands. "She—"

"That's all right, Papa! I don't think I need to

know," his daughter interrupted. Hastily, she grabbed her knitting. "Look! I'm making a scarf. The stitches are bumpy looking, but good!"

Owen came closer. He dropped to a crouch beside Élodie's chair. His daughter knit feverishly. She did not look at him.

Cautiously, Owen put his hand on her arm. "I'm sorry, Élodie," he said again. "But Miss Walsh is gone. She had to…leave unexpectedly. She'll miss you and never forget you—"

His daughter's shoulders bunched. Her face scrunched up, too. Valiantly, Élodie tried to keep on knitting.

"Miss Walsh was very sorry she couldn't stay longer." Owen swallowed hard, still hurting. "But it was time for her to go."

Élodie's needles quit moving. She let them fall to her lap.

When she looked at Owen, her eyes were filled with tears.

"Couldn't you have just said yes?" she demanded to know, her voice choked. "Couldn't you have just told her you'd go with her? It wouldn't have killed you to attend one stupid picnic!"

Confused, Owen examined Élodie. Then he remembered the way she'd stared at the poster for the Independence Day town picnic.

"You think I refused to take Miss Walsh to the picnic?"

"Of course!" Élodie's chin wobbled. She shrugged off his hand, then jumped up from her chair. Her knitting dropped, uncared about, onto the rug. "Miss Walsh was fixing to ask you to escort her. That's why she went downstairs to see you!"

"To ask me about the Independence Day town picnic?"

His daughter nodded. "It was very brave of her, too. I've been sitting here with my fingers crossed, on account of how risky it was. Everyone *knows* you don't go to social functions, Papa. Miss Walsh thought maybe *she* could change your mind. But if you told her no—" Élodie sobered, appearing to realize something more. "Miss Walsh already thought you couldn't love her—because of me!—and now she *knows* you don't! She knows it!"

That Élodie is right, Owen recalled Daisy telling him days ago, *and you'll never love anyone, ever again.*

"Élodie," Owen asked sharply, "what did you tell her?"

His daughter sniffled. "I didn't tell her anything."

Pushed to his limits, Owen tried again. "What did you tell her?" he asked more sternly. "What did you tell Miss Walsh?"

"I told *Miss O'Neill* that you wouldn't ever love

her," his daughter confessed in a defiant tone, "because you already *swore* you wouldn't ever love anybody ever again! And it worked, too! Miss O'Neill was rightly scared off. And I was glad, too. Even if it meant I never ate spiced apple butter ever again! Only—" Élodie gulped. "Only Miss Walsh overheard me, so *she* knew it was true, too." She cast him a guilty glance. "Oh, Papa! Now Miss Walsh is gone," Élodie wailed, "and it's all my fault! It's all my fault Miss Walsh gave up on you, and after only three tries!"

With a piteous sob, she started to cry. Owen felt knifed clean through. Not sure what to do, he tried to equate this new information with Daisy's leaving...and came up entirely blank.

What "three tries" was Élodie talking about? And why had his daughter found it necessary to have "scared off" Miss O'Neill in the first place? Owen felt powerfully befuddled.

"It's not your fault," he declared even more sternly than before. He hugged Élodie close. "Don't ever say that, you hear?"

Obediently his daughter nodded. She seemed unconvinced.

"I told you I wouldn't ever love anyone in the same way I loved your *maman*," Owen felt compelled to clarify. "I told you I wouldn't ever be able to replace your *maman* in my heart." For good measure, he placed his hand on his heart. That was a mistake. It felt empty and aching. As best he could, Owen forged on. "Or in your heart, where you'll always keep your *maman* safe with you. But that doesn't mean I'll never love *anyone,* ever."

Élodie brightened. "Then you *do* love Miss Walsh?"

Pricked with guilt, Owen hesitated. Then he swore beneath his breath. What would be the harm in being honest now?

"I do love her," he said. "I do love Miss Walsh. When I'm with her, I feel warm again. I feel like the mountain rocks in the sunshine. I didn't think I would ever warm up again, but I did when Miss Walsh was here with us. I do love her. I do."

His daughter gave a solemn nod. "Well, everyone in town *does* say you're flinty and immovable." Improbably, her pert little smile bloomed. "So I guess that's fitting!" she teased.

Wholly unable to grin back, Owen reached down. Tenderly, he thumbed away the tears from Élodie's cheeks. Then he kissed her.

"Yuck!" Élodie giggled. "You kissed my nose, Papa!"

"I must have missed," Owen joked. "Let me try again."

"No! You'll kiss my nose *again* if you try!" Giving a girlish shriek, Élodie ran. "You'll have to catch me first!"

Shaking his head, Owen watched his daughter frolic away. In her turn, Élodie pulled a funny face, brazenly challenging him to catch up with her. As bad as things were, at least Élodie would be all right, he reckoned. That meant the world to him.

From near the fireplace, Élodie's smile glowed with a decidedly mischievous aura. "You won't get away with this forever, Papa," she cautioned when he still hadn't chased her. "When it comes to this nose kissing, I'm going to warn my new baby brother ahead of time, so you'll never catch him unaware!"

Uh-oh. At that, Owen went still. Visions of the life he'd begun to dream of—but hadn't yet dared to share with Élodie or Daisy—tumbled through his mind. Him, with *two* young-uns by his side, toddling hand in hand. Him, cradling a baby boy in his arms…gazing with wonder at Daisy as they chose a fitting name.

In his privately sentimental moments, Owen had favored—

Well, his favorite name didn't matter now. What did matter was Élodie. Apparently his daughter believed that love would conquer all—and that her "new baby brother" would be home with them soon. Owen didn't see how he could accomplish any of that. Not now. Not now that Daisy was gone…and lost to him forever.

This was the harm in being honest about his feelings, Owen realized too late. *This* was the harm in having feelings at all.

I do love her. I do. What a fool he'd been to say so.

Clamping down on those selfsame emotions for the final time, Owen shook his head. He gave Élodie a harsh look. "I don't have time to play anymore," he said. "I have work to do."

Then, doing his best not to see his daughter's disappointed little face, Owen made himself stand. He crumpled up the poster for the Independence Day town picnic and tossed it in the fire. Then he took himself back to the life he deserved—a life without a loving woman, a life without joy…a life without smiles.

He'd borne up under it once. He'd damn well do it again.

Chapter Twenty-Eight

"Thank you, Gus." With relief and chagrin, Daisy took Gus's hand in hers. She shook it. "I truly appreciate your help."

"Pshaw. T'weren't nothin'," Owen's helper told her. "I'm happy to help you bring over your things from the stable." He aimed his jaw toward the trunks and crated books he'd helpfully delivered to her at Mrs. Sunley's home, where Daisy had been staying. "You're welcome anytime. If you need anything else, you just call on Gus Winston. I'll come a'running straight over."

"I strongly doubt Miss Walsh intends on needing anything more from *you,* Mr. Winston," Mrs. Sunley said from her perch in her favorite chair. Regally she dismissed him. "But you may continue to flatter her at will, if Miss Walsh agrees to it."

Daisy couldn't help blushing. Mrs. Sunley could be blunt at times, and even quite salty in her remarks. But she was also remarkably kindhearted. Mrs. Sunley's crusty demeanor hid a gentle and compassionate woman of some means—a woman who had, surprisingly, been the first to offer Daisy lodgings when she'd arrived, forlorn and tear-stained, at Thomas's offices a few days ago. Since then, Daisy had grown very fond of Mrs. Sunley.

"See that?" Mrs. Sunley pointed at Daisy. "You've already put some color back in her cheeks. Hurry up!" she instructed Gus. "Do it again! Flatter her some more, you dimwit!"

The poor stable helper stammered, clearly at a loss.

"That's all right, Gus," Daisy said, coming to his rescue as best she could. She released his hand. "You've done enough."

"Hmmph. You deserve a lot more, is what I say." Hat in hand, Gus eyed her compassionately. "After the low-down way Mr. Cooper treated you, I reckon you might need some mollycoddling."

Unfortunately, his remark only reminded Daisy of the kind things Owen had done—bringing her hot ginger tea, hauling wood for the stove, rubbing her feet after a long day's tutoring.

With a frown, she shook herself from those recollections. They wouldn't do her any good now. Now everything had changed.

Maybe she should have stayed at the stable a bit

longer, Daisy thought bitterly. Maybe she should have stayed to hear Owen enumerate all the reasons he could not love her. Maybe then she would have found it easier to carry on without him.

"That's quite enough, Mr. Winston," said Mrs. Sunley.

"All I mean is, everybody was plumb happy a week ago," Gus went on, undeterred, "and now everyone's wretched miserable!"

That piqued Daisy's interest. "Owen is miserable?"

"I'll say!" Gus nodded fervently. "He's ornery like the last bear at a honeycomb, too. Grumbles like there's nothin' but bees in his life." The helper shook his head. "And poor Élodie—"

"Well, *do* have a fine afternoon, Mr. Winston!" Mrs. Sunley bustled toward him, literally herding him toward the door with her impressively unfurled fan. "Thank you again! Goodbye!"

Concerned, Daisy followed them. "'Poor Élodie'?" she repeated. "What's the matter with Élodie? Is she all right?"

On the front porch, Gus faced her. He cast a tentative glance at Mrs. Sunley, then put on his hat. "That little girl just misses you sorely, Miss Walsh, that's all I meant," he said with noticeable kindness. "I ain't never seen Élodie take a shine to nobody the way she did you, and that's the truth."

"Élodie will be fine!" Mrs. Sunley boomed. "Off you go!"

As though fearing for his manhood, Gus legged it back toward the stable. Watching him go, Daisy sighed. It was bad enough that she missed Owen. Missing Élodie was terrible, too.

When she'd left Owen's home, Daisy had been too distraught to properly consider Élodie. Now Daisy wished anew that she'd talked with Élodie herself. She wished she'd told the little girl that she loved her and would miss her. She wished she'd apologized for everything...everything that might have been for all of them, and now would never be.

"You know, I'd actually begun to think of us as a family," Daisy confided to Mrs. Sunley in a wistful tone. She clutched the porch railing, remembering. "Me and Owen and Élodie, I mean. I know it's silly. I scarcely spent two weeks in their company! All the same, I can't help wishing we could have—"

"Thinking about what might have been is no good for anyone," Mrs. Sunley announced. With fierce practicality, she strode back inside. At the doorway, she noticed Daisy hadn't followed. She doubled back. "You've got to go on with your life, child." Her voice softened. "Anything less will ruin you."

At Mrs. Sunley's insightful tone, Daisy started. She glanced at her companion, belatedly remembering that Viola had outlived both her husbands.

Undoubtedly, those difficult times had taught Mrs. Sunley a few things about being resilient.

"Besides, any man who wants you ought to earn you," the older woman went on, aiming a puckish glance in her direction. "Unless Owen Cooper can conjure up a powerfully impressive show of love and devotion, I guess he's already had his chance."

"Well, you do have a point there." Daisy couldn't deny that. She couldn't think of anything Owen could do that would restore her faith in him. Her trust had been sorely damaged. "But we oughtn't bandy that about *too* much, lest we tempt fate. Mr. Cooper *can* be mighty persuasive when he wants to be."

Thanks to his scoundrelly, too-charming past.

She'd truly believed that past was behind him, Daisy couldn't help remembering. How could she have been so wrong?

Drawing in a bolstering breath, Daisy put her hand on her belly. She *had* been wrong, she reminded herself. She guessed she'd have to live with that. Thanks to Owen, she now knew she was strong enough to do that…even if she didn't want to.

As she turned to go inside, a glimmer of movement caught her eye. Daisy squinted. Far down the street, she glimpsed a familiar red-haired woman getting into a hired carriage. At her side, a nattily dressed man with a bowler hat helped her alight.

"Mrs. Sunley…" Daisy pointed. "Isn't that Miss O'Neill?"

The widow looked. "Hmmph. Maybe. It's no concern of ours."

What a peculiar reply. "Who's that man with her?"

"Some highfalutin fellow from the East." Mrs. Sunley's disparaging sniff made her opinion plain. "Astair Prestell."

Astair Prestell. Fascinated, Daisy stared. She'd expected to catch a glimpse of that renowned speaker when she'd gone to collect her earnings from Conrad at the Lorndorff Hotel. Then, she'd been disappointed. Now, she kept watching.

"Have Miss O'Neill and Mr. Prestell been spending a great deal of time together, then?" she asked. *Maybe that meant,* Daisy thought, *that Miss O'Neill had decided against setting her cap for Owen.* "Mr. Prestell *does* seem quite Miss O'Neill's type."

"Male? Unmarried? Upright and breathing?" A head shake. "Yes. He quite does." Mrs. Sunley gestured. "Come along now."

"I wonder where they're going in that carriage?"

"You won't have to wonder for long," Mrs. Sunley opined. "Miss O'Neill has a mouth on her like a roadrunner has feet. By nightfall, the whole town will know where she went and why."

Daisy grinned. "I thought Miss O'Neill was your friend!"

"She is." Mrs. Sunley folded her fan with a snap. "That doesn't mean I can't see what's right in front of me. I like *you* all right, too, but I can still see you're addlepated over Mr. Cooper."

Daisy winced. She clenched the porch rail more tightly.

"*And* I can still see you've got a hopeful future," Mrs. Sunley added in a gentler tone. "Why don't I make us some tea?"

Decisively, Daisy straightened. "No, thank you. I've just decided—there's someone I need to see."

"Not Owen Cooper, I hope! I used to like *him,* too, until—"

"No, not Mr. Cooper," Daisy assured her. She hurried to Mrs. Sunley, then gave her a hug. "Thank you. For everything."

The older woman blinked. Then she bristled. She brandished her fan, waving it like a weapon. "Off! Off! That's enough."

Smiling to herself, Daisy ended her embrace. Then she went inside to fetch her hat. Within moments, she was on her way.

"And so that's why," Élodie told an astonished-looking Mrs. Archer, "we need a new plan, to set things right again."

"I see." Mrs. Archer glanced around Élodie and Papa's front room, taking in the unread newspapers, cast-off clothing and haphazardly abandoned home-keeping projects that Élodie and her father hadn't had the vitality to take care of. "Evidently, I missed a great deal while I was away visiting in Avalanche."

"Yes, you certainly did!" Élodie assured her. "While you were spending time with your sister, Papa fell in love with Miss Walsh. Miss Walsh fell in love with Papa. We all started thinking up names for my new baby brother. I learned to sew, knit, embroider and even cook soup! But then Miss Walsh left us." She heaved a sigh, still feeling poorly about that. "I *told* Papa he could fix it. Because he can fix *anything!* But he only gave me a hug, with those faraway eyes of his, and he told me, 'Not this time, *mon petit chou*,' even though I *know* he could do it."

"Yes." Mrs. Archer frowned, appearing deep in thought. "I believe he could fix things, too. The question is… Should he?"

Élodie frowned. Loyally, she said, "Of course he should!"

"And you say you're getting a new baby brother soon?"

"Well, I think it will be a baby boy. Papa does, too," Élodie confided, feeling relieved to have someone to unburden herself to. Papa was awful these days at listening to her. All he did was mope around and work at the stable from dawn till dusk. "Miss

Walsh said we had at *least* six or seven months to wait before we found out for sure."

"Six or seven months?" Mrs. Archer looked at her piercingly. "Are you sure she said 'six or seven months,'? Not longer?"

"I'm sure. Because when Miss Walsh told me that, I remember feeling sorry we might not have the new baby in time for Christmas." Suddenly remembering something else, Élodie drew in a sharp breath. Her eyes widened. "Only I wasn't supposed to tell anybody about that! About the baby, I mean. Oh, no! I—"

"I wouldn't worry about that, dear," Mrs. Archer gave her a warm smile and a pat on the hand. "I'm not just 'anybody,' after all. And you had to tell me so we could make up a new plan."

Excitedly, Élodie sat up. "Then you've thought of one?"

"Yes. I've thought of one." Wearing a decisive expression, Mrs. Archer cast a thoughtful glance toward the stairs leading to the stable. Her gaze shifted to the shuttered window, beyond which Morrow Creek went about its usual workaday routines. "But it will require *very* careful handling this time—more so than even our last plan. Do you think you're ready for that?"

"Oh, yes!" Feeling more eager by the moment,

Élodie smiled. "If it will make Papa happy again, I'm ready for anything!"

"Good." Mrs. Archer nodded. "Then here's your part…"

Chapter Twenty-Nine

Upon reaching the door of his office at the *Pioneer Press*, Thomas waved his hand. He showed Daisy inside. "Here we are!"

"Thank you, Thomas. I'm so happy you could see me."

"Naturally I could see you! You're my sister." Trying not to show his concern at Daisy's increasingly careworn appearance, Thomas perched himself casually on his desk, in a pose suggested by Miss Reardon. She had mentioned that his employees and visitors might find him less "stiff" if he came out from behind his desk occasionally. Thomas had learned to enjoy his new stance. He adjusted his spectacles. "Is everything all right?"

"Fine! Fine," Daisy assured him. "I'm very well."

Thomas didn't believe her. It didn't take a man of huge intellect to glimpse the dark shadows under her eyes…the lines of fretfulness on her face and the paleness of her complexion.

In the days since Daisy had arrived at his office, upset and essentially homeless, his sister had only gotten worse, it seemed. Further worried by that fact, Thomas crossed his arms.

"So…everything is fine. You're well. And you decided to pay me a visit to assure me of that? That's very thoughtful."

"Yes." Daisy gave him a wan smile. She folded her hands in her lap. "I was talking with Mrs. Sunley today—don't make that nasty face, Thomas, she's a lovely woman!—and something she said gave me an idea. An idea I'll need *your* help with executing."

"Anything you want." Thomas meant it. "After all, it's because of me that you're here in Morrow Creek at all."

Unhappily so, too, Thomas thought, feeling partly responsible for that, as well. He knew that Daisy had left her publisher, Barker & Bowles. He knew that she'd parted ways with Conrad Parish, her former speaking-engagements tour manager. He knew that she'd suspended her cross-country speaking tour.

He knew, most remarkably of all, that she was having a *baby,* because Owen Cooper had told him so. What Thomas *didn't* know was when Daisy would tell him that extraordinary news herself— when she would confide in her elder brother as she ought to do. The fact that she hadn't yet upset and worried him.

At first, Thomas had thought he'd understood everything. Especially after Cooper had corralled him in his stable and delivered him an unstinting message *not* to upset Daisy. Thomas had thought it patently obvious: the two of them were in love.

But now, since Daisy had abruptly left the Coopers' home, Thomas felt much less certain about his original assessment—and much more apprehensive about his sister's future prospects.

"All right, then." Brightly, his sister eyed him. "Here it is—I'd like a job, Thomas. A position at the newspaper, to be precise." Daisy sat up straighter. "I could write about home keeping! With recipes! You said yourself the raffle was absurdly popular. Surely your readership would enjoy learning more."

"I'm sure they would." Worriedly, he gazed at her. "You are a wonderful writer and a talented homemaker, with a great deal of expertise to share. But is now truly the best time for this? You seem so—" *Miserable,* Thomas thought. *Hopeless.* He tried again. It was no use. "You seem so very unhappy."

Daisy appeared stricken. "Well, that's why I want to keep busy. That…and the fact that I can't rely on Mrs. Sunley's kindness forever. Nor can I stay stuck in one place, refusing to move ahead. I'm moving on! That's why I want your help."

"And what do you think Owen Cooper would say about this?"

"Owen?" Daisy's mouth dropped open. She shook her head. "He has nothing to do with this. This is *my* life. My life alone."

My life...on my own, Thomas heard, and felt doubly sorry.

How would Daisy manage with a baby...and no husband? Thomas had to tread carefully though, lest he upset Daisy even further.

"Mr. Cooper wants to take care of you," he said gently. "I realize you're having some...troubles right now, but surely before too much longer you and Mr. Cooper will reconcile?"

"I can't imagine it. The fact is, you're wrong, Thomas. Owen never wanted to take care of me." Daisy stared at her hands, twisting them in her lap. "I realize it may have seemed that way at first. It did to me. But Owen had...other plans."

Baffled, Thomas watched her. "He had plans to marry you."

His sister scoffed. "Please. I seriously doubt that. I realize Owen Cooper can be powerfully persuasive at times, but—"

"He asked my permission to marry you," Thomas insisted, certain on the matter. "That day in the stable? Remember? That's what he wanted to talk to me about. He wanted to ask for your hand in marriage. Since I'm your nearest male relative, I was in a position to—"

"Owen asked to *marry* me?" Daisy appeared dumbfounded.

"Yes." Her gob-smacked expression made him grin. "He did."

"When?"

"That day, in the stable, a week or so ago." Thomas frowned, not understanding why his sister was so surprised. Surely Cooper hadn't kept his intentions to himself? "The day you served us lemonade and jumble cookies, and Miss Reardon came with me to call on you and Mr. Cooper, with Miss O'Neill."

"Why?" Daisy's astounded gaze swiveled to his. "Did Owen say why? Did he think I had a huge dowry? A family fortune?"

At that, Thomas laughed outright. "Quite the opposite. In fact, Owen spent much of his time assuring *me* he could provide for *you,* should the need arise. He seemed…unsure how you would respond. He seemed to be under the impression that you and Mr. Parish had some sort of connection to one another. But if that wasn't the case, Owen said, he hoped to beg for your hand himself."

Feeling frightfully curious, Thomas peered at his sister, trying to gauge her expression. He'd discussed this matter at length with Miss Reardon, during which time they'd concluded that Daisy could not possibly have been attracted to someone like Conrad Parish…but she could definitely love Owen Cooper.

"So," Thomas probed, "which man will it be? Mr. Parish? Or Mr. Cooper?" He considered things further. "If it's Mr. Parish, then you'll have to catch a train to chase him, because he's already left town. According to the frightfully loquacious Miss O'Neill, Mr. Astair Prestell dismissed Mr. Parish on very short notice. Miss O'Neill says that Mr. Prestell has agreed to speak at the Independence Day picnic, which is why he is still here in town. It will be quite a coup for us all!" Thomas blinked, belatedly realizing he'd lost the thread of his conversation. He regrouped, then smiled at Daisy. "If it's Mr. Cooper who's your choice, then… Well, no worries at all!"

"No worries?" Daisy quirked her lips, appearing deeply regretful. "I wouldn't go that far."

"Why not? As Virgil said, 'Love conquers all things,' does it not?" Thomas angled his head at her. "*I* think it does."

"Leave it to you to offer up ancient quotations."

"Daisy…" Patiently Thomas waited until she looked at him. "Do you love Mr. Cooper? If you do, that's truly all that matters. From there on, all you need is the courage to act."

"Aha. 'Fortune favors the bold,' then?"

"See? Mr. Virgil has much to offer us all."

Daisy smiled. "But *I've* never been bold, Thomas. Never."

"Hmm. I don't know about that." Thomas mulled it over, chin in hand. "You wrote a cookery book of your own. You left home and embarked on a cross-country speaking tour. You jumped off a train and came here. You took on the challenge of tutoring a little girl and her curmudgeonly father." He couldn't help grinning at that. "And you just barged in here and demanded—*demanded!*—that I give you a position at my newspaper. If those aren't bold actions, I don't know what are."

"But I didn't do any of those things for *myself!*" Daisy protested. "I did them for Barker & Bowles. Or for Conrad. Or for Élodie and Owen. Or for—" She broke off, cradling her belly. Then she glanced up at him. "The point is… I'm afraid."

"Everyone is afraid sometimes." Thomas smiled at her as encouragingly as he could. "You mustn't be too hard on yourself for that. Besides, you're living in the Wild West now! There's no place like this territory for being bolder than ever before."

"You're always the optimist." Appearing unconvinced, Daisy shook her head. "But because I was *so* afraid before, I think I misjudged Owen horribly. And now it's too late to fix it."

"It's never too late," Thomas promised her. "Never."

His sister seemed to consider that for a moment. Then she gave him a teasing smile. "Really? It's never too late?" Daisy asked. "Is that what you tell yourself when you delay, yet again, with telling Miss Reardon how you truly feel about her?"

Caught, Thomas fussed with his trouser braces. "Well…" He grinned at his sister. "Let's tackle one issue at a time, shall we? Exactly how," he pressed, "will we cope with Owen Cooper?"

Chapter Thirty

With all his strength, Owen hoisted a fresh beam into place. He squinted at the stable's ceiling, gauging the beam's positioning, then nodded to himself. Everything looked fine.

He'd been planning to make some improvements to the place for a while. Now, faced with the need to stay busier than ever before, he'd decided this week was an appropriate time to act. Already sweating in the July heat, Owen tromped back to his work area. He gathered some nails, preparing for his next task.

Maybe if he labored hard enough, he thought, he would stop thinking about Daisy. Maybe if he strived and hammered and cut, he would cease feeling lonely without her. Maybe he would stop listening for the sound of her laughter. Maybe he would no longer hope to see her, stirring a pot upstairs, at the end of the day, with a welcoming smile on her face and a kiss for him.

Maybe those things would happen, Owen reasoned as he stared at his next length of lumber and prepared to measure it. Or maybe he would simply lose his wits while hoping for them.

Either way, he couldn't bear to be idle. So he worked.

"Yoo-hoo!" A knock came at his stable door. "Mr. Cooper!"

With a disgruntled frown, Owen glanced up. Miss O'Neill strode down the hay-strewn aisle toward him. Her fiery hair looked as recognizable as her toothy grin and flirtatious wave.

"I'd *hoped* I'd catch you here today!" Stopping in front of him, Miss O'Neill touched his arm, ostensibly to steady herself. "With all the hullabaloo outside, I'd worried I'd miss you."

"Do you have laundry to deliver?" Owen asked, perplexed.

"No, silly!" She gave him a playful wallop. "I'm not making deliveries *today*. It's Independence Day! Did you forget?"

Owen reckoned he had. "I've been busy. Working."

"So I see!" She sent an unmistakably admiring gaze toward his musculature. "I guess I ought to have known you wouldn't take a day from your stable—at least not without some coaxing."

Her hinting could not have been broader. Owen did not have the patience to indulge her. "Was there something you wanted?"

"Why, for you to stop working and escort me to the annual Independence Day town picnic, of course!" Companionably, Miss O'Neill looped her arm in his, trying to lead him away from his work area. "I know you don't usually attend, Mr. Cooper, but since we've gotten so much *closer* over the past few weeks, I—"

"I'm not attending." Purposefully, Owen disengaged her arm from his. He patted her hand for emphasis. "I have work to do."

"Surely *today,* of all days, you don't!" With a coquettish smile, Miss O'Neill tried again. "Please come with me. I've been so counting on it! Now that Miss Walsh is no longer here—"

"The answer is no. Independence Day is one of my busiest days here at the stable. Whether Miss Walsh is still here or not is—" At the thought of her, Owen felt his heart turn over. He wished Miss O'Neill had not mentioned Daisy. "No. Just…no."

"Are you *sure?*" Miss O'Neill simpered. "Last chance!"

"I assure you," Owen told her. "You're a very charming woman, but nothing could pull me away from my stable today."

"Nothing?" She sighed. "Truly? Not even a willing woman?"

Damnation, she was brazen. That was hardly like

her. Granted, Miss O'Neill could be forward, but... "No. Nothing."

"Well, all right, then." A pout. "Goodbye, Mr. Cooper!"

With that, Miss O'Neill sashayed out. For a long moment, Owen watched her leave, wondering if he was a fool to refuse her invitation. He'd already lost Daisy...but he'd remembered, despite himself, how nice it could be to have a woman around. Miss O'Neill had made it more than plain that she wanted him. He had every opportunity, he realized, to move on with a new life.

But if that new life couldn't include Daisy, Owen knew, he didn't want it. Those were the facts. So he went back to work. Putting Miss O'Neill out of his mind was easy. Forgetting Daisy was not. Somehow, Owen would have to do it all the same.

Downstairs outside the stable, Élodie waited with bated breath for Miss O'Neill to emerge. The moment she did, Élodie and Mrs. Archer both surged forward, eager for any news.

"Well, Abbey?" Mrs. Archer asked. "What did he say?"

"He said no." Miss O'Neill grinned at that. "I swear, I did my best to offer a winning invitation, but he was adamant. I may as well have been a horse myself, Owen was so uninterested."

Privately, Élodie felt reassured by that fact. When Mrs. Archer had announced this portion of their plan to her, she'd been justifiably skeptical. But it appeared to have worked.

"I almost overplayed my hand," Miss O'Neill confessed. "I was *quite* forward. But I assure you, Owen wants no other woman."

"Excellent." With her usual pride in a scheme well executed, Mrs. Archer nodded. "I wouldn't take his rebuff too much to heart, Abbey. We all know you're a fine woman."

"As long as Mr. Prestell knows it, that's all I care about!" Miss O'Neill crowed. "Speaking of whom… I must dash! Astair and I have important plans together. I mustn't be late."

She exchanged goodbyes with Mrs. Archer, then hurried away. Watching Miss O'Neill leave, Élodie bit her lip.

"All right, Élodie." Mrs. Archer turned to her. "Are you ready for your turn? Do you remember what to say?"

Earnestly, Élodie nodded. "Yes, I do. I'm ready."

Then she drew in a steadying breath and headed inside.

On the day of the Independence Day town picnic, Daisy opened the door at Mrs. Sunley's home to find her brother and Miss Reardon both standing on the porch, wreathed in smiles.

"Hello!" Thomas said. "Are you ready to go?"

"No." All the same, Daisy opened the door wider. She gestured for them to enter. "I'm not at all sure about this."

"That's why we made a plan!" Thomas said. "Remember?"

"I know, but…" Daisy wrung her hands, casting a faltering glance at Miss Reardon. She and her brother truly did make a handsome couple—whether they realized it or not. "I don't think it's a *good* plan. I'm no good at subterfuge to start with—"

"It's not subterfuge," Miss Reardon chimed in. "It's strategy. And although I wish we'd had time to bring in Mrs. Archer and Miss O'Neill, for their expertise with tactical details, I truly believe time is of the essence. You must act!"

Thomas's gaze dipped to Daisy's growing belly. He did not have to add a similar exhortation. Daisy already knew how her brother felt about her delicate condition—and her best chance of continued happiness, too. During their talk at the *Pioneer Press* offices, Daisy had finally confided in Thomas about her baby—and her fears that she'd ruined her chances with Owen, besides. To her relief, her careful and conservative brother had become her greatest ally…even going so far as, with Daisy's permission, to bring in Miss Reardon to help them plan.

Now their strategy was set to come to fruition—but Daisy had begun having second thoughts. "I know we agreed that I would attend the Independence Day town picnic with you today. But I still don't understand how that will help me reconcile with Owen. He won't even be there! Everyone knows Owen doesn't—"

"He'll be there," Thomas interrupted, full of certainty.

"Leave that to us," Miss Reardon promised. "All right?"

Still, Daisy hesitated. After her talk with Thomas, she'd realized that she'd been wrong about Owen. She hadn't needed strength enough to *leave* him; she'd needed strength enough to believe he wouldn't hurt her, the way Conrad had, to believe that Owen *must* have had another reason for behaving the way he had.

Now Daisy *did* believe that. All that remained was finding Owen and telling him so…at the Independence Day town picnic.

At least, that's what Thomas and Miss Reardon assured her.

Doubtfully, Daisy gazed at them. Then she lifted her chin. If nothing else, she reasoned, Élodie would be at the picnic. Daisy could find Élodie, apologize for leaving so abruptly and maybe assure herself the little girl was doing fine. That way, even if Owen wasn't at the picnic—and she personally doubted he would be—the event wouldn't be an utter loss.

"All right!" Daisy said. "Let's have ourselves a picnic!"

Chapter Thirty-One

Swearing under his breath, Owen glared at his most recently placed beam. It looked crooked. Hellfire. He guessed this was what he got for trying to work while his heart was broken.

With the stable bustling around him, he put his hands on his hips, feeling exasperated. Down the aisle, Gus placed the next boarding horse in a stall. He saw Owen watching, tipped his hat with a downright sullen motion, then kept on working.

Evidently, Gus was still irked at him over Daisy's being gone. Well, Owen thought, Gus could go on being irked from now till next Sunday. There was no undoing what was already done.

With a sigh, Owen swiped his arm across his brow. His stable was already half-full. Business promised to be especially profitable this year. That should have pleased him. It did not.

"Papa?" Élodie approached, looking somber. "Are you busy?"

"Nope." Deliberately, Owen dragged himself from his own bad temper. "I'm never too busy for you, *mon petit chou.*"

His daughter appeared tentative. Also, troubled. By now, it occurred to him, she and Mrs. Archer should have been on their way to the town picnic. Maybe Mrs. Archer had canceled today?

If so, Élodie would be powerfully disappointed.

"What is it?" Owen pressed. "Is something wrong?"

"Well, I was just wondering…" Élodie's innocent gaze lifted to his. "What's a bastard? Because I heard some of the ladies at the pharmacy saying Miss Walsh was having a bastard baby." She inhaled a gulp of air. "But when I asked Mrs. Archer about it, she only shushed me." Owen felt himself gaping. Élodie cast him an inexplicably…wily?… glance. "'Course, she was one of the ladies saying those gossipy things, so maybe that's—"

"Mrs. Archer said—" Owen broke off at a sputter, feeling wrathful enough to spit nails. "They said Daisy's baby was—" He rounded on the empty space surrounding him and Élodie, needing a target for his rage. He stumbled for more words, fists clenched.

"I'm sorry, Papa!" Élodie put up both hands in a peaceable gesture. "I didn't mean to make you angry. I only thought—"

"I'm not angry," Owen said to reassure her. Then he realized the truth. He *was* angry. Damn angry. He was angry enough to raise hell with the whole town. "I'm furious."

"Why? Is a bastard baby a bad thing?" Élodie pulled a face. "Because it *sounded* like a bad thing, the way those ladies were all whispering about it. I felt plumb sorry for Miss Walsh."

Owen growled at the thought. If people in town had been slandering Daisy… Well, they'd have him to answer to. The whole all-fired lot of them. He knew just where to find them.

At the annual Independence Day gala town picnic.

"That's why I reckoned I'd better ask you," Élodie said. She gazed up into his face. "I knew *you'd* know what to do."

Surprised and humbled by her constant faith in him, Owen gazed down at her. Looking at his daughter's earnest face and loyal demeanor, he was startled to feel…remorseful.

He'd spent so much time trying to ensure Élodie's future, it occurred to Owen just then, that he hadn't spent enough time seeing to her days as they were right now. He'd labored so hard, for so long, to free his daughter from the potential heartache in her future that he'd overlooked the very things that were happening to her right at this moment—like listening to a person she loved be maligned for being brave enough to have a baby all on her own, in a town where she scarcely knew anyone.

Poor Daisy, Owen thought. Even if he couldn't be with her the way he wanted to be, she damn well deserved to be treated with respect and kindness. She deserved…more. More than this.

"If you don't know what to do," Élodie said further, balling her fists in perfect imitation of his fighting stance, "then I'll bet *I* do! I'll tell off those ladies, but good! If you say that's a bad name to call someone, Papa, I'll do it!"

Shaking his head at her pugnacious demeanor, Owen put his hand on Élodie's shoulder. He gave her a comforting squeeze.

"That won't be necessary. I'll take care of this."

"You will? Are you sure?" His daughter appeared relieved, yet still fretful. "Because it's a mighty big problem. As near as I could tell, *all* the ladies in town were talking about it."

At that, Owen closed his eyes. *Daisy needed him,* he realized. He'd be damned if he would let her down. If no one else would defend her, he swore to himself, Owen Cooper would.

"I'm sure," he told Élodie. He hugged her. "You put that word clean out of your head, you hear? You won't ever need it."

His daughter smiled. Vigorously, she nodded. "All right."

"Now, run upstairs and get your parasol and your fancy shoes and…and whatever else people take to the Independence Day town picnic." Helplessly, Owen gestured. "Hurry, or we'll be late."

Élodie's eyes widened. "We're going to the *town picnic?*"

Her excited squeal drew all eyes to them. At first, Owen scowled. Then he nodded firmly. "Darn tootin', we are."

"Hurray!" Waving her arms, Élodie ran upstairs.

From the nearest stall, Gus led in another boarding horse. Then he leaned both arms on the gate. "You ain't leavin', boss," he drawled. "Tell me another stretcher, 'cause I ain't buyin'—"

"You put up a sign, lock up the place and go home, Gus." With an expansive wave, Owen added, "Hell, go to the picnic!"

"What? You're pullin' my leg!" His helper gestured. "I'll be damned if there ain't folks lined up down the street, wanting to board their horses and park their buggies here. If you don't take their money, they're liable to head straight on down to—"

"Don't care. Let them leave." From a nearby peg, Owen snatched up his hat. "Some things mean more than money."

Gus boggled. He grinned. "All done savin' up for

a rainy day, boss? Fixin' to enjoy yourself in the sunshine a spell?"

"Something like that," Owen allowed, then grabbed his coat.

With her heart pounding in excitement, Élodie raced upstairs. Once there, she flung open the window shutters. She leaned out to give Mrs. Archer their prearranged signal.

On the street below, Mrs. Archer beamed. She signaled too. Then she picked up her skirts and bustled to the square.

Everything was set! Nearly overcome with excitement, Élodie hurried to her bedroom. In a trice, she'd assembled her parasol, her best ruffled gingham sunbonnet, and a necktie for Papa. Downstairs, he'd looked handsome, of course—as usual—but Élodie reckoned this occasion called for something a mite fancier than his usual homespun attire.

Clutching those items, she hurried back to her father. She still didn't know what a "bastard" was, it occurred to her on the way. Miss O'Neill had suggested the correct vocabulary for her talk with Papa, and although Mrs. Archer had shied away from that particular term, in the end the two older women had agreed.

Doubtless, Élodie reasoned, that word meant something scurrilous. She wasn't stupid; she'd seen the look of ferocity on Papa's face. But Élodie couldn't understand what a tiny, innocent baby could do to deserve to be called names. Besides, by this time next year, Élodie's new baby brother wouldn't be worried about that. He'd be enjoying the town picnic, too!

Heartened by that thought, Élodie flew downstairs. It had been a near thing, her misunderstanding Papa's notions about loving someone again—and Élodie spilling the beans about that misunderstanding. But now, things were almost fixed. Élodie had *not* ruined things between Miss Walsh and her papa—and she'd have herself a brand-new family by the end of the day to prove it!

Humming with excitement, Élodie spotted Papa waiting for her in the stable. She headed directly toward him. They might never have gone together to the Independence Day town picnic before...but judging by the determined look on Papa's face right now, their first visit would be *plenty* memorable.

With Daisy securely hastened off—in Mrs. Sunley's capable company—to the Morrow Creek town square for the picnic and all its frolics, Thomas took Miss Reardon's arm. Together, they left in the opposite direction to finish their part of their scheme: making certain that Owen Cooper wound up at the picnic, too.

"Oh, dear!" Miss Reardon blushed with the effort of walking quickly, her breath coming faster. "I *do* hope we haven't set ourselves too difficult a task! Mr. Cooper can be so troublesome at times. If we can't convince him to come with us, so we can present him to Daisy, as we've promised...we're sunk!"

"Don't worry, Mellie," Thomas told her. "We'll do it."

"But how can you be sure?" She turned her beautiful gaze to his, her skirts swishing along as she moved. "We shouldn't have promised! We should have waited for Matilda and Abbey to help."

"I don't need help," Thomas proclaimed. "I'm sure."

"But the situation is so significant!" Miss Reardon said. "We *cannot* fail. There is nothing more important than love."

"That's right," Thomas agreed, reveling in the feeling of her arm in his. "Love is absolutely the most important thing."

And that's when it struck him: here he was, chasing through the streets like a madman to assure his sister's loving union with Owen Cooper...when his own potential love stood ignored, right beside him! Abashed to realize it, Thomas stopped.

"Thomas, what are you doing? Come *on!* We must hurry."

Pulled back by his arm, Miss Reardon stopped,

too. She gazed at him, with her merry eyes and her arresting demeanor, and Thomas knew right then that he could dawdle no longer.

"You're right," he agreed. "Time is wasting. That's why I have to say, I'm wild about you, Mellie. I think about you all the time. I want to be with you night and day. And when all this is finally finished," Thomas swore, "I promise I will love you—"

"I already *do* love you," Miss Reardon declared. Then suddenly, with full measure of wonderment and delight, she was kissing him. She was kissing him as Thomas had dreamed of kissing her, so often, if only he could find the courage.

It was marvelous. Better than all his dreams combined.

"There." She smiled at him. "It's about time we had that settled between us. We'll talk more later. You can tell me again how spoonily you think of me." Another impish grin. "In the meantime, let's hurry. There's the stable, straight ahead!"

Miss Reardon grabbed his hand. Thomas let himself be led, dazedly feeling like bursting into poem or song. *Mellie had kissed him,* he thought in a dither. *Mellie properly loved him!*

By his side, she appeared lively, too. Surely this was a good omen for the day. But then they reached the stable, Thomas tried the door...and all his good cheer faded into dust.

"It's locked." He looked around, baffled. "The stable is closed." Thomas chased the perimeter. "No one is here at all."

"But how can that be?" Miss Reardon asked, following him.

"I don't know. Owen Cooper nearly never leaves here."

Thomas scratched his head, pondering it. Miss Reardon gazed at him in equal befuddlement. Almost at once, they came to identical—and identically worrisome—conclusions on the matter.

"If Mr. Cooper isn't here," Mellie fretted at the stable door, "then how can we bring him to Daisy at the town picnic?"

Sobering quickly, Thomas frowned. "We can't."

At the thought of his sister, alone and expectant at the gala town picnic—at *his* urging—Thomas wanted to groan with dismay. What had they done? Worse, what were they to do now?

Chapter Thirty-Two

At the grassy square in the center of Morrow Creek, the whole place buzzed with frivolity and laughter. Red, white and blue bunting stretched from pole to pole at the entrance gate. Townspeople milled about, dressed in their most sporting garb, chatting with their neighbors and waving souvenir flags. The town band played a patriotic tune, festively arrayed on the same stage where, later, Astair Prestell was scheduled to appear.

BARKER & BOWLES PRESENT: THE LITERARY FIGURE OF OUR AGE! ASTAIR PRESTELL AND HIS ELUCIDATING OBSERVATIONS... TODAY ONLY!

Gazing at the sign and stage, Daisy felt at first wistful, then accepting. She would have liked to have spoken at the town picnic. But with everything else that had gone on...

Well, maybe next year, she reckoned as she

scanned the crowds for signs of Élodie—or Mrs. Archer, who was supposed to have brought her here.

Unfortunately, Daisy glimpsed neither of them. There were plenty of children present, but none of those children sported twin coppery braids, an elfin smile and a lovable demeanor.

Determined to enjoy herself all the same—because, after all, Morrow Creek was her home and her baby's home now—Daisy turned to Mrs. Sunley, who'd accompanied her here. She smiled.

"My goodness! I think the entire town is here."

"Pshaw," Mrs. Sunley scoffed. "You haven't seen anything yet. This place is only half-full right now. By nightfall, it'll be downright rootin' tootin'!" She gave Daisy a fond smile. "Good luck on your mission, my dear. I'm off for some mescal."

Left on her own, Daisy watched as her friend toddled off to enjoy what had become—apparently—a yearly tippling tradition.

Standing there alone amid the frolicsome antics of the Independence Day celebrants, Daisy sighed. She hoped Élodie hadn't decided to stay home this year. She hoped Thomas and Miss Reardon were correct, and Owen would be at the picnic, too. She hoped… She hoped she wouldn't lose her nerve when she saw him, and fail to tell him all the things that were in her heart.

She'd never been brave, Daisy knew. All her life,

she'd relied upon happenstance to guide her. If not for her newfound friends here in Morrow Creek, she would never have met Owen Cooper. She would never have known Élodie. She would never have had cause to question Conrad's behavior, to acknowledge her baby and her changing future…to risk loving someone with all her heart. Thomas, Miss Reardon, Mrs. Sunley and everyone else had seemed to discern that about her. Their very necessary urgings toward a new, more complete life had brought Daisy very far.

Now all that remained were a few more important steps. The only question was, could Daisy take those steps on her own? Could she claim the man and the life she wanted and make amends for her mistakes in the process?

Daisy didn't know. Just then, surrounded by everyone she knew in town and a great many more people she did not, she feared the answer was no. Panicking, she hoisted the freshly baked pie she'd brought, then turned away from the crowd altogether.

Upon pushing his way into the town square, Owen spotted the group of gossipy troublemakers he sought almost immediately.

With Élodie's small hand held firmly in his own, he beelined toward them, making his way to their gathering point at the popular booth hosted by a local mescal distillery.

With every step, his focus narrowed, blotting out the cheery hellos of his neighbors, the flapping flags and signs, the bunting and the band. With every step, his teeth clenched more tightly, causing his jaw to ache. With every step, his resolve strengthened. He intended to defend Daisy or die trying.

"You." Owen reached the group at last. He swept them all with his most fearsome gaze. Shaking with anger, he honed in on Mrs. Sunley, Mrs. Archer and Miss Reardon, specifically. He reckoned Miss O'Neill ought to have been included, but she was nowhere in sight. "You ought to be ashamed of yourselves, slandering Daisy the way you did! How you could treat a good, kind, gentle, *caring* woman that way is beyond reason! I never—"

Mrs. Sunley raised a glass. "Mescal, Mr. Cooper?"

Owen gaped at her. "Do I *look* as though I want a drink?"

"You look as though you want to murder someone," the widow said. "A drink generally helps calm down folks who are tetchy."

"Tetchy?" Awash in amazement, Owen scowled. "Damn right, I'm 'tetchy'! I'm mad as hell!" He pointed. "You three are—"

"Language, Mr. Cooper." Miss Reardon tsk-tsked,

aiming a meaningful glance at his daughter. "There are children present."

Frustrated, Owen glared at them. "You don't even have the decency to be ashamed of yourselves! I heard what you said about Daisy. It's reprehensible. Don't you know the damage that can—"

"Hello there, Mr. Cooper!" Thomas Walsh had arrived, appearing chirpy and pleased—and not the least cowed by Owen's fury. "It's about time you came to the picnic. You led us on a merry chase."

Owen didn't know what Daisy's exasperating brother was blathering about, but the sight of Thomas made him even angrier. The least the man could have done was stand up for his sister.

"You will all *stop* spreading malicious gossip about Daisy!" Owen said, coming clean to the point. "You will shut your mouths and not say a single word more! Otherwise, I promise I'll—"

To his amazement, Mrs. Archer—his longtime friend—laughed.

"This isn't *funny,* Matilda!" Owen felt his brow crease.

"I'm sorry, Owen. But it rather is." Mrs. Archer sent Élodie a comforting glance, along with—Owen would swear—a very conspiratorial grin. "You are properly formidable and quite terrifying in your protectiveness, I assure you. It's most impressive. Truly! But we have *not* been slandering Miss Walsh," she said in a more serious tone. "It was all a ruse," she confessed, "concocted deliberately to bring you here today."

Flabbergasted, Owen stared at them. The foursome nodded.

So did Élodie. "It's true, Papa. We all conspired to do it, because we all wanted you and Miss Walsh to be happy together."

Even *Élodie* had schemed to bring him here? For Daisy?

"We knew the only thing guaranteed to bring you out of your hidey-hole was making you think that Daisy needed you to defend her," Miss Reardon admitted cheerily. "So we made it all up."

Still smarting over *hidey-hole,* Owen frowned. He gestured at the town picnic. "This is all one of your irksome schemes?"

"Well, not the picnic itself," Élodie clarified. "But otherwise…yep. It's a scheme. Just like the bride raffle was."

The bride raffle, Owen remembered. *The very thing that had brought him and Daisy together.* Discomfited at the memory, he had to admit the truth: if not for his interfering friends and neighbors, he might well have missed meeting the woman he loved.

But that didn't mean he had to *like* their damn meddling!

Grumbling, he gave them another scowl, just to

assure they knew it. "Daisy never heard a cruel word against her?" he asked.

"There was never an unkind word spoken," Mrs. Sunley promised. With a twinkle in her eye, she added, "If you're so hell-bent on protecting her, maybe you ought to consider why."

Wholly taken aback, Owen did. He did consider it.

"And when you're done doing that," the meddlesome widow added, "maybe you ought to tell her. She's right over there."

Helpfully, all three women, one bespectacled man and one little girl pointed in the direction of the pie-contest table.

Owen swiveled. He couldn't see Daisy. But he could see a flashy BARKER & BOWLES PUBLISHING sign. He could see a stage. He could see his future—alone and bleak—if Daisy left town again.

"Mr. Astair Prestell won't be speaking today," Mrs. Archer informed him, misinterpreting his interest in the signage. "Apparently, he and Miss O'Neill eloped by rail this afternoon."

But Owen didn't care about clandestine weddings or hearing a famous author speak. All he cared about was finding Daisy before it was too late. To that end, he turned to the group.

"Mrs. Archer, can you please watch Élodie for a minute?" Owen asked. "I'm sorry about before."

Contritely, he gestured. "I didn't mean—well, I was all fired up, is the thing. And—"

Matilda smiled. "Of course I'll take care of Élodie."

"Oh, no, you won't!" his daughter declared. She clenched his hand in a viselike grip. "I'm not missing this! Let's go, Papa!"

Recognizing the mulishness in Élodie the same way he did his own, Owen nodded. "All right. But we'd better hurry."

Chapter Thirty-Three

She should have known better than to hope this scheme would work, Daisy realized as she stood, still alone, in the square. Apparently, Thomas and Miss Reardon were wrong. Owen had not come to the town picnic…and neither, it seemed, had Élodie.

Disheartened, Daisy mustered up a smile for a group of passing children. She waved at Molly Copeland, whom she'd met at the sociable sightseeing outing, and her sisters, Sarah and Grace. She glanced at the lemonade stand…

…and would have sworn she glimpsed Owen standing there.

Surprised, Daisy stood on tiptoe for a better look. She knew she shouldn't hope. Still, her heartbeat increased a notch.

No. Now there was no lanky, broad-shouldered,

handsome man with a little girl by his side. All she saw were strangers.

But then, near the starting line of the three-legged sack race, Daisy could have sworn she caught sight of Owen *again.*

She couldn't be sure, because the picnic grounds were packed cheek by jowl with revelers. If it *had* been Owen, Daisy discerned, he appeared to have been searching for someone.

But whom? And why? And could she even be sure it was him?

Everyone knew that cantankerous Owen Cooper didn't waste his time over "social silliness." Not for any reason. And yet, there he seemed to be *again,* peering over the crowds…at *her.*

Their eyes met. Jolted by that contact, Daisy blinked.

It *was* Owen. It was! He was here. He was looking for her.

Hardly able to fathom it, Daisy looked around. She didn't know where to go, what to do, how to behave. Her mind whirled.

Never at a greater need for clarity, Daisy could suddenly find none. Thankfully, her feet were not similarly confused. They took up walking, heading directly across the green to Owen.

An instant later, Daisy lost sight of him. More picnic-goers clogged her path and her view. She walked faster. Where was he?

Then, with blissful suddenness, he was there. *Owen.*

He stopped right in front of her, appearing tall and proud and serious and wonderful and smart and loyal and fierce and beloved and sorely, deeply missed. Near him, Daisy trembled.

"You look like ten kinds of wonderful," she blurted, aching to touch his bristly unshaven cheek—wanting to assure herself that he was real…really there, next to her, all over again.

Remarkably, he smiled. "You look like all I ever wanted."

At that, Daisy nearly burst into tears. Maybe she *hadn't* ruined everything, she thought. Maybe there was still hope.

"Owen…I'm so sorry!" Daisy said, making herself stand still and straight. "I'm sorry I didn't give you a better chance to explain. I was scared and alone and shocked, and I know that's really no excuse for all the terrible things I said—"

"You said a lot of good things, too." Owen's solemn, dark-eyed gaze met hers. "You *did* a lot of good things. You showed me a side of myself I didn't even know was there, Daisy, and I—"

He broke off. Beside him, Élodie urgently tugged his sleeve. With an apologetic smile, Owen leaned down. He conferred with his daughter. When he rose again, he was wearing a necktie.

On him, it appeared beyond handsome—even if it didn't quite match with what seemed to be a hastily pulled-on shirt and coat.

Eminently satisfied, Élodie rocked back on her heels. She cast Daisy a smile. Relieved that she seemed to be fine, and assuring herself that she would hug Élodie twice as diligently later, to make up for their separation, Daisy winked at her.

"I'm sorry, too," Owen said. "I'm sorry you had to see me and Conrad that way. I'm sorry I didn't think about what you needed more than what I wanted to give you. I'm sorry I didn't try harder to explain!" His gaze pleaded with her to understand. "Everything you said about me… It was everything I feared was true. I couldn't stand hearing it. Not from you. So I—"

"It *wasn't* true!" Daisy interrupted, impassioned with a need to make him understand. She couldn't help grabbing his hand. "I *know* you couldn't have wanted to hurt me. You don't have it in you, Owen. You're not mean. You're sweet, especially to me. You *are!* I should have remembered that. Only—"

"I *didn't* want to hurt you." Owen's voice was hoarse with needfulness. "I never wanted that. I only wanted you to have—"

"A nest egg. Like Élodie's!" Daisy squeezed his

hand, heedless of the curious picnic attendees who'd begun slowing, stopping, even gathering near their meeting place. "I thought about it later, and I knew that must be it. You wanted to give me a steady future. That's a noble gesture. It truly is."

"It's a *necessary* gesture," Owen disagreed. He swallowed, his gaze still fixed on hers. "Being with me hurts. It was bad for Renée. I didn't want it to be bad for Élodie—or for you."

"Is that what you think?" Daisy shook her head, brimming with compassion for him—a big, strong man who'd shouldered this fear alone. "That you're *dangerous* to the people who love you?"

Owen looked away. He seemed unable to speak. He nodded.

That brief affirmation nearly broke her heart again.

"But it's not true!" Daisy swore. She squeezed his hand to make him look at her again. "Owen, being with you is the best thing I've ever done. When I was with you... I felt special. I felt understood and accepted and loved. *Loved!*" Shaking her head, Daisy smiled. "Do you know how rare that is? To feel that you make someone truly happy? To feel that every day is brighter when that person is in it? To feel that the whole world was constructed just so you two would wind up together, as one?"

At that, Owen grinned. His smile dazzled her. "I

have a small notion of what it's like to feel the whole world turning around you, just to make something particular happen. I do."

Belatedly realizing he was talking about their scheming—but well-meaning—friends and neighbors, Daisy smiled wider. "Thank heavens. Otherwise, I might never have found you. Both of you!"

She beamed at Élodie. The little girl smiled back.

For an instant, Owen merely gazed at Daisy. He took in her smile, her face, her bearing and her whole being…and he smiled. Daisy smiled back at him, feeling positively beguiled.

Élodie cleared her throat. She elbowed her father in the ribs. "Not now, Papa!" she said. "You can't be tongue-tied *now!*"

All three of them laughed. Then Owen took hold of Daisy's other hand. He pulled it to his chest, where she felt his heart beating a steady rhythm. He squeezed her hand tightly.

"I came here to defend you, Daisy," Owen said. "I came here to make damn certain the world was treating you fairly. But along the way, I realized I wasn't treating you fairly."

"Owen, no. That's not true! You're—"

"I wasn't treating you fairly," he persisted, wholly undeterred by her protest, "because I never told you the truth. I never told you I love you. But I do, Daisy. I love you with all my heart and soul combined."

His gravelly voice deepened, roughened with emotion. "I love you today, and I know I'll love you even more by tomorrow. And if that sounds impossible—" Owen broke off, his face finally glowing with a rascally smile. "Well, then that's entirely appropriate. Because you made me believe in miracles, Daisy. Just by being with me, you made me believe in *myself.* You made me hope again. You taught me to open wide and take in my life. I'd plumb forgotten all that. I had. But it's so sweet, and *you're* sweet, and I…I know that if you don't say something soon, I'm going to turn into a gibbering fool, Daisy. Maybe I'm a fool already! Lord knows, I'm pretty far gone. But I need you to understand. I need you to *need* me. I need you to please, *please* forgive me. Say we can try again—"

"We can try again," Daisy said, tears welling in her eyes.

Owen seemed taken aback. "We can?"

"Of course!" Daisy said—and this time, those tears fell. "What do you think I've been trying to tell you?" she blubbered, not caring who heard her. "I *do* need you, Owen! I need you like flowers need rain. Like bread needs butter. Like soup needs salt." Seeing the perplexed look on his face, Daisy laughed. She had a lot to teach him. "Those are good things!" she explained. "They're good like *you.* Like me. Like us, together." Drawing in an emboldening breath, she gazed straight at him. "I love you, Owen. I love you with everything I am," she dared to tell him. "And if you say that's enough for you, then I believe you—"

"That's enough for me," he said, voice choked with tears.

"—and I would like to come back and never leave again."

"As far as I recall," Owen told her, "you never left. Because you were always in my heart, every moment. I love you. I love you!" He swept the enraptured crowd with a redoubtable glare. "And I don't care who knows it. I would marry you today—"

"Today?" Daisy breathed, gazing up at him. "Now?"

"—if there was someone here to marry us. I promise you," Owen said, "I will love you and protect you, no matter what."

"Marry me?" Daisy asked again. "Today? Here? Now?"

Owen nodded. Solemnly, he dropped to his knee. Daisy felt her mind whirl anew—and this time, her heart joined in, too.

"I've never said a word to you I didn't mean," Owen told her, "and I mean this now—I love you, Daisy. If you will honor me by becoming my bride, I will spend my life making you smile."

"Well—" Daisy sniffled "—if I could accomplish

the miracle of making *you* smile, I guess I can do anything." She lifted him up for a kiss. "Yes, Owen! I *will* marry you. Yes, *please!*"

As they came together for that kiss, all the Independence Day revelers cheered. The band struck up a tune. Daisy blushed, Owen tried to glower— and failed—and Élodie whooped with joy.

Someone else stepped forward. He cleared his throat. "I'm Reverend Benson," he said. "I can marry you today if you'd like."

Someone in the crowd guffawed. "Called your bluff, Cooper!"

Daisy would have sworn she recognized Gus's joking voice, making that gibe. But she didn't have time to ponder it for long. Because in the next moment, Owen looked at her. She looked at him. Élodie watched them both, then they nodded as a trio.

Jubilantly, Owen kissed her again. "Let's do it!" he said.

"Let's!" Daisy agreed. "Only…" She cast a longing glance at the starting line of the three-legged sack race. "Do you think we could indulge in one tiny race together first?"

Owen raised his eyebrows. "You want me…to do that?"

Biting her lip, Daisy nodded. "I've always wanted to."

"Do it, Papa!" Élodie urged. "It will be fun!"

"I'm just dying to see Cooper do a three-legged race!" put in a tipsy-sounding Mrs. Sunley from the sidelines. "Do it!"

Reverend Benson stood by. He grinned. "I *do* have all day."

With that, it was settled. There was a three-legged sack race for a starter, a break for pie in the middle, a hurried change of clothes and assembling of rings to follow, and then...

"Owen Cooper," Reverend Benson intoned once they were all gathered near the hastily repurposed stage in the town square, "do you take this woman, Daisy Walsh, to love and cherish, with all your heart and soul, to be your wife, now and forever?"

Owen glanced sideways—undoubtedly at the reverend's liberties with their vows. In a booming tone, he said, "I do!"

At the same time, Daisy felt...something. Startled, she clutched her belly. It felt like a flutter. Like a gentle wave. Like...a teeny-tiny baby delivering her his very first kick!

With her eyes wide, Daisy signaled Owen. She took his hand. She lay it on her middle. An instant later, another kick came.

This time, Owen's smile was downright euphoric. Feeling, with him, as though they had an unfair quantity of wonderfulness to look forward to, Daisy faced the reverend again. He repeated their vows, this time with Daisy in mind. "...now and forever?"

"I do," Daisy promised. She sneaked a glance at Owen. "And I think," she added in a more private tone, "my baby does, too!"

"*Our* baby." Owen pulled her close for their first wedded kiss. His gaze touched hers, making her feel safe and beloved and wonderfully secure. "*Our* family, together, now and forever."

Happy and radiant, Daisy nodded. "*Our* family," she agreed, knowing it was true. She'd taken a chance on being brave, and now she had more to look forward to than she'd ever dreamed of.

Hand in hand, she and Owen turned to face their friends and neighbors. The town square resounded with applause and cheers.

Some of that enthusiasm was doubtless owed to the copious quantities of mescal that had been donated by the distillery. Some of it was owed to the overall mood of celebration in the air on this, the most festive of all summertime holidays. But a part of it, Daisy knew, was owed purely to the power of love...a power she'd had cause to doubt once, but would never doubt again.

Especially not while she had herself to depend on, a family who loved her and now a new daughter to shower with affection.

"Élodie!" Daisy swooped down for a hug, laughing with glee.

The little girl hugged her, too. Shyly, she asked, "Can I call you Mama now? It's not like Maman, but it's still special."

"I'd be honored," Daisy said. Impulsively she kissed her.

"Arrgh!" Élodie cried with a giggle. "Not another nose kiss!" With girlish exaggeration, she pretended to be thoroughly exasperated. "What am I going to do now? I'm doomed!"

"Doomed to be loved, you mean!" Owen chortled.

Laughing, he looked at Daisy. She looked at him. At the sudden thought of the wedding night still to come, Daisy felt a frisson of excitement shiver through her. Then, by mutual unspoken agreement, they both turned their attention to Élodie.

"First one to catch her kisses her nose!" Daisy said.

"I'm first!" Owen vowed. "I'm bigger and stronger!"

Élodie yelped. Squealing with laughter, she ran across the green—with her new mama and her papa in headlong pursuit. As Daisy chased after her, she could have sworn she heard the trio of Mrs. Archer, Miss Reardon and Mrs. Sunley laugh, too.

"That's one more successful scheme!" Mrs. Archer declared.

"Hurrah to us!" Mrs. Sunley cheered. "We triumph again!"

"Whoever," Miss Reardon asked, "shall be next?"

But Daisy didn't have time to linger over their gossip. She had a wonderful new life to catch up with... the sooner the better, and forever after, just as she'd always hoped for.

* * * * *

Discover Pure Reading Pleasure with

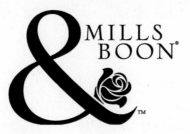

Visit the Mills & Boon website for all the latest in romance

 Buy all the latest releases, backlist and eBooks

Find out more about our authors and their books

Join our community and chat to authors and other readers

Free online reads from your favourite authors

Win with our fantastic online competitions

Sign up for our free monthly eNewsletter

Tell us what you think by signing up to our reader panel

Rate and review books with our star system

www.millsandboon.co.uk

 Follow us at twitter.com/millsandboonuk

Become a fan at facebook.com/romancehq